The Helping Heart

SISTERS OF STELLA MARE BOOK 4

ANNIE M. BALLARD

DEVON STATION BOOKS

The Helping Heart

Print ISBN: 978-1-7782367-5-4

Ebook ISBN: 978-1-7782367-4-7

Published by Devon Station Books, Fredericton, New Brunswick, Canada, E3A 2Z8

Copyright © 2024 by Leslie Ann Costello, writing as Annie M. Ballard

Book Cover by Claire Smith, BookSmith Design, Sydney, AU.

Editing by LZ Edits, Orlando, FL

Contents

Return to Stella Mare

Helen stepped out of the empty townhouse, glancing right and left. As she picked her way across the slippery pavement, she tucked herself deeper into her long black coat. Collar up, hat and scarf and sunglasses firmly in place, she felt nearly invisible, if a bit cold. The early morning sun was strong, but the wind blew icy, even in March.

It was just a few steps to the Sunshine Diner. Just a few incognito steps and she'd find coffee. Slipping in without anyone recognizing her would be perfect. Nobody needed to know she was in town. Not yet.

Not her father. Not her sisters. Nobody.

They'd be annoyed, of course. Maybe even angry, because she usually kept everyone apprised, especially since her visits had been few except for the recent past. She'd been in town last fall twice, maybe a third time, too. She had trouble remembering details through the smoke of devastation of the rest of her life.

They could all be mad if they wanted. This was different. This wasn't a visit. She was here and not going back. Walking down the sidewalk, she lifted her chin. The thought of explaining everything to her father made her stomach hurt. Even though it had to happen sooner or later, she preferred later. Much later. When she had everything figured out.

She felt safely anonymous on Water Street. She'd been away twenty years, practically a lifetime. Nobody would recognize her. Where the sidewalk was well-plowed, she picked up the pace, head high. She'd have breakfast at the Sunshine Diner, get a few groceries at the Save Mart. Then, maybe, afterwards she'd call her father. Maybe.

She almost made it to the Sunshine.

Near the diner, another long black coat turned her way, blue eyes peering over her knitted scarf. "Helen Madison!"

Helen stopped.

"It is you," the woman said with satisfaction. "What are you doing here? Without letting anybody know you were coming?" The woman in front of her was as covered up as Helen, but there was no mistaking her. She looked enough like Helen's mother to be her, except Agnes had died six years ago.

"Hi, Corinne," Helen replied. "I was going to the Sunshine. Want to join me?"

"Will you fill me in there?" Corinne demanded. "Maybe I'm the only one who didn't know you were coming. James usually tells me, though."

Helen shook her head slowly. "Nobody knows." She lifted her shoulders and dropped them, resigned. "Come on, let's get some coffee. Maybe you can help me."

Once they chose a booth in the steamy diner, Helen peeled off her scarf and shed her coat. She gazed at Corinne. "You've always been more like a sister than an aunt. Except you're less judgmental than my sisters."

Corinne scoffed. "I appreciate the sentiment, but I don't find the girls to be too judgy. Besides, when did you ever worry about them judging anything you do? They adore you."

Helen sat up a little straighter. "Well, thanks for that."

"So why are you here? I'm desperately curious. Which one of the girls is in trouble now?"

"Is that how you see me? I show up when somebody's in trouble?"

"Well, the last time you came unannounced, it was to help Rett get through her deposition."

Helen nodded slowly. "I guess so. I was doing some other things at the same time, though. I just didn't tell anybody."

"The suspense is killing me, really," Corinne asserted. "Tell Auntie Corinne. What's going on?"

"I rented a house."

"Really? I always hoped you and Reg would get a summer place here. Are you finalizing the deal this week?"

Helen shook her head. "Not a summer house. A house. I'm moving in."

Corinne's mouth dropped open, but no sound emerged.

Helen would have laughed if she wasn't so upset. "I shocked you. Sorry about that."

Corinne spluttered. "I am shocked. I had no idea. You're moving here? You and Reg and Jake? Your practice? You can't just move a law practice, can you?"

Helen's coffee threatened to come back up. "This is just what I hoped to avoid," she said, wiping her lips with a napkin. "This feels like the third degree."

Corinne narrowed her eyes. "You can hardly expect any less."

She stirred with the spoon still in her mug. "I guess. I just want the questions to be over."

"Because?"

She put the spoon on the table with a clang. "Maybe because I don't really know the answers. Or I don't know the answers I want to tell people. Corinne, you have to keep this private. Completely private, especially from Dad."

"Private from your father? Helen, you're asking a lot. He'd be hurt if he knew I was keeping something from him about one of his girls."

"He's going to be some annoyed at me for keeping all of this from him anyway," she acknowledged. "I really need a friend in this mess, though. I need somebody I can talk to who won't share what I say. Can you be that?" She looked up imploringly. "I understand if you can't."

Corinne shook her head. "Helen, you never get yourself in trouble. I can't imagine that you're in any mess that we haven't seen or heard about before. But okay. Yes. I will keep your confidence, even from your father. It goes without saying, but I am saying that I won't talk to the girls or anyone about you."

Helen leaned back in her chair. "Thank you."

"Tell me," Corinne insisted.

"Reggie and I are separated. Since the new year."

"You didn't tell anybody?" Corinne's shock was clear, but then her good manners prevailed. "Oh, Helen. That's too bad. I am so sorry."

"Yeah, me too. Or it would be me too, except he's already moved on. To Juliet, just as sweet as her name." Helen couldn't help it, her lips twisted with anger as she said the words. She opened her eyes wide and adopted a neutral expression.

Corinne looked thoughtful. "Juliet, eh?"

Helen sighed. "It's not entirely what it sounds like. We really did grow apart. Nothing in common, really, except for the obvious things."

"Obvious things like having a son and working in the same law firm?"

"No, Reg left a few years ago. Didn't you know that? He moved to another firm with the blessing of the partners, and now we refer to him for particular types of intellectual property cases."

"So you weren't working together."

"No, not for years. You knew Jake was going to hockey school, right?"

"Yes. We talked about it at Christmas, that he was admitted for winter term and how unusual that was. Does he like it?"

Helen shrugged. "I guess it's great." She remembered their recent, painful conversation, just last night. "He's not talking a lot to me right now. More to Reg."

"Jacob isn't talking to you?"

Helen's chest was very tight. She looked out the window by their booth. "He's taking this separation kind of hard," she said. "Reg says he's adjusting well to being at boarding school, and the competitive nature of the place suits him just fine. He loves working out and practising morning, noon, and night, and he's never had any academic trouble. He'll be fine, I think. The only challenge is that his classes are in french, but he's been in immersion all along, so he'll be fine." She looked up. *Maybe if I can convince Corinne, I can convince myself.*

"I'm glad his school is going well," her aunt said. "I am never sure if going away is really okay for kids who are only, what, fourteen?"

"Jake is sixteen now," Helen corrected. "He's been pretty independent for a long time, and he's so committed to hockey that he'll do anything it takes to succeed. Remember when he was little, he would get himself up for early morning practice, then get his father up to drive him?"

Corinne mused. "I do recall you telling us about that. How has it been for you?"

"Am I being too dramatic to say awful? I knew Jake was going to grow up and go to away to school, of course. I just thought we'd have a few more years before he moved out."

"I imagine the house felt empty."

Helen thought briefly of the house, outside of Ottawa - all glass and wood. It had felt empty even when all three of them were still there. "It was empty, yes," she said.

"Jake's off at boarding school, but why are you here?" Corinne's voice was soft but insistent. "Sorry about the questions, but this really isn't clear."

Helen shrugged. "It seemed like the thing to do. I let my partners buy me out of the firm, and Reg bought me out of the house, and I sold it." She thought through the conversation with Reg about the house. The thought of Juliet and her two kids tumbling around the glass-and-wood tabernacle of her defunct family life had made her physically ill, so she insisted on getting the house. Now none of them would have it.

Corinne looked out the window. "You're here for good. Jake is away at school, you and Reg have separated, you sold your practice, and now you are here."

"That's the short, painful version," Helen agreed. It didn't sound so bad when you put it that way. Succinct, anyway. Nobody was really at fault.

"The short version," Corinne repeated.

"There are details," Helen said vaguely. "You've got the big picture, though."

"James knows none of it?"

"I arrived last night. Only my rental agent even knew I was coming."

"I'm kind of surprised the news didn't travel," Corinne said. "You know how this place is."

"I swore her to secrecy. Told her I was a big city lawyer." Helen allowed herself a small smile.

"I'm sorry for being indelicate," Corinne said, "but what are your plans? That will be James's first question."

"I know what Dad's like," Helen said. "That's why I didn't talk to him in advance. Now I've got a house and my furniture is arriving on Friday, so that's a plan, right?"

"What are you going to do for work?"

Helen shrugged. "Selling the practice bought me breathing room. I can take some time. I'm just going to settle in here for now. Maybe Dad needs my help."

Corinne scoffed. "There's nothing helpless about that old man."

"But he's got diabetes now, right? And he's not great about his exercise and diet."

"He does okay," Corinne corrected. "You'll get yourself in some trouble there, if you start bossing James around. Your sisters have tried."

"Well, they're not me," Helen said. "I'm the oldest. I have some license that the others don't. Anyway, I came to Stella Mare because I can help my family best by being here."

"I'm not buying that story," Corinne said. "It's a strange time to come home. We've all adapted to your mum being gone, and the girls have all gotten themselves straightened around. Everybody's finally on a good adult life track, you know?"

"Is that so? That's not how I heard it," Helen disagreed. "I heard that Rett's taken a dead-end job at the downtown clinic, Evie wants a PhD, like she's capable of that, and Dorie's planning to marry a guy with no prospects."

Corinne barked out a laugh. "Well, that's a uniquely critical perspective. You won't win any popularity contests with that position."

"I know," Helen said. She leaned across the table and covered her aunt's hand with hers. "I disappeared to Ottawa a long, long time ago. In a lot of ways, I regret being a long-distance sister and daughter. I know I missed out. But now I'm here, I'm in a position to help and I can see my help is needed."

In the silence, she felt the weight of Corinne's gaze, blue eyes boring into her. Like they could see into her soul. Shifting in her seat, she changed gears. "You know, you look just like Mum right now."

Corinne dropped her gaze with a smile. "That's funny. I was just thinking about what your mother would say about having you back in Stella Mare. All her girls back in the village."

"What would she say?"

"Well, she'd be pleased on the one hand, but you know Aggie. She'd also be poking at you about your life goals, how you're coping without your family, and of course whether you're going to get a dog."

"A dog! Yes, that would be Mum." Helen relaxed into a smile. "Are you wondering those things, too?"

"Well, probably not the dog part." Corinne chuckled.

"I'll be honest, but again, please don't share this," Helen said. "Right now, I don't have life goals. I have day goals and week goals. Things work if I don't think about stuff too much." Especially that last interview at work. Or her recent visit with Jake. Her face warmed. "No dog, either. Dorie doesn't need to palm any animals off on me."

"I don't think she's in that business, exactly," Corinne said. "I'm sure you need to take some time. You've been through a big transition. It takes a while to get your balance back."

"Always a social worker," Helen said, drawing her hand back. "Thank you for hearing me. But I really don't want anyone here to feel like they have to take care of me, so please, please don't tell them. Or better yet, tell them I'm great. Feeling terrific, can't wait to start over in Stella Mare, looking forward to a new beginning." She put on a big smile.

Corinne reached over to touch her hand, resting on the table. "It's okay to be struggling. You've been through a lot."

Helen's shoulders sank as her eyes filled, but she pulled herself upright immediately. "Thanks, but I really do have things managed. I do."

Corinne pulled her hand back and fussed with her buttons. "Of course you do," she said, glancing back up at Helen. "You always do. You always have."

"Yes," Helen agreed. "Well, this has been nice, but I've got to get going. Come for dinner on Friday. I'll have my furniture then and we can all get together at my new place."

"Why don't we just go to James' like always? You don't need to be unpacking and making supper at the same time. Let's just tell your father you're here and he'll make the plans."

Helen shook her head. "You tell him I'm here. Then I'll invite him to dinner."

Corinne glared. "Absolutely not. I won't let you put me in that position. Oh, by the way, James, your eldest and possibly favourite daughter is in the village and she didn't let you know? That's not fair to anybody."

"I thought it was worth a try," Helen said, offering an impish grin, feeling considerably lighter. It had felt good to tell someone.

"Oh, you!" Corinne swatted at her with her scarf. "That's totally not going to happen. I'll keep your secrets, but I'm not going to take the brunt of your father's reaction to you avoiding him. It's disrespectful."

Helen sighed. "Well, when you put it that way, I guess you're right. I just wanted to avoid his reaction myself."

Corinne raised her eyebrows. "It's your job to tell him you're here. Unless somebody in this town has already alerted him."

"I haven't seen anybody but you," she objected.

"That doesn't mean nobody has seen you," Corinne said. "Call him now or he'll be hearing it from Josiah Steeves or something. I bet you've been in the Save Mart."

"That was next on my list," she admitted. Maybe she'd have to see Dad instead. "Okay. I'll call Dad. Or stop by."

"You do that," Corinne agreed. "I expect there will be hell to pay, but the sooner you get that over with the better."

Coming Clean with Dad – almost

She walked home to get the car to drive to Dad's house. It wasn't far, but she had to shop after her visit. She needed things for the house that would not be on the moving truck.

When she pulled into the driveway, she saw only her sister Evie's little car, and breathed relief. Dad's truck was nowhere to be seen. Boots slipping on the icy pavement, she walked around the car to the back of the house, the same way she'd gone home every day after school until she was eighteen. She could walk this way with her eyes closed. For a moment, she did close her eyes, but when her left arm brushed an unfamiliar object, she opened them immediately.

Something was parked behind the house in a temporary shelter. She looked under the canvas cover. Oh, Dad's truck. But why on earth did he have this fabric thing going on? He'd said for years he wanted to build a garage to replace the shed where he spent a lot of time and also keep the snow off his vehicles, but he had never quite made it happen. Maybe this was his interim step? Helen wasn't sure she liked it.

The back steps had been neatly shovelled, and the small porch held the remains of a Christmas tree, leaning against the house, yellowed needles carpeting the porch floor. She gave it a critical glance as she pulled open the storm door and pushed on the knob of the inner door.

The kitchen was quiet and dim, though the morning light filtered across the sink from the backyard window. She slipped off her boots, grateful for wool socks, dropped her puffy coat on a kitchen chair, and headed for the counter. The coffeemaker was still on, with half a pot in the carafe. She poured herself a cup.

"Dad?" Seeing nobody, she called again, a little louder. Two vehicles in the yard, yet nobody was home. She looked around, curious.

The house was tidy. Well, it had mostly always been tidy, even though full of things; furniture, decorative and useless objects, books, extra clothes, boots, dishes, the things that families collect over lifetimes. However, Evie had spent last summer clearing out, so the house felt unfamiliarly spacious, even the old kitchen. The same scarred oak table was there, with only four chairs. The sideboard, instead of being piled with mail, Dad's newspapers, and assorted sweaters, held framed photos and a book. Her glance skimmed the girls' high school graduation pictures, and then landed on a larger framed shot of the four sisters with Mum at Helen's university graduation.

There they all were: she and Rett, alike as sisters could be, Evie, shorter, rounder, darker and curlier, and Dorie, a mere baby at the time of the picture but already looking like Helen and Rett, though she hid behind her mother's skirts. Mum, tall and willowy like her daughters. Her open smile struck Helen like a fist. She swallowed hard.

Snapping her gaze away from the photo brought her to the ancient-looking book. The textured cover drew her, and she stroked a finger across the embossing. Opening it carefully, she caught her breath. Mum was everywhere. Here was her handwriting, that careful Palmer Method script. Notes were inscribed into the margins, corrections marked in recipes. The family cookbook, her mother's and handed down from her mother before her. Trust Evie to make a display of it. It probably warranted a display, given it held so much of the family history. Helen giggled a little. Other families kept a family bible, but the Madisons had a cookbook. Given how important food was to them, that was about right. She closed the book reverently.

Her gaze slid up the wall to a stunning watercolour seascape painted by Evie for some parental anniversary. Even way back in high school, Evie's paintings were distinctively hers. Her talent had meant nothing to Helen, but she could appreciate it now.

Leaving the sideboard and its memories, she walked into the living room and plunked herself onto the squishy couch. Nobody was home, that was for sure, because the dogs weren't even there. Her father kept two massive hairy creatures her mother had loved. They were a fixture around the house, so it was rare to walk into the Madison family home and not be draped in dog hair and drool. That was a disloyal thought, but Helen allowed herself to have it for a moment. Dogs were wonderful, but maybe they were not for everyone.

Sitting on the couch gave her a great view of the wall over the television. Dad probably watched too much TV, she thought. Maybe he needed a push to get out more. She resolved to be just that push, but as she gazed, her perception narrowed and sharpened. What was on that wall? She squinted at the framed certificates and photos.

Rett's certificate of achievement in high school sciences. Rett had swept all the academic awards for science her last year. That intellect was being wasted as a nurse in a little community clinic. That girl had a good brain not being used only checking ears and throats. Helen huffed in irritation.

The next thing on the wall was a photograph she didn't recognize. It drew her off the couch to look. She lifted it from the wall and carried it back to the couch where she clicked on the lamp and peered. Suddenly, her stomach gave a lurch and a wave of nausea washed through her. With a gasp, she dropped the photo as if her fingertips burned. She backed away.

Deep breaths. Here and now. It was just an old photograph.

A kerfuffle came from the kitchen and Dad's big furry black dogs, Custard and Mallow, scrambled in from the kitchen to greet her. She pulled her legs up on the couch to protect her coffee from their welcome, reaching to scratch an ear with her other hand.

"Loretta? That you? What are you doing here?" Footsteps followed. She turned toward the kitchen.

"Not Rett, Dad," she called back. "It's me, Helen."

"Helen?" He came around the corner into the living room. She had her hand in one dog's big ruff and held him in front of her as if for protection. "Helen, really?"

"Hi, Dad," she said. She felt about twelve years old and caught out. How was it possible to feel so much like a bad kid when you came to see your father? Lifting her chin, she noted his expression. Anger? No, not exactly. Surprise and confusion. Now she didn't feel like a kid, but more like a grownup with a child. She set down her mug and gently pushed Custard away with her knee so she could stand. Dad looked old. Older than she'd ever seen him look.

She moved swiftly to give him a hug, then stood back and smiled. "Aren't you happy to see me?"

"Of course I am," he said firmly. "Helen, it's good to see you. Here, let's sit down." He headed for his recliner while she returned to the couch. "Did I know you were coming?" he asked quite seriously.

This was not the greeting she expected, and not what Corinne had told her to anticipate.

"No, Dad, probably not," she said. "I didn't tell anyone."

He looked pleased. "So it's a surprise visit. That's wonderful. Have you seen your sisters? Who picked you up from the airport?"

This might not be as hard as she'd expected. "I drove this time, Dad. The only person I've seen is Corinne, and that's just because I ran into her. You're the first."

"It's nine in the morning," he said, confused again. "Did you drive overnight?"

Before she could formulate an answer, she heard another arrival at the back door. "Oh, Evie's here," she said and headed for the kitchen, where her sister Evie and her boyfriend Stephen were shedding outerwear.

"Hey, you two," she said, anticipating their surprise.

"Helen!" Evie dropped her coat on the floor in the rush to give her a hug. "Oh, what are you doing here? It's so good to see you."

"Hey, let me breathe!" She backed away from the hug. Evie tipped her chin up, dark hair curling around her smiling face.

"You're still tall," Evie said.

"You're still short," Helen retorted, in their habitual greeting. "Hi, Stephen."

Evie's boyfriend was hardly a boy. At least forty-five, he was a semi-employed artist-writer-historian from somewhere in the States. Nice enough, Helen thought. He smiled at her as he picked up Evie's coat and hung it with his. "James must be pretty pleased," he said.

"He's in the living room," she said. "I just arrived. Come on in."

"I live here," Evie reminded her, as she headed back toward her father.

"I know," she said airily. "Of course."

When they were all settled, Evie asked, "Why are you here?"

"Well, that's kind of the news," Helen said, looking at her father. Thank goodness Evie was here for this part. "I've moved here."

The silence was broken only by a dog licking his big paw.

"Well? Aren't you going to say something?" This lack of response was worse than what she'd imagined.

"Uh, but why?" Evie asked.

Helen fingered the diamond tennis bracelet on her left wrist, tucked under the sleeve of her sweater. "I should have told you." She brushed her hair away from her face and lifted her chin. "Reggie and I have separated." She looked past Evie's stricken face to focus on Stephen. The only non-family member, he just looked kind, not shocked.

James pushed himself up out of his recliner and walked over to the window. Helen looked at his slightly bowed back, and said rapidly, "We decided last fall, and we knew Jake was heading to hockey school. Well, at least we thought he would be, and Reg moved out and Jake moved out, and that house, well, it was just, it was just...."

James leaned his head on the window as Helen's voice petered out. "Dad?"

Evie reached to pat her knee. "I'm so sorry, Helen. What a terrible time you've had." Her sympathetic expression reminded Helen Evie had broken up with her long-term partner less than two years ago. Of course they hadn't been married, so it wasn't the same. But it was still nice to hear a little sympathy.

"It's been hard," she agreed. "I decided to come back to Stella Mare." She stared at her father's back, willing him to turn around.

The ticking grandfather clock marked the silence.

"Dad, I should have told you," she said again. He turned and started back toward his chair.

"Yes, you should have," he said heavily. "You have a family here, you know. Family helps when there's trouble."

Maybe. Or maybe they just judge. "I didn't want you to worry," she said. "There wasn't anything to do. I figured I'd get here and then let you know."

"And so you did."

A heavy silence filled the room. Stephen asked, "Tea?" James and Evie assented quickly. Stephen headed out toward the kitchen.

Helen tried to assess the situation. Her father was hard to read. "Dad?"

James stood by the recliner, looking off into the distance. "Times I never thought I'd see. Families breaking up." He turned his blue gaze on her. "What happened, Helen? How's Jakey?"

She took the easier question first. "Jake's living the life, Dad. He loves hockey school. He does his favourite thing twice a day, and all the people there just live and breathe hockey, so even school is a treat."

"That's not what I meant," James said, narrowing his gaze. "How's he doing with the breakup of his family?"

Helen's eyes suddenly filled and spilled over. A sob caught in her throat.

"Little girl." James reached for her, and she tumbled into his arms, tears flowing freely now. He patted her back as he held her, leaning slightly on the recliner. Evie slipped out toward the kitchen.

She clung and sobbed for a moment, but then recovered herself, stood up and held her father by the shoulders. She remembered her sixteen-year-old satisfaction when she was finally tall enough to do that, but it was even easier now as Dad seemed shorter. "I'm okay," she said, dashing her hand across her face. She headed back to the couch. "Thanks."

James scoffed but sat in his chair. "You're here now."

She nodded. "I am."

Stephen returned, setting a tray on the coffee table. Evie poured from the old brown teapot. "Here's your tea. Cookies, too. Dad?"

James reached for the cup she offered. "Thank you, Evie. No cookies for me."

Helen lifted her coffee mug and said, "No tea, thanks, but a cookie sounds great. Nothing like coffee and cookies to soothe the heart."

"Spoken like a true Madison sister," Evie said with a smile. "We can feed any feeling."

James was not distracted. "What happened? People don't just separate after almost twenty years. Something happened." He was adamant.

Her prepared response slipped out easily. "We just grew apart, Dad. We were too young when we got married."

"Too young? You were a lot older than your mother was."

Helen shrugged. She'd said all she was going to say about that.

"What are you going to do?" James wanted to know. "You must have a plan. I have never known you to be without a plan."

"When I was here helping Rett in the fall, I checked out a couple of small law firms," she said. "My partners bought me out, so I thought I'd buy a practice that's already up and running."

"What? You sold your practice?" Evie's shock was obvious.

"They wanted to buy me out." Helen shrank back from the question.

"That's not much of a reason. You've been building that practice your whole career. Your life was in that work. What made you do that?"

Dangerous ground. "I was ready for a change," she said smoothly.

"What kind of change?" Evie persisted. "If you buy a practice here, you'd still be practising law."

James looked puzzled. "Did you say you're buying a practice in Stella Mare? There's not a lot."

She shook her head. "No, not in the village, Dad. Maybe in Saint Jacques. It's only an hour away, but I want to live here."

"That's too far to commute," Evie said. "You can't do that all winter."

Squaring off against her sister, she contradicted, "Sure I can. Ottawa has the most snow of any national capital in the world. I know how to commute in snow."

"Not in New Brunswick," Evie said grimly. "I assume in Ottawa a lot of people travel. The roads are ready for rush hour and all that."

Stephen laughed. "Rush hour? I'd forgotten that concept."

"It's when more than four people line up at the traffic light," Evie said, "or all day long during tourist season."

"I haven't made any decisions about work yet," Helen insisted. "Selling the practice means I can take some time to choose the right thing. Most people don't get to re-imagine their career at my age. I'm going to get reacquainted with my home village and province."

"Sounds like Jakey going to school was a change, and Reggie moving out was a change," James mused. "You were already dealing with a lot of change. Don't know why you'd sell your practice."

She had to stop this questioning. "I needed to leave," she said plainly. "So I did."

"Needed to?" James couldn't let it go. "Why did you need to?"

Increasing the volume, she said, "You're right, Dad, everything went wrong. I just made a break. I'll probably start practising again as soon as things get organized, but right now I'm taking some time."

She lifted her chin. It was all under control. She had to sound like it was all under control.

It worked. Her father backed down. "I knew you'd have a plan," he said, satisfied.

Evie was less easily convinced. "That's a pretty loose plan," she said. "Hang out for a few months and then decide what to do?"

Helen sharpened her gaze. "Isn't that what you did after Jase threw you out?"

Evie pulled back like someone had struck her. Helen, suddenly remorseful, folded her lips into a grim line. Stephen reached for Evie's hand and said mildly, "Sometimes it takes a while for a new direction to appear. I've been through periods like that. Maybe that's where you are, too, Helen."

Feeling marginally better, she nodded. "Maybe. Sorry, Evie."

Evie sniffed and nodded, then took her cup out to the kitchen. Stephen followed.

"Are you girls fighting?" James asked. "Already?"

"Dad! We don't fight."

"Oh, you used to have some doozies," he said. "Before you left."

"We were kids then," she objected. "Kids fight with each other."

"Well, the other girls used to fight even after you left," he said, reminiscing. "But they figured it out after Aggie died. It was like they made a pact to do better. Rett gave Dorie some grief, though, before she got the Sanctuary started."

"A dog sanctuary," Helen said. "How is that any kind of real job? She's always going to be scrambling for funding."

James' look sharpened. "You be careful. You've been away for almost twenty years. Everybody's not going to want to play by your rules anymore, Helen."

She scoffed. "Come on, Dad. I don't expect that."

"That's what you say, but I know you, my girl."

She folded her arms and narrowed her eyes. He could have a point. Or not. They might need her broader perspective. Stella Mare was a very small place.

Not Exactly Mother of the Year

The movers arrived with a beeping truck backing into her court at six thirty am. Relief that her furniture had arrived mitigated Helen's annoyance at being awakened. She threw on sweats and headed down to open the front door. How many of her neighbours were now awake and annoyed at the new person? Well, it wasn't her fault.

The truck groaned to a stop. A man emerged from the passenger side to rattle the big rear doors while the driver approached Helen.

"Ms. Madison?" His eyes and mouth were lined with fatigue. He held out his clipboard. "Here's your manifest. This is you, right?"

She squinted at the document. "Yes. That's my signature. How long do you think this will take?"

"We're unpacking you, too, so probably at least until noon. I've got a local guy coming to help with the lifting. But we should be on our way by lunchtime, I think."

She nodded stiffly. "Good. Let me know if you need anything." She watched him head toward the truck, where his colleague had climbed in the back, sorting through blanketed furniture and cardboard boxes. There was a lot of stuff in that truck, and it wasn't all hers. She had no idea how they could keep track. She'd have to watch them closely.

A kid showed up about eight. Lanky, with dark hair hanging into his face, he carried a stack of moving boxes into the kitchen.

"Who are you?" Until he appeared, she'd forgotten about the 'local guy' and besides, this was a kid, hardly a guy.

He looked uncomfortable. "Chuck. I'm helping."

"Oh, right. Well, Chuck, be careful. That top box is full of breakable stuff."

He looked around, unsure, and she snapped, "Oh, just give it to me. I don't want to worry about it." She grabbed it from him, registering his shock. He looked barely old enough to have a part-time job, no older than her Jake. His embarrassed flush poked at her. Maybe she'd been a bit harsh. She hardly saw him the rest of the morning. Perhaps he avoided her.

By eleven, her furniture was in place and she'd had time to realize just how small her new home was. The dining room table nearly touched the walls. Her bedroom was claustrophobic with furniture. She sighed. There was nothing to do about that now.

The men were full of questions about where to put things, questions she couldn't answer. Her shoulders tightened painfully and watching them emptying the boxes made her teeth hurt. The counters and tabletops were piled high, and clothes had been dumped on her bed when she reached her limit. No more hands on her things.

"You can go now," she said to the driver. "I'll finish up."

He eyed her doubtfully. "You specified unpacking. We're supposed to unpack you and take the boxes."

"I know," she said, reaching for his clipboard. "I'll sign. All the boxes arrived. The furniture looks okay except for that scratch on one chair, and I'll take responsibility from here."

"I'll need you to document that, Ms. Madison," he warned. "If you find any breakage, you'll have a different process to make a claim."

"It doesn't matter. You've done your job, all I need you to do, so let's wrap this up." So you can get out of my house, she thought, but had the wherewithal to keep to herself.

"Okay," the driver said, scribbling on his paper. "Now if you decide you need more help, Chuck here is a local lad. He could probably help you out." He nodded toward Chuck, and Helen's gaze followed. Chuck looked profoundly uncomfortable.

"Sure," she agreed absently. "Chuck, leave me your contact information. I probably will need some help around here." She looked back at the driver. "Is there anything else?"

"We'll gather up the empty boxes and make sure we've taken all our stuff, but nope, that's it. I hope you enjoy your new home."

She nodded. "Me, too." She watched the truck drive down her court toward Water Street. A moment later, Chuck followed on an old bike, bouncing over the ruts and ice. She closed the door firmly and turned the deadbolt.

Even though she'd been eager for them to leave, the house became too quiet after the door closed behind them. It was different now with furniture in it; her steps didn't ring hollow, but it was still new. The table was familiar, but the space wasn't. It was way too quiet. She pulled out a kitchen chair to sit at the laden table and listen to the silence in her new house. Listening became remembering.

Jake would never be as awkward as that Chuck. Hopefully, Jake would never need to work as a labourer. With snappy customers. Briefly uncomfortable, she thought about her son. He should be here.

She'd invited him, riding a wave of mother's hope, but he was too busy. Maybe something more than busy.

Her mind floated back to her recent visit to the Quebec town that housed his boarding school. On her way to her new home in New Brunswick, she spent a night at the shabby little motel that catered to hockey school parents. They offered a teen-friendly buffet for week-night dinners, perfect for visiting families.

He sat across from her as he always had at home, but she couldn't stop staring at him. How much could a boy change in a couple of months? There was something in the set of his jaw that looked different. Not so young. "What's the best thing about your school?"

He looked up from his plate. "Well, not the school part," he said with a little grin. "Hockey, obviously."

"Why is that obvious?" she retorted. "I'd like to think there are many things that could be good about this school."

He wiped his mouth with his napkin and leaned back. "Yeah, probably. But you asked what was best. I like playing the best."

"Are the other boys good? Is there competition?"

He laughed. "Yeah, very good. Very much competition until we get a real opponent on the ice. Then we're a team."

Helen puzzled over that. "I don't see how you can switch like that. If you're in competition for resources, just having a common enemy won't make you less competitive."

"We're not competing for resources, Mum. This isn't some roleplay game. We're competing to see who's the most skilful, the toughest.

The hardest worker. When we have a team to beat, all those things become assets for the team. All for one, and one for all. Like that."

"It seems to me you have to be a team even when you're not playing against somebody else," Helen argued. "If you can't get along with your teammates off the ice, things won't work very well when you're on it."

"Nobody said we don't get along," Jake said irritably. "We're just competitive. There's a pecking order, like."

"How do you know about those things?" she asked. "Pecking orders?"

"Oh, that's Dad," he said. "He talks like that."

"Hmm."

There was a moment of quiet before he went on. "You sold the house?" His voice was tight.

"I told you. I sold the house. Renting one in Stella Mare. I might move there permanently."

"I don't get it. Don't you have to work?"

"Jake, we went over this. Sarabeth and Jeremy bought me out. I'm no longer employed, I sold the house, and I'm going back to New Brunswick. The moving van picked up the furniture last week and I've been in transition for days. That's why I'm here, to see you on the way."

"It was pretty sudden."

Helen's stomach sank. "Jake, do I really have to draw you a picture? Your Dad moved into Juliet's place, you left, and there I was."

"In the house you loved," he said, pain crossing his face.

She shrugged. "Turns out I didn't love it so much when I was alone there." And didn't have a job, she had added silently. "Besides, you always complained about that house."

Jake narrowed his eyes. "I did not. That was Dad."

"Well, the house was mine in the separation and I sold it."

He stared at his plate.

"Listen, Jake, there wasn't really any option," she started.

He jerked up to look at her. "It was my house, too. You could have told me before you did it."

"Maybe. But what's done is done." Her tone changed as she considered her case. "I want you, no, I expect you to come to Stella Mare for Easter break. You haven't seen your Madison family for a long time."

Jake was already shaking his head. "No. Just because you move to the middle of nowhere doesn't mean I have to. I'm staying with Dad and Juliet. In Ottawa I can see my friends. Hang out with Sasha and Vicky."

"Juliet's kids? I thought they annoyed you."

He shrugged. "They can be fun."

"We can have fun in Stella Mare."

He looked at her blankly. "If Stella Mare was so much fun, why haven't I been there since Grandma died? You can go, do whatever, but I don't have to."

"Jake," Helen began, but he cut her off.

"I'd like to go home, please."

"That school isn't your home."

"Well, it's what I've got."

"You always have a home with me, Jacob."

"Out in the wilderness, some place I've never seen."

He had a point. She was silent.

He took a breath. "Mum, why did you sell your practice? I don't get it."

"It was time," she said, her heart pounding.

He gave her a hard look. "It's true then. You had an affair."

Her eyes watered, but she lifted her chin. "Do not confuse me with your father, Jake. He had an affair, right out in the open. I don't know who has said what to you, but I wish you'd ask me directly."

His voice was thick. "I am asking you, Mum. Why did you sell our house? Why are you moving when you said you'd never leave Ottawa?"

"It's complicated, Jake."

"So? Don't I deserve to know?"

When her silence continued, he choked down sobs. Dropping his napkin on the table, he stood. "Just drop me off at school, please. I'm done."

A stony silence lay between them in the car. Nothing she could tell him would make sense to a teenage boy, at least not without destroying his idea of family. As she pulled up at his residence, words gathered in her throat, but he slipped out of the car muttering, "Bye," then jogged to the building.

Choking back tears, she watched him pull open the big wooden door and slip into the light inside. She wiped her eyes before pointing her car down the long driveway. Autopilot took her back to the motel. Sitting in her car to text him, she wrote, *you can believe whatever your father tells you, but it's not true.* Shaking her head, she deleted it. Jake didn't need her calling Reg a liar. Instead, she wrote,

It was time for me to leave my practice. I'm sorry you're upset about the changes. It's not easy for me, either.

Stomach in a knot, she sent it off. Reg had been trying to brainwash Jake, obviously. No surprise there. She was shocked, though, Jake would think ill of her. After everything she'd sacrificed for him.

In the motel room, she had thrown herself onto the bed, wriggling to find a comfortable spot, but nothing worked. Instead, she pulled on her coat and hat again, and headed out into the cold Quebec night. Walking might clear her head.

Still thinking about Jake, she walked under tall pines laden with late winter snow. The moon was nearly full, casting light bright enough to see the way, but she still felt wrapped in darkness. She walked fast, arms pumping, fists clenched, fingers firmly, imaginatively gripped around Reg's chicken neck, but as she approached the old brick shops, she slowed a bit. It wasn't really late, but everything was buttoned up tight. A noise in an alley to her right made her jump and glance over. A dark shadow loomed, leaning closer to her, heavy, and a smell like wet wool filled her senses. The moon tilted. Her throat held a scream as her heart nearly burst.

Just as it seemed the terror would overtake her, she spotted a woman walking a small dog down the sidewalk in her direction, the moon settled back into the sky, and she could breathe again. Whatever that had been, it was unpleasant.

A loud beep made her jump. Startled out of her reverie, she slapped the kitchen table. Here and now. That was over, and here she was, in her new house. Jake would come for Easter. He had to. She would not be stuck here in Stella Mare without her son. In the meantime, she had plenty to do, and she needed the right music to make it happen.

She looked for her speaker. Her "Future Me" playlist had been getting heavy use. She needed to hear those songs, the ones she'd chosen to help keep her pointed forward. No time now for looking back. That was over.

She cranked up the music and started putting away dishes in her new cupboards. Only a hundred boxes to empty today. She could do it.

By evening, she was nearly ready for the family. "Come in, come in!" Helen gestured, holding open her front door. "It looks like everybody arrived all at once."

Evie looked behind her. "Oh, there's Rett and the kids," she said.

"And Dorie's truck," Helen added. She held the door as her family tumbled in, one after the other, kids squabbling. Soon there was a pile of boots in the hallway and coats piled on the living room sofa. The house was suddenly full of sound and life.

"Daughter," James said, giving Helen a hug in the kitchen. "You going to show your old man around?"

"Sure, Dad. Let's go upstairs." She led the way, and not only James, but Evie and Dorie followed.

"Let me see what I can aspire to," Dorie said with a grin. "Wow, that's an amazing view from your bedroom."

Evie wandered from window to window in the main suite. "Even winter looks beautiful from here."

"Big bedroom," James said. "Hard to heat?"

Of course Dad would wonder that. "No, Dad, new construction is tightly insulated. Come on, you can see my office and the guest room."

Following the sound of running feet, Rett's twins appeared in the upstairs hall. "We want to see too!" Callie shouted.

"Come on in," Helen said. "This is my bedroom."

Maggie gave a huge leap into the middle of Helen's bed, and before anyone could say a word, Callie was there, too. "Can we jump?" she asked.

"No," Helen started, but the little girls were already bouncing up and down. "Oh, well," she said, and led the way to the other rooms.

"Ahoy!" Corinne's voice came up the stairs. Helen heard Rett and Chad talking, too.

"We're upstairs." She leaned over the hall railing to call downstairs. "Come up if you want the tour." She returned to her father and Evie.

After everyone had wandered through the house at least once and the twins had tried jumping on all the beds, they returned to the kitchen, and Helen wheedled Dorie into helping her serve dinner.

"Hey, I thought I was going to be a guest," Dorie mock-complained.

"You get the good job," Helen said. "Everybody's happy to see dinner served." She gave Dorie a small push toward the dining room where her younger sister made a show of putting the big casserole on the table.

"I don't know what it is," Dorie said in response to a question. "Helen just handed it to me. Smells good, though, doesn't it?"

Helen came in holding a tray full of bowls. "It's tortilla casserole," she explained. "You'll love it."

"I'm sure I will," Corinne said, picking up a spatula. "How did you have time to cook while unpacking?"

"It's a superpower," she said modestly. "Excessive organization."

"Well, I'm impressed," Corinne remarked. "Do you want me to serve?"

"You've got a nice place here," Chad said while the food was being passed. "I didn't know these townhouses were so fancy."

Helen scoffed. "I wouldn't call it fancy," she said. "It's serviceable."

Evie raised her eyebrows. "That bathroom is pretty darn nice."

Rett was busy putting food on her children's plates, but she chimed in. "Yeah, your bathroom is the size of my dining room, and I live in a single-family house. New is pretty nice."

"I figured a townhouse would do for someone who lives alone," she said. She appreciated her sisters' approval, but she wasn't sure she agreed. This house was fine, sure, but it couldn't hold a candle to the wood-and-glass place she'd had in Ottawa. She didn't want to seem ungrateful, so she didn't make that comparison for her family. Of course, none of them had ever seen her house, except Dad, and he was singularly unimpressed by ostentatious display. Not that her house had been ostentatious. It had been just, well, spacious. Modern. Big.

"It's a nice house, Helen," James said heavily, as if making a proclamation. "You've got a good view of the water, and you're right downtown here in the village. Not too big, but not squeezed, either. When Jake comes to stay, it'll feel just right."

Dad knew how to put a point on it. Helen's eyes watered. "I hope he comes soon for a visit," she said thickly. It was weird to live in a house Jake had never seen.

Dorie busied herself pouring wine. James waved her off, brandishing his sparkling cider.

"A toast," Helen's youngest sister suggested. "To Helen's new home!"

The family lifted glasses, including the children who hoisted cups of milk. Helen gazed at them and got misty all over again.

"Thanks, you guys," she said. "It's so nice to have you all in my house. That's never happened before."

Evie looked a little shamefaced. "I'm sorry I never visited you, Helen. There's no excuse. I'm glad you're here now, but I wish I had been better about travelling to see you."

There was a chorus of agreement and finally Corinne said, "It's a good day when all four Madison girls are at the same dining table. James, you are a fortunate soul."

"I think maybe I am," James said. "Now if you girls can just keep getting along, things will be wonderful."

"Dad!" Helen objected. "How can you even question that? We're all adults here. It's not like it was when we were kids."

Rett lifted her chin, but she said nothing. Evie glanced toward the floor. Dorie, oblivious, was chatting to Mason about dogs.

"Right?" Helen insisted, looking at her sisters.

"I hope so," Rett said soberly.

Evie nodded silently, and Dorie said, "What did I miss?"

"Nothing, really," Corinne told her. "We're just welcoming Helen home."

A Little Bit Like Home

As Helen pulled into Rett's driveway, she got a good view of the house. Old, for sure, ramshackle, too, and in desperate need of renovation. How Rett could put up with such a home was beyond Helen, but she was determined not to criticize. She walked around to the patio door and let herself in.

"Good morning," she chirped, walking into the kitchen where Rett was up to her elbows in bread dough, her long light hair tied back.

"Hi," her sister said, glancing up. "Coffee's over there."

She hung her coat by the back door and filled a mug. "What are you doing today? We could go to Saint Jacques. Shop, get a late lunch, and there's a new show opening at the Carteret Gallery early this evening."

Rett, scowling, dumped dough onto the counter and started kneading. "I don't know what world you think I live in, but I have kids, Helen. Homeschooled kids. I can't just drop everything and head out for all day and all night."

"You don't have to get all huffy about it. I'm a mother, too," Helen shot back. "I just thought you could use a change of scene. Dorie will babysit."

Rett's scowl got deeper. "You didn't ask her, did you?"

Helen looked away, slightly stung. "Well, I might have mentioned it. What are you so annoyed about? I'm just helping."

Rett pounded the dough with a fist, then looked up. "What did Dorie say?"

"She said she thought you needed a break, too, and that she'd be over around three. At three-fifteen, actually."

Rett stopped kneading to look at her. "That's very precise. Precisely when they get back from the library."

Helen smiled. "Exactly. She'll be here when the van drops them off. So we can go now. Get a new perspective. Maybe even get you a new outfit."

Rett glanced down at her flour-dusted leggings and sweater. "What, you don't like my style?"

Helen raised her eyebrows. "It's very cute."

She got a brief grin from Rett, who conceded. "Okay. I probably need a break. But I can't leave. If I don't finish this bread, I'll have wasted the ingredients."

"Let's take it over to Dad's. He'll be happy to bake it for you. Or Evie? Somebody must be at home over there."

"Are you for real? Nobody's hanging around waiting to watch my bread rise. I can't just dump it on Dad."

"Come on, everybody likes to help. You can ask, can't you?"

Rett sighed. "No, I can't. If you want this so bad, you do the asking. I'm just here baking bread." She pulled the dough pile toward her, shaped it into a mound, and covered it with a tea towel.

"Okay." Helen, unperturbed, pulled out her phone. "I'll ask."

Rett slapped butter into a bowl and rubbed it around, chin stuck out. She dumped the dough in and tucked the towel over the top. Still grim, she scrubbed her floury fingers in the sink. By the time her hands were clean, Helen had it all worked out.

"Dad's there, and he's willing to stick around to bake, if he can have a loaf of bread out of it," she announced. "So go get yourself ready to head out on the town."

Rett shook her head. "Out on the town of Saint Jacques on a Tuesday morning. You've got a vivid imagination, Helen."

Helen sipped her coffee with a little smile as Rett stomped up the stairs. Rett definitely needed to get out more.

It was nearly seven p.m. when Helen and Rett pulled into their father's driveway. In the full dark and snow cover, Rett pulled her shopping bags out of the backseat, saying, "Thanks, Helen. See you later."

"Wait!" Helen called as her sister headed toward the tree line behind the house. "I'll drive you home, just wait. You've got to get your bread."

"No, I'm good," Rett called back, moving fast. "Tell Dad I'll see him tomorrow."

Helen gazed after her. It wasn't far to her house, but the walk went through the woods. Why did she have to rush home? A ride would be safer, smarter. Her kids had been fine all afternoon, so why did Rett need to get there right now? Sisters.

Helen headed for the back door of her father's house.

The porch light was on. Dogs scuffled on the other side of the door. She knocked and called out, then pushed in the kitchen door, gently shoving a huge canine greeting committee member aside. "Move it, Custard," she muttered, and the big dog backed away, still wagging. His sibling, Mallow, head-bumped Helen's thigh. She reluctantly patted his head with her free hand. His silky warm head felt good, and she scratched his ear, then unzipped her coat.

"Dad?" she called. "Evie? Who's home?"

The house was quiet, but a noise on the porch activated the dogs again and Evie came through the door.

"Hey," Helen said. "Welcome home."

Evie did not look happy. "You're in my parking spot," she said. "How long are you staying?"

"Well, that's not very nice," Helen admonished. "Why not, 'hello, dear sister, it is so good to see you?' That would be good."

Evie petted a dog, not looking at Helen. "I'm tired and hungry and you're parked in my spot. I'm happy to see you, but now I'm going to have to go out in this cold again."

"So sorry, baby sis," Helen said. "I know you're kidding. Besides, I'll move your car for you if the cold is a big problem. Or Dad will do it."

Evie looked at her and said nothing.

"Come on, Evie, lighten up. I'll move your car. Besides..." Helen rummaged in one of her shopping bags. "Rett and I went to Saint Jacques today."

"I heard," Evie said dryly. "Dorie told me you pressured her into babysitting." She slipped out of her boots and pulled off her coat.

"No pressure," Helen said blithely, sorting through items in her bag. "She was happy to help. Where is that...oh, here it is!" She pulled out a length of silky fabric in a wash of golden yellow, deep oranges and soft browns. "Isn't that gorgeous?"

Evie came closer, running her hand over the cloth. "Oh, it really is."

Helen draped the fabric across Evie's shoulders. "It's perfect," she said smugly. "Your eyes, your hair, your skin...look at that. Perfection!"

"What is it?"

"A shawl, I guess, or you could wear it as a scarf. Doesn't matter, does it, when it's so gorgeous? It's so you."

Evie took the length of material in both hands, spreading it across her front. "Or an overskirt. Or draped, like this." She tossed one end over her shoulder. "Where did you find it?"

"Thrift store," she replied succinctly. "Rett knows all the good ones in Saint Jacques. I had no idea what you can find if you look closely. This is for you."

Evie looked up, eyes wide. "Really? Thank you. Now I feel bad for being so crabby about my parking spot."

Helen laughed. "So you should. Anyway, that's all. I'm going home, so grab your coat and keys and we'll switch places."

"I'm sorry," Evie said, fingering the shawl. "Thank you. Thanks for thinking of me."

"Yeah, well, I'm always looking for blues and greens, like Rett and Dorie and I might wear, but those colours just looked like you."

Evie's smile dimmed slightly, but she turned obediently to get her coat and the two left the kitchen.

Helen backed out so Evie could drive in, then she drove toward the water, heading home, humming. When she turned the last corner to see her townhouse, the lighted windows offered a welcome. The house might be empty, but it didn't need to be dark. Those timers were such a good idea.

All it needed was music. As she unlocked the front door, the fragrance of Italian herbs floated toward her. So smart to put dinner on a timer, too, she thought smugly. Almost like coming home.

Almost! Her traitorous heart lurched, but she firmly tamped it back into place. This was home now. There was a place to hang her coat; her slippers waited in the closet. It was cold comfort, but comfort nevertheless.

She thought about Rett going home to a house warmed by a wood stove, surrounded by her kids, and Dorie at her own house with all those animals. About Evie alone at Dad's until Dad came home. Jake at school. He had called it home. Was it really now? Her heart squeezed at the thought, and she quickly sent him a text.

It's Mum. Thinking of you. Hope you're having a good night.

Despite herself, her mind turned to Reggie and Juliet, imagining them at home for a late dinner. Reg mooning over his new woman and laughing with her children. Her lip curled, but her eyes filled with tears, and she hurried into the kitchen.

She slid the chicken parm onto her favourite plate and tossed the salad. She lit candles for the table, then poured wine when she sat before her tidy meal. Lifting her glass, she whispered, "to home." She looked away from the mockingly empty chair across the table. What was home, anyway?

Tonight, this was it. She sipped, then gently set the fragile glass on the table. Alone or not, she needed to eat.

Running Into the Past

Helen had seen little of Dorie, so she was pleased when her baby sister called later that week. Maybe Dorie wanted to go out for lunch.

That wasn't it.

"Come on out to the Sanctuary," Dorie invited. "Chad's here and we're getting a litter of puppies that are going to need foster homes. They're going to be so cute. You'll love them."

"I thought you helped old dogs," Helen objected.

"We do," Dorie agreed. "That's why this is such a big thing. We hardly ever have puppies, and right now it's only because the County Rescue is over capacity and Mike, the director, thinks I can place them as fosters. In the meantime, things are going to be really fun this afternoon."

"No, thank you," Helen said pertly.

"Puppies? You can say no to puppies?"

"Maybe the kids would like them," Helen demurred. "I don't think it's for me."

"What happened to you?" Dorie demanded. "You used to love dogs even more than me. I remember Maple always slept on your bed. It made me so mad when I was a kid. I wanted him, but he wanted you."

"Dogs are fine," Helen said, brushing at imaginary dog hair on her trousers. "I like them fine. I just think Rett's kids would like your puppies more. That's all."

"I already invited them," Dorie said with some satisfaction. "I just thought it might be fun for you, too. Especially with the kids here. Come on. Be Auntie Helen and play with some puppies."

"No, thanks," she said.

"Well, come over anyway," Dorie insisted. "Rett and the kids are coming for lunch and we're going to have a fun afternoon. I thought you came back to reconnect with the family, and you've hardly spent any time with the kids."

"I certainly have," Helen retorted. "I'm busy this afternoon."

"I just thought you'd like to be invited. Since you're here all alone."

Helen narrowed her eyes. "I'm doing just fine. Thank you, but maybe another time."

"Okay," Dorie said lightly. "Your loss."

The click in Helen's ear sounded snippy, but that was hard to tell. Dorie could be snippy if she wanted. Helen wasn't going to mess around with a bunch of puppies. Puppies would remind her of Mum, and that was a dangerous place right now. Besides, she was going to the gym. Or for a run. Or something. She didn't need her baby sister to make up a social life for her.

No, not the gym. The sunshine drew her outdoors to soak it up, even though it was still wintry cold.

She pulled on layers, starting at the skin and working her way out. All the insulation was making her overheat, so she quickly grabbed gloves and keys and went out. On the porch, she locked the door and tucked the key in the mailbox (nobody would ever look there, she thought, when everyone else in town puts their key under a rock).

A brisk breeze smacked her in the face as soon as she stepped off the porch. Walking quickly down her court, she broke into a slow run when she hit Water Street. The icy air swept by. Her first steps felt uncertain on this snowy mess of pavement. The spectre of falling hit hard, but she was prepared with her mantras: *The first part is the worst part. My body is adjusting. Adjustment isn't danger.*

Running south down Water Street felt terrible, but five minutes later she cut off onto the trail where the packed snow and flat surface allowed her to lean into a familiar rhythm. Right foot, left foot, pounding the trail, one after the other, on and on. Here and now. She warmed enough to partly unzip her jacket without losing her rhythm.

She'd forgotten her music, but that allowed her to pay attention to her surroundings. Along the trail, the mysterious evergreens reached high toward a narrow strip of blue, and the woods resounded with chickadees, crows, and the occasional complaining squirrel. Only the footprints of humans, dogs, and snowshoes were reminders of the village.

One foot, then the other foot, in a soothing rhythm. Here and now.

Unfortunately, she couldn't outrun her thoughts. She had to face this dog thing directly. It was really about Maple. Maple and Mum.

Feet hitting the snowpack one after the other, her mind floated past Dorie's annoyance and back to childhood.

Mum hadn't intended for Helen and Maple to become inseparable, but it happened. The dog arrived by happenstance when Helen was painfully trying to find her place in middle school. The dog became the friend she needed. Later, when newborn Dorie arrived, creating chaos right from the start, Helen took complete responsibility for Maple.

The dog had been a funny one, one ear sticking straight up and the other one bitten off in some early-life dog fight they'd never know about. He'd had short hair but shed as much as those big black behemoths currently at Dad's house. Profoundly attached to Helen, he had slept in her bed as Dorie said, waited with her for the school bus, and hung out by the front door whenever Helen was due home. Even when her teenage life required unusual hours, the dog waited. Mum remarked on it often, but to Helen it was just how things were, she and Maple. She'd had no idea how rare this relationship was, or how much she had counted on it.

In grade twelve, upon her return from the provincial debate team competition, she went to bed for a week. The dog stayed with her. She didn't, couldn't, talk to Mum or anyone about what happened, so she just said she was tired. The experience of the competition was so tainted that she couldn't even acknowledge the win. She felt no pride in helping her team to come in first. Instead, she stayed in her bed, curtains drawn, arm wrapped around her dog.

Her tears wet his fur, and he snuffled closer and licked her face. She had stifled her sobs in her pillow but told the dog everything. He'd keep it quiet; she knew that. You could trust Maple.

Rett had been solicitous at first, giving Helen space by camping out on the living room couch. She became annoyed as Helen's isolation continued. Helen recalled her words as if it had happened yesterday.

"You know I live here, too," Rett shouted through the bedroom door. Their mother replied with something soothing from the hallway, but Rett was unappeased. The door opened and Rett flicked on the light.

"Get out," Helen said automatically.

"What's your deal? I'm just getting some clothes."

Helen pulled the duvet over her head, Maple snuggled under it with her. She heard Rett banging drawers and the closet door, and footsteps approached the bed. "Tomorrow. This is it. I'm back in here tomorrow."

Rett stomped out the door, but Helen's mother's footsteps approached. Helen peered over the top of the duvet. Her mother was looking down at her.

"Whatever it is, you're going to have to face it," she said. "You can't hide in here forever."

"Yes, I can," Helen said fiercely. "I don't, I can't..."

"You can do whatever you have to," her mother said firmly. "What happened in Fredericton?"

Helen swallowed hard. "Nothing." Her chest felt weighted; a giant's palm pressing down, squeezing.

"I understand you don't want to talk about it. That's your choice. But you need to remember that whatever happened is over."

A moment of relief that Mum would not insist on hearing the story opened into a flicker of hope.

"It's over, Helen. You're here now. You're right here." Her mother patted the bed. "Right here, and right now."

Helen's chest eased. Mum was right. What happened was over.

"Here and now," her mother said again. "We both know something happened, but it is over now."

"Right," Helen said weakly. Here and now.

"You don't have to talk about it. You do, however, have to get up and go to school. Tomorrow morning. Got it?"

"Mum..."

"School. Tomorrow." Her mother patted her knee. "Now come downstairs and have some breakfast. The other girls will be out the door for the bus in ten minutes."

After she left the room, Helen burrowed back into the bedclothes, wrapped around Maple. There was no way she could go to school tomorrow, but when Mum said you had to, she usually meant it. The dog licked her ear. Maybe Maple could come, too. Didn't they have dogs to help people?

Going back to school felt hard, but once she got there, it was a non-event. She withdrew from the debate team, citing too much homework, and focused on getting into university so she could get out of New Brunswick. Her fights with Rett escalated.

Rett was just so irritating. They had nothing in common anymore. Rett was a star on the field hockey team, but Helen couldn't stand watching the sport. Rett played basketball in the winter, but Helen went to the library to study. With some shame, Helen remembered snapping at Rett about a book she recommended.

"You should read it, Helen," her sister urged. "You'd love it."

"That's just childish," she snapped at her. "I'm reading classics."

Rett made a face. "Boring."

"You watch. I'm going somewhere. I'm not staying in this crummy place."

By the following August, she'd made good on that promise, heading to Halifax for university. She'd left her connection to her sister long before.

She left them all, including her beloved dog. At eighteen, she imagined her whole life ahead, somewhere else. Someplace with big buildings, lots of people. Anonymity. Starting with going to Halifax for university.

Maple.... What had happened to him? She remembered climbing into the minivan, Dad driving, Mum in the passenger seat, ceremoniously driving her to university, a province away. She had gazed back once toward the house. Maple sat on the porch with Corinne, Rett, and Evie. Dorie, little Dorie, was on her knees hugging the dog, no doubt crying. Dorie, nearly three, cried a lot and adored her biggest sister.

Helen always thought of Dorie and Maple together, not only because Maple sparked Dorie's affection for dogs, but because they were the two creatures in the family who loved her without expectations. That was true love, Helen thought now. Too bad she'd not realized how rare it was.

That glance had been her last glimpse of Maple, who died before the Thanksgiving holiday. Age-related causes, Mum had said. Nothing anyone could do. Helen had a hole in her chest for a while whenever she thought about Maple, so she did her best to avoid thinking about the dog. Instead, she focused on her studies and besides, she met Reg when she went back to uni. Having a boyfriend helped take her mind off the loss.

Now on the trail, her pounding steps slowed with fatigue despite her busy mind. Walking briskly, she tugged her zipper down further. Dear Maple. She'd not thought about that dog for years. There had been other dogs; her mother always had dogs around the house. None of them measured up to Maple. There would be no more dogs for her. Losing dogs hurt.

Jake had asked for a dog. She vetoed the idea, though Reg had wanted to consider it. She knew neither Jake nor Reg would follow through to walk it, take it to the vet, figure out what kind of special food it needed. All of that would end up on her plate, and she wasn't up to it, no matter how much Jake begged. Now, though, she wondered if things would have been different if they had let Jake get a dog. Jake would enjoy Dorie's puppies, but that thought brought her right back to puppies in general.

She'd rather run than let puppies drool all over her, but the memory of the sweet softness of puppy fur made her catch her breath for a moment — or maybe that was a result of running. There was no point in getting all mushy. Maple was a memory. Puppies were a non-starter. In any case, right here, tired from her run, this was where she'd rather be, not at Dorie's barn covered with puppies.

The cold began to penetrate, so she picked up the pace to an easy jog.

Puppies made her think of Mum. Dad's house was so empty, even with Evie and Dad both there. If Mum hadn't died what would she say about Helen's current predicament? With a sudden burst of fear she thought, *if there is a heaven, Mum is there and she most certainly knows everything that's happened. Everything I've done.* Then the fear subsided into the rhythm of the run, the thump, thump of her feet on the packed snow, the sound of her breath, the occasional caw of an avian sentry and a flurry of white cascading from the big pines overhead. Here and now.

She had a moment of being present to the running, the cawing, the snow falling, and then she was back again — to Reggie's face as he told her he was moving in with Juliet ("I just can't take the coldness anymore..."), to Jake's haunted look when they told him about the separation, and his most recent final words to her about the move. Slipping further back, she recalled her last dinner out with Jean-Louis. He'd held her hand over the crème brûlée and slipped the diamond tennis bracelet on her wrist. The sparkle of the jewels repeated in his eyes, wreathed in wrinkles, his grey mustache hovering over his smile.

Jean-Louis. At least he had wanted her around.

It's true he was an old man, an old man who was her partner's client, and of course she should not have been going to dinner with him. Or drinks. Or for long drives in the country. But he made her feel good during a time when she was sure she'd never feel good again, and so she did those things. Not proud but not ashamed, either. Well, not entirely ashamed, until — well, until later. Clamping down on the flow of memories, Helen brought her attention back to the trail, her legs, and her lungs. Here and now. Here and now.

Fatigue sent palpable waves through her legs. She stopped again and reached for the bottle attached to her belt. Swigging water, she checked her wristwatch to see she'd already gone seven kilometres. She could turn around now and call it a pretty good day. Or go a little further and make it a solid fifteen after the turnaround. Casting a glance behind her, she headed further down the trail. After all, nobody was waiting for her at home.

Dad Tells It Like It Is

Monday morning, early, James called Helen. "I want you to come over," he said bluntly. "I need to talk to you."

"What is it, Dad?" she asked while frantically searching for her bag. "Is something wrong? Can I call an ambulance?"

"Geesh!" James exploded. "Helen, I'm fine. Would you for Pete's sake just come on over here? I'll make you coffee."

Helen thought about her father's stovetop percolator. "Maybe just a cup of tea," she suggested. "I can be there in twenty minutes." That would give her time to pick up a treat for them to share. Diabetic-friendly, of course.

"Just come," he said sharply. "You don't need to bring anything."

Was he a mind reader? "Sure, Dad, got it."

The screen door off the back porch was unlocked. "Dad!" she called as she entered the kitchen. The electric kettle was steaming on the counter.

James walked in from the living room. "Helen," he said. He wasn't smiling as he went to the counter to pour hot water into the old brown betty teapot. Helen recalled her mother making tea just that way every morning of her childhood. James slipped the cozy over the pot and carried it to the table.

"Get yourself a cup," he said, nodding toward the cupboard.

"Sure," she agreed. "One for you?"

He shook his head. "I'm onto coffee already." His mug was on the table. "Sit," he said, taking a chair himself.

Helen's stomach was tight. "What's going on, Dad? Are you feeling okay?"

He gave her a look of exasperation. "I told you, I'm fine. It's you I'm wondering about."

"Me?" Confounded, she frowned. "There's nothing wrong with me."

"That's not how I hear it," he said grimly. "If there was nothing wrong, why don't any of your sisters want to spend time with you?"

She scoffed. "Dad, I don't know what you're talking about. I see a sister at least once a week."

"That sounds like a program," he said, still grim.

"Well, it is a kind of program," Helen admitted. "I like to be systematic about things. If I plan to see one sister weekly, then I won't be too far out of touch."

James gazed at her with that look she remembered so well, the one that made her keep talking. It still worked.

"I never lived near family, so I have to program this stuff into my schedule," she explained, despite feeling like she was digging herself a hole. "It's good to spend time with family members every week, so that's what I'm doing."

"Whether you like it or not?" James' eyebrows raised even as he sipped his coffee.

"Of course I like it," she protested. "They're my sisters."

"And there's something wrong with every one of them, isn't there?" he asked, still not smiling.

"Dad, I thought you'd appreciate my support for their issues."

"What issues are those, Helen?" James' normally mild tone sharpened. "You see issues with your sisters, and you think I want you to do something about that?"

"Look at what Rett's doing. I mean, come on. She's ruining her career, with that part time stopgap job at the Downtown Clinic. They're paying her practically nothing. She could do so much better." She stood and paced the kitchen as she talked. "I had no idea she considered moving back here to be a good move. I just thought it was a temporary fix. There's no life for her in Stella Mare. She's too good for the jobs here. And that house. It's awful."

James, eyes narrowed, sipped away.

"Evie thinks she needs to go back to school to become, what? An academic? Like what kind of idea is that? Do you know how hard it is to get an academic job? Tenure is becoming extinct and besides, she's not the brightest bulb in the box, is she?"

Her father sat in silence.

"Evie was never good in school, Dad, you have to remember. Why does she think this is even possible now?" She turned at the kitchen sink and leaned back on her elbows. "I can't believe both of them have made such poor decisions. Throwing their lives away." She made an impatient noise, a harrumph.

"And Dorie? How are you judging Dorie?" James asked after another silence. "I assume that sister isn't doing the right thing either."

"Don't be mad," she implored, heading for the table. She slid back into her chair. "I just hate to see my sisters ruining their lives."

"Ruining, eh? What about Dorie?"

"Dorie's going to marry a man who doesn't even have a job, Dad. He's the most socially awkward human I ever met, and she spends her days cleaning up after a bunch of old dogs. What kind of life is that? What kind of career is she making? I just think she could do so much better."

James set his cup on the oak table with a distinct thunk, then he leaned his chair back so it rested on two legs. When he looked at her from that distance, she felt about twelve and like she'd done something very wrong. Like Dad could see right into her heart where there was a black mark. A mark that told everyone she was a liar, or maybe a cheater, or she'd been mean to her sisters. Or worse. Much worse.

"I think you're wrong about your sisters," he said, "but they aren't the issue. What really happened in Ottawa?" Now his voice was typical Dad, mild yet penetrating. "What made you come back at this stage of your life, Jake in high school, Reg's business taking off, and you doing so well in your practice? Seems like a strange time to cash out your partnership and hightail it for New Brunswick."

"I told you," she said, heart pounding. "With Jake living away at boarding school, I realized Reg and I had grown apart. It's that simple."

Her father sat forward, the chair legs clapping on the tile floor. "Big life changes are never simple," he said. "You can tell the story like it's simple. It's never simple."

He was right. All the other stuff, the details, the half-truths, the assumptions and attributions, the horrible shame, the guilt... Her field of vision shrank. She drew a choking breath. "Dad..."

"No, you listen to me. You were always the golden child, Helen, our first daughter, so special and so smart that we told you the world was yours. You could do anything you wanted to do. So you did. You went away to Halifax for university, even though your mother wanted you closer to home, and you went off to law school in Toronto, and then you and Reg decided on Ottawa, even though you were both Maritime kids. You did whatever you wanted to do, and you did it well. And yes, we were proud of you and your successes."

There was a moment of silence. Wondering what she should say, Helen offered, "Thank you."

"Yeah, well," he went on. "You stayed away, kept yourself to yourself. That way, you were always our golden child."

"I was far away," she protested. "I had a practice to build, a child to raise."

"I'm not criticizing, daughter. I'm just observing. You're here now, and you've given me some things to observe."

Helen felt a flash of anger. "I'm not perfect. So what?"

"You don't have to be perfect," he said. "But you have to trust that we'll still be here even if you're not."

What was he talking about? "I know you're here," she said querulously. "Where else?"

"When you're ready to tell me why you're actually back here, I'll be here. But in the meantime, I have a bone to pick with you."

"A bone? What are you talking about?"

"Your sisters love you. They're all happy you came back. But somehow you've annoyed each one of them enough that I've heard about it. I suspect it has something to do with your idea that they need fixing, but maybe that's just an old man talking."

"Who's annoyed with me?" She was irritated at the very thought. How dare they?

"Everybody. Even your sister Evie, who never complains about her sisters. I expect you've even got some ideas about how I should live my life."

He really was a mind reader. "Of course not, Dad. You're fine," she said, but she couldn't meet his eyes.

"Something's happened between you girls and I expect you to put it right," he said. "Just fix it."

"Is this why I had to come over right now?" She was incensed. "I thought there was an emergency."

He glared at her. "This is an emergency. You left here twenty years ago. You couldn't wait to see Stella Mare and your family in your rear-view mirror."

"That's unfair!"

"You left and you didn't come back, and that was your choice, your decision." James spoke heavily. "There are consequences to every decision, though. You could think about that while you're planning how to revamp your sisters' lives."

Helen's eyes smarted. "You are accusing me of something and I don't even know what."

James' face softened. "Just think, Helen, how you'd feel if your sister Rett showed up in Ottawa to tell you all the ways you'd screwed up your life."

She opened her mouth to protest, but then closed it. That was a terrible thought. "You might have a point," she conceded.

"You've been under our radar, and I guess I didn't even realize it," he added. "I believed everything was great, but now you're here in Stella Mare and not talking about why. Maybe, just maybe, things were a dite more challenging than we all realized."

She sank into her chair, hands over her face. "You have no idea," she murmured. Challenging? A wave of despair washed over her. Dad could never imagine the mess. The last four months had been enough to make her question her survival. Or her sanity. Tears seeped through her fingers.

"Aw, now, Helen." Her father lumbered to his feet and rounded the table to pat her shoulders. "It must have been hard." He handed her a paper napkin.

With an effort, she pulled herself back to the old kitchen. He was trying to help. She sniffled and wiped her eyes. "When I got here, I realized Mum's really gone."

"What? It's been over six years. I know we all miss her, but time passes."

"Not for me," she said thickly. "It was one thing to visit for a couple of days. I could pretend she was in Saint Jacques or Fredericton, visiting. But living here, I can't fake it anymore. She's really, truly gone."

She swiped at her eyes again. Dear Mum, the touchstone, who could keep you on track just because she was alive, even far away. This sudden realization was like a breeze blowing through her mind. Maybe that's part of what happened, she thought. I lost my guiding light.

Best keep that one to myself.

James walked toward the counter, where he leaned on his palms to look out the window. He gave a sniff. "I never thought about that," he said. "It's almost like a new thing for you."

She made a sound halfway between a giggle and a sob. "Kind of silly, but it's really hit me since being here. Every time I walk into this house, I expect to see her. Hear her voice."

He turned back toward her and leaned back against the counter. "Getting over that took me a good long time," he said. "I don't feel it all the time now, but it was hard when you got here and I had all my girls together. All four of you and Corinne, and only Aggie was missing."

"Oh, Dad." She got up to embrace him, feeling his hard palms gripping her biceps. Then he pushed her away and looked into her eyes.

"You see, you have to fix things with your sisters. I can't have you four girls here not getting along."

She nodded. She got it. "Okay. I'll figure something out."

Snow and Sisterhood

Would spring ever come? The St. Patrick's Day blizzard arrived a little ahead of schedule, followed by a warming trend that left ice everywhere. Despite being only days from the vernal equinox, it was decidedly winter.

Helen was about done with the Maritimes. She'd had plenty of snow in Ottawa — it was supposedly the snowiest capital in the world — but this unrelenting icy, sleety, messy stuff left her with grey days, freezing rain on top of soggy snow, then a cold snap that resulted in sleet icing everything. When the power went out for the fourth time in a week, she reached her limit and called Rett.

"Can I come over?" she asked. "It's miserable here. I'm so cold I can't function and besides, my laptop battery ran out."

Rett was mildly welcoming. "Sure you can. Just remember that there's a lot going on here. You might not like the chaos."

"I'll appreciate your woodstove, though," she said. "Besides, I'm a lawyer. I can tolerate chaos."

Rett snorted. "I always figured you were a lawyer because you hated chaos, and it was a way to make all the pieces fit."

Helen huffed. "Shows what you know about my job," she said, but with good humour.

She considered driving the short distance to Rett's house, but decided exercise would be better, so she walked the kilometre, muttering under her breath each time she slipped on the icy sidewalks. Across Water Street and around the corner on Prince, a bucket truck from the power company was at work cutting branches away from the power lines. She waved to the worker directing traffic and kept her distance.

The insidious sleety mix penetrated her outerwear, slipping inside her collar. She shrugged and tried to hurry, but the treacherous footing kept her slow. "Well, this is miserable," she muttered, now wishing she'd taken the car. When she got to Rett's street, the scent of wood smoke buoyed her along. Just a few more houses to get to Rett's driveway. Taking the moral high ground about getting exercise was not her smartest move. Maybe learn something, Helen. A sleet storm is not the time for a walk.

The latest snow banked the sides of the driveway a little, so she climbed up to tread on the snow-covered lawn instead of the pavement. At least here she could feel a bit of traction. Sweat gathered in the small of her back as she stared at the goal: Rett's front door. Just a few more steps. Never had the ramshackle old house looked so good. As soon as her foot hit the porch, the front door creaked open.

Mason, Rett's nine-year-old, shouted, "Aunt Helen's here!"

She breached the door with relief, met with the fragrance of freshly baked bread, wood smoke, and coffee. She couldn't wait to shuck her wet clothes and have a hot drink.

"Did you walk?" Rett asked, horrified. "It's awful out there."

"Yes, it is," she agreed, taking off her coat and holding it at arms' length. "Where do you want me to put this thing?"

"Is there ice on it?" Mason wanted to know.

Rett looked closely. "Well, look at that. Ice forming on your coat, Helen. Next time, use the car." She draped the coat over the back of a chair near the wood-burning stove.

"I was just telling myself that," she agreed. "I don't know what I was thinking."

Rett looked quizzical. "Maybe hotshot lawyer from Ottawa shows the provincial locals how to handle winter weather?"

Helen sighed. "Yeah, maybe a little of that. The lawyer from Ottawa seems to have forgotten that she used to be a girl from the Maritimes."

Her sister looked amused. "Funny. Get those boots off and I'll get us some coffee."

"I smell bread," she said.

Rett turned back, eyebrows up. "Bread, Helen? You'd eat bread?"

"To heck with carbs," Helen declared. "I narrowly escaped a Maritime winter sleet storm. I need sustenance."

"What did you escape?" Her six-year-old niece, Callie, was intrigued. "What was out there?"

"Something scary?" asked Callie's twin, Maggie, always ready to be frightened.

"Just the sleet," Helen said. "Cold and messy and slippery."

"Oh," Maggie said, bored, and turned back to her toys.

Helen followed Rett to the kitchen, where an old camping lantern cast a weird glow. "How do you have coffee?" she asked. "Wood stove?"

"Well, I could, I guess," Rett said, "but I'd just made a pot when the power went out, so I poured it into the big Thermos." She handed over a mug.

"Ahh." Helen relished the scent and the warmth on her hands, then sipped appreciatively. "Where's that bread?"

"Right." Rett pulled a checked tea towel from a partial loaf on the counter. "Butter?"

"You bet," she said. "I'm going to enjoy this."

The sisters sat at the kitchen table while Helen sank teeth into the warm bread with melting butter. The sleet clattered against the big windows, and it was so gloomy outside Helen could barely see the shed where Rett kept chickens and goats.

"What do they do on a day like this?" she asked, jerking her head toward the backyard. "You must have been out there to feed them, right?"

Rett scoffed. "Oh, yes. Milked the nanny goat, too, and picked eggs. Life goes on even when there's a storm and the power is out."

"How about Dad? Is he okay?"

"You can ask him," Rett said. "I'm not the keeper of information, you know."

"Right," she agreed, and pulled out her phone. She called the landline first, but got a message about the circuits being out of service, so sent him a text.

"He says they're fine," she reported, phone in hand. "Warm enough."

"Then I guess everything is just fine," Rett said with a smile. "Look, I'm going to put this pot of soup on the back of the woodstove. It's frozen now, but it'll be ready for lunch."

"You're really good at this emergency homemaking stuff. How often does the power go out?" Helen asked.

"Often enough," Rett remarked dryly. "You'll get used to it. You grew up with it."

Helen could barely remember. She followed her sister back into the living room where the girls were playing school with their dolls, and Mason was fitting Lego pieces together.

"Mum, can we watch Frozen?" Callie asked.

"Power's out," Mason reminded her.

She started to complain, but Rett interceded. "Nobody loves it when the power goes out, but we're like pioneers here. We have firewood so we're warm and dry, we have lots of food, you kids have toys and books, and now we have Aunt Helen visiting. You can watch Frozen another time."

"Did the power go out when you were kids?" Mason asked from his Lego table.

"It must have, but I don't really remember," Helen said. "Rett?"

Rett considered. "I remember only one time, but I'm sure it happened a lot more than that. But this one time, we were still in high school, Helen. It was out for a week."

Helen pondered. "Really? A week? You'd think I could remember something like that."

"Of course you can. The storm lasted two days, but it took five before they restored power to our street. Remember Mum kept inviting the neighbours in because we had the woodstove? Old Mrs. Lewis next door, Brenda Smithers and her girls. Didn't Billy what's-his-name come over? That guy who had a crush on you?"

"Billy who?" Helen licked the melted butter off her fingers. "I don't remember a Billy. But I remember those little kids, Aurora and Honey Smithers."

"I work with Honey now," Rett reminded her. "She's the receptionist at the downtown clinic."

"Oh, that clinic," Helen disparaged. "How long do you plan to be there?"

Rett stuck another log in the stove after poking the coals. There was a long moment before she turned back to Helen. "Let's not go there, okay? We're going to be here for a while, so let's avoid problem topics."

"Agree to disagree? I can do that," Helen said. "If I must."

Rett looked amused. "You must. At least for the duration of this ice storm, while my bad choices are providing you with warmth and shelter and homemade bread."

"Okay, I get it. Please stop."

"I'm not asking you to stop giving advice forever, you know. I do need my big sister at times."

Helen knew she did. Rett hadn't hesitated to call her for advice all last fall. She resisted the urge to point that out and took her dishes to the sink. "Do your kids know how to play charades?"

"They're kind of little for that, but I bet we can get a whopper game of Go Fish happening."

The games were over and the kids snoozed, wrapped in blankets in front of the wood stove.

"When does winter end here?" Helen asked. "It's been March forever."

"June is coming," Rett said, cocking her head. "I'm sure you remember."

"It's probably been too many years for me to really remember," she said. She tried to recall long June days, daylight persisting until after ten pm, and birdsong heralding the dawn before six. Imagining it during a wintry storm was hard, though. "I'm complaining again, aren't I?"

"You are," Rett agreed. "But everybody complains about the weather this time of year."

"I guess it could even snow on Easter."

"It could, and it has. I think Dorie's having Easter dinner this year."

"That's good. I'm going to tell Jake to come. He hasn't been to Stella Mare for a long time."

"Dad would love it," Rett said with a grin. "All the rest of us, too."

Helen thought about 'the rest of us.' It was a motley crew, not like Ottawa. "He's never met the twins, and Mason was only two the last time he was here," she said. "It might not be on the top of his list, but I think it would be good for him to come."

"Good for you, too."

"Yes. I miss him," she said simply. "I'll tell him once I can email again."

By late evening, the power flickered back on, lights brightening the kitchen and living room, where the kids and Charlie the dog were asleep under a pile of blankets in front of the stove. Rett and Helen had been sitting on the couch. Rett got up and stretched. "Let's get the chickens into bed," she said.

Mason sat up and rubbed his eyes. "Is it morning?"

"Not yet," Helen told him. "It's time to go to bed, though. The power's back on." She helped him gather his blankets, then hoisted Maggie to her shoulder. The little girl squirmed to settle herself against Helen, head tucked into Helen's neck, still clutching a blanket. Helen wrapped the trailing corner around the child with her free hand, then headed for the stairs. It had been a very long time since she'd carried a sleeping child. In fact, she couldn't remember doing it with Jake, but she must have.

She tucked Maggie into the bed she shared with Callie and brushed a strand of hair off the child's cheek. Sweetness, that's what sleeping children were. She turned to see Rett tucking in Callie. Was it so long since she and Rett had shared a bed? Mum coming to read stories, hear prayers, tuck them in? It felt like forever, but Rett's eyes in the dusky gloom were just the same now as they had been so long ago. Helen slipped quietly into the hall, leaving Rett to finish settling her children.

A kerfuffle drew her to the next room, though, so she stuck her head in to see Mason and Charlie the dog sorting themselves out on the bed. "Everything okay?" she asked quietly, stepping forward to pull the blanket up to Mason's chin.

"Mmm hmm," he murmured. "Charlie's here." His eyes fluttered closed. The dog groaned out a sigh and stretched out back-to-back with the child.

"Goodnight, Mason," she whispered, and backed out to the hallway and down the stairs.

When Rett returned to the living room, Helen handed her a glass of wine. "I should probably go home," she said.

Rett laughed. "You poured yourself a glass, too, didn't you? You're not going anywhere."

"Right. It's not sleeting anymore, but the walking will be awful."

"Better in the morning when you can see, at least," Rett agreed. "But the only place to sleep is right here, on the couch. Hardly luxury accommodations."

"When have I ever needed luxury?" she demanded. Rett just raised her eyebrows. "Well, okay, I appreciate luxury, I'll give you that. But I don't require it."

"Right. The couch is yours."

"Thank you. Good night."

A Chat with Evie

By mid-morning the roads had been cleared and sanded, and even the sidewalks were safe for walkers, so Helen returned home. Back to business as usual, whatever that was.

Her email to Jake went unanswered all day, so she sent a text. He read the text, but didn't answer, so she sent another. This time she got a terse reply.

I'll talk to Dad.

Scowling, she texted Reggie.

I invited Jake for Easter but he says he has to talk to you. What's up?

No answer. She sent another, then got a note that Reg had turned notifications off. "Frig!" She tossed the phone on the couch in her living room. The weather was still miserable, her son was cryptic, and her ex-husband was incommunicado.

Only one thing to do. Well, she could go for a run but the trail was likely to be icy, so she grabbed her ever-ready gym bag and headed out to move some iron. That's what she needed. When everybody in the world was trying to keep her from her goals, it was time to push some heavy weight around. At least this way she might avoid yelling at her sisters.

An hour at the gym cured a lot of ills. Leaving the gym pleasantly tired, she stopped at her father's house on the way home. She rapped once at the kitchen door, and then pushed it open. Mallow and Custard rustled from the living room to wag a greeting and got an absent pat. Evie looked up from the table where she was gazing at an old book.

"Hi."

"Is Dad here?"

"Hi, Helen," Evie repeated. "Come in."

"I'm in," she announced. "Where's Dad?"

"Is he expecting you? I don't know where he is," Evie said.

Helen stuck her face in the doorway to the living room. "He said he'd be here."

"Well, he's not."

Her head snapped around at Evie's uncharacteristically sharp tone. "What's got into you?"

"You could notice I'm here," her sister said tiredly. "Have a conversation."

Helen lifted her chin, marched to the table, and sat. "Okay. I'm here. What do you want to talk about?"

"This will not work." Evie closed her book. "I'm sorry I brought it up." She slid back her chair.

"No, wait." Helen put out a hand. "What's that you're reading?"

Evie touched the book's cover. "Just something for my project. About women's work in the nineteenth century."

"Women's work!" Helen scoffed. "Come on, Evie. Is anybody interested in that stuff, really?"

"I am," Evie said, injured. "But obviously you're not."

"Well, what do you expect? Nobody lives like that now."

Evie's face grew red. "Do you have to be so nasty?"

"I'm not nasty," Helen declared. "I just tell the truth."

"I shouldn't have expected anything." Evie sighed. "You never liked me, so I'm not surprised that you still don't like me. I am surprised that it still hurts."

"What? Where did you get that idea? What did I ever do?"

Her sister looked at the floor. "You were always too busy, too smart, too whatever, to bother with me. When you went away, you never got in touch with me. You didn't come to my graduation, from high school or university. You never called me. It was always Helen and Rett. You and Rett were a pair. And then Dorie. She was always your baby. Yours and Mum's. Like everyone just skipped over me, the third girl, the extra one."

"I had no idea." Helen propped her chin on her fist. "You were skipped over?"

"The one that didn't belong," Evie said grimly. "I still don't belong."

"What are you talking about? Of course you belong. That doesn't make sense."

"Look at me. I don't even look like a Madison. And you and Rett have kids. I don't have kids. Maybe I won't ever get to have kids."

"Of course you look like our family. You look just like Grandma Sarah."

Evie's face relaxed a bit. "I thought so, but it's only from looking at old pictures. You're the first person to say that."

"Don't you remember Grandma?"

Evie was quiet, then said, "Maybe? Not really."

Helen leaned back in her chair. "She had dark hair like you. Not when she lived here with us, but when she was young. Dark, curly hair.

Mum didn't look like her at all; Mum looked a lot more like her Aunt Hannah, or whatever her name was."

Evie looked excited. "Aunt Hannah. I read her journal. She's the reason I've gotten into domestic artifacts, like Great-grandmother Leonie's hooked rugs. She was tall and light, like Mum and the rest of you."

"Those genes came from somewhere, but who knows?" Helen said lightly. "So you are a Madison. You just reflect a different part of the family."

"I suppose."

"I never didn't like you," she said, clumsily. "I like you just fine. I guess I don't know you very well."

"Maybe that goes both ways," Evie said.

"Probably."

A moment passed.

"Can I ask you something?" When Evie nodded, Helen drew a breath. "If you want a baby, why are you going to graduate school? You're not so young anymore."

Evie sighed. "Thirty-six. I know."

"What's with that boyfriend of yours? Can't you light a fire under him to get the baby thing going?" She poured more tea into her cup. "You can go back to school later."

"I don't know about that," Evie said. "Stephen and I are still new, you know. Babies are not exactly on the agenda."

Helen looked up. "Then put them on it! How are you going to get what you want if you don't go for it?"

"I don't know, Helen," her sister objected. "That's not how things work with us."

She scoffed. "Well, babies get harder to make as you get older, and PhDs are a dime a dozen, as Mum would have said."

Evie looked horrified. "Mum would never have said that about a PhD. She respected education. Look how she supported you."

Helen, taken aback, got quiet. "Did she? I don't remember that."

"She told everybody about her daughter going to law school, doing the family proud." Evie spoke as if telling a story. "Her Helen, a lawyer. Nobody in the family had ever been a lawyer before. Nobody except Dad ever went to university, really, except Aunt Hannah went to Teacher's College, but that was back in the day."

"Well, Corinne," Helen corrected. "She went to university to be a social worker."

"Right," Evie conceded. "I always think of her as part of our generation, though, not Mum's, even though they were sisters."

"It's the age gap," Helen agreed.

"And the fact that she lived with us while she was a teenager," Evie added. "Sometimes she feels like an aunt, and sometimes like another sister."

"She was like a sister to me," Helen agreed. "We're only twelve years apart in age."

"Just like me and Dorie," Evie noted. "Only we're in the same generation."

Helen reflected for a moment on families. "Families are shrinking," she said. "Grandma Sarah was one of twelve, and she only had eight. Mum had four."

"The fourth one being a bit of a shock," Evie said with a grin. "But don't repeat that to Dorie."

"I remember." Helen smiled. "I remember Mum and Grandma and Corinne all laughing about how things carry down a generation. Corinne arriving when Grandma was over forty, and then Mum doing the same."

"Maybe over forty will be my time, too," Evie said, a bit sadly. "I didn't want to wait so long, though. I expected Jase and I would have a houseful by now."

Helen scoffed. "Jase. He was never going to work out."

Evie looked up, surprised. "Did you think that before? Why didn't you tell me?"

"Oh, you know," she demurred. But she wondered if she really had thought that before. Or maybe she was so far away, she didn't waste thought on her sister's choices in men or otherwise. Well, now she was here. Things were different now. She could take an active role in her sisters' lives.

"I think you should give Stephen an ultimatum," she said firmly. "A baby or you're done."

"You're out of your mind," Evie said. "I'm waiting to hear about grad school for fall, and you think I should argue to start a family immediately? That's just nuts."

"Tick, tick, tick." Helen gave her best clock imitation. "That's your biological clock."

Evie frowned. "I get the reference."

"I'll help," Helen offered. "I can make suggestions."

Evie stood up, shaking her head. "Absolutely not. Do not talk to Stephen about this. Are you hearing me?"

Helen hummed a little tune, sipping her tea.

"Helen, I mean it," Evie warned. "That's a bad idea."

"Okay, okay," she agreed. "Your way."

A scuffle of dogs from the sunporch announced a new arrival. The big black dogs hit the kitchen about the same time James pushed open the outer door.

"Daughters!" he said, cheerily. "Good to see you." He bent over to greet Custard and Mallow, who accepted his caresses, then wandered back through the living room. James hung up his coat. "Any supper for an old man?" he asked with an impish grin.

Evie scoffed. "Leftovers."

"Leftovers are great," Helen enthused. "Let's see what's in here." She opened the refrigerator and started pulling out containers.

"If you're doing that," Evie said, "I've got some things to finish up for work." She headed toward the little room off the kitchen that had become her office. Helen hummed tunelessly as she checked for food.

"Look at this! Salad makings, leftover roast chicken, and even some rice. Excellent."

"I guess you're staying for supper, then," James said.

She threw him a quick look. "If that's okay with you."

He shrugged. "Always good to see you. Besides, Corinne might show up, like as not."

"Great. I'd like to see her." Helen busied herself with the food. "You could call her, maybe."

"I could," James said, "but I'm not going to. She comes when she wants to."

"You don't want to plan?" Helen asked, plaintive.

"Plan what? You're cooking leftovers," he reminded. "Besides, family gets to just show up. Like you did."

"I guess," she said. "But I would like to know how many plates to put on the table."

James chuckled. "That sounds a dite like your mother. She loved having people just show up, but sometimes she stressed a little about making sure everyone had what they needed."

"Hmm," Helen murmured. She remembered her mother inviting everyone and his brother to the house for meals. She used to say they could always add another potato to the pot. It was fun when they were little, never being certain who would show up, especially for Sunday evening, when Agnes cooked a big pot of soup or chowder and baked bread. She remembered, too, during her last year in high school when the uncertainty was overwhelming, and she often stayed in her room to study when the house had unexpected guests. She felt a little annoyed. "Mum cared more about strangers than the people who lived in the house," she said a little sharply.

"Prob'ly seemed like that to you girls, betimes," James said placidly. "Aggie cared a lot about everybody, and it wore her out."

Soothed, Helen continued to set the table. "I'm going to put a place for Corinne," she decided, "and then she'll be welcome if she shows up."

James got heavily to his feet and patted her shoulder. "You're very much like her," he said, and headed toward the living room, leaving Helen to gaze after him, plate in hand. He was clearly losing it. *I couldn't be more different from Mum.*

Dinner Conversation

Helen, Evie, and their father, sat in the kitchen in the lingering light of the early spring evening, passing food. When Corinne arrived on the back porch, James cast Helen a meaningful glance.

"Come in," Evie said. "Helen made dinner."

"I made leftovers," Helen demurred.

"Food is food," Corinne said with a smile. "Thanks for the welcome."

After dinner, Evie pulled rhubarb squares from the freezer and made a pot of tea. "They'll take a few minutes to thaw out," she said, "but we can chat. Stephen's coming over, too."

Corinne leaned back, pulling her tea mug closer. "How's the adjustment, Helen? How are you doing?"

"I hadn't thought about it," she said, surprised. "Okay, I guess. I've been running a lot."

"Running? Away or toward?" Corinne smiled as she posed the question, but Helen knew it was a serious inquiry.

"Ah, that's still unclear," she said. "I don't know what's next yet, if that's what you mean. I could be running in circles. Not really getting anywhere."

"Where do you want to get?" Evie asked.

Helen shrugged. "I don't know. I'd like to feel more at home here, I know that."

James frowned. "You are at home. This was your home for your whole life."

"Not the last twenty years, Dad," she reminded him.

"Oh, well, twenty years is nothin'," he scoffed; Corinne choked on her tea. Helen caught Evie's eye with a tiny smile and shake of her head. Dad was always Dad.

"It's not nothing, Dad," she reminded.

"Well, maybe it seems long to you girls. Half your life, and all that."

"To an old guy like you, it's short," Corinne said, grinning. "Even to me it doesn't seem like a very long time, but it's Helen's entire adult life."

Helen felt those words like a weight on her back. "Makes me miss Mum," she said quietly. "Might be why I keep trying to give everybody advice they don't want." She shot a glance toward Evie.

"Still the big sister," James agreed.

She was the big sister, the one who had left to create a fulfilling life elsewhere.

Fulfilling. Ha. If her life was so fulfilling, why was she back? She shook it off. "I don't know about work, but I know I'm here and I'm staying. Maybe I'll be lawyering, or maybe something else."

"Like what?" Corinne asked curiously. "It's a big deal to change professions."

Shifting uncomfortably in her chair, Helen said, "But look at Evie. She's shifting careers and doing it well, right?"

Evie looked at her. "Thanks."

"It's true," James added. "Going back to school isn't an easy decision when you're what, twenty-five?"

"Dad," Evie said impatiently. "You know perfectly well I'm thirty-six."

"Whatever." He was genial. "You know us old guys. We don't have a good sense of time anyway." He grinned at Evie and winked at Corinne. "I know how old you are, Evelyn. It's a good thing to learn something new. Even us old guys can learn something new."

"Thanks, Dad," Evie said. "Why are we talking about me? I thought we were talking about Helen's future."

"Because I don't have a clue about my future," Helen said wryly, getting up. "How are those rhubarb squares doing?"

After Stephen joined them, they lingered at the old table, chatting. This kind of thing hadn't happened in Ottawa. Nobody came for leftovers and stayed to just hang out. At least not in Helen's experience. She leaned back in her chair.

The old house had its own noises, barely registered under the conversation; the roar of the furnace in the basement, creaks from the eaves. James' big dogs, banished to the sunporch, snored in tandem. Helen leaned further to look toward them, noting the long light still glowing through the living room. Daylight lasted longer now that it was April. Long days didn't seem to change the wintry weather, though. She sighed. Spring couldn't come soon enough.

Her phone pinged. "Sorry," she said, gesturing. "I've been waiting to hear from Jake." She clicked on the notification, but the text was from Reggie, so she shut it down.

"Did you know Evie's going to North Carolina?" James asked Helen and Corinne.

"For Easter," Evie put in.

"That's great," Corinne said, sounding approving. Helen was less certain.

"She gets to meet my family and see my university," Stephen put in. "We'll visit the place where I teach."

Helen was confused. "You teach there still? I thought you moved to New Brunswick. Between positions."

He laughed but gave her a quizzical look "I'm on sabbatical," he said. "so I'm fully employed. I have been considering seeking a local position, but now Evie might go to the States for school, so a lot of things are uncertain."

This was all new. "Really, Evie?" Helen asked. "You might go to the States?"

"I should hear any day now, but I'll go wherever they'll take me," her sister said.

Helen snorted. "Don't devalue yourself. I'm sure everybody will want you." Or at least her tuition dollars.

Evie looked a little cheerier. "Thanks, Helen. Admission isn't a personal thing, though. There are only a few places and there might be a lot of candidates."

Helen looked at her father. "What do you think about Evie leaving the province?"

James' placid face gazed toward Evie. "I think Evie is going to find the perfect place for her. I'll miss her, and she'll come back when she can, but everybody's children leave sometime." Evie glowed and smiled back at her father.

"You weren't so happy when I left for Ontario," Helen said sharply, fidgeting with her glass. She stood abruptly and started stacking the dirty dishes.

"Let that go," James said. "Sit down. We'll get the dishes. It's just nice to have all of you here."

Corinne patted her chair and Helen slowly returned to sit. "I invited Jake to come for his Easter break," she said. "Sorry you won't be here, Evie."

"Oh, darn it!" Evie looked concerned. "I haven't seen him for a long time, except on video."

"You guys never came to visit," she said. "Did you ever see my new house in Ottawa?"

"I visited before you moved into the new place," Corinne said.

"Your mum and I went every year," James said stoutly. "Until she took sick."

"True," Helen agreed. "You did. Mum came on her own, too, remember?"

"I remember," Evie said, her mouth grim. "Dad kept calling me to help with Dorie. When Jake was born, right?"

James scoffed, but Helen spoke over him. "She saved me. Maybe Jake, too. What did I know about a baby?"

Evie leaned toward her. "Tell us. Tell me." Stephen watched, a faint smile curving his lips.

"Oh, well," Helen demurred with a glance in Stephen's direction, but Evie stared intently into Helen's face.

"Tell!"

Helen gazed at the ceiling. "It wasn't fun. I was so, so tired. So much crying. So little sleep. The baby cried, I cried. I dripped with everything; sweat, milk, baby vomit."

"But the baby," Evie protested. "The baby must have been fun."

"Not at first," Helen said. "I had no idea that my life could become such chaos with one six-pound addition. Mum saved us. She took to him like a pro."

"She was a pro even before you girls came along," James said. "She was the oldest girl in her family."

"She always said I broke her in," Corinne said, smiling. "I called her Mum until I was four."

"Well, it worked. But then she had to leave. I couldn't believe I was going to be on my own, me and Reggie, but that was what happened. I couldn't wait to go back to work."

"No!" Evie was aghast. "Didn't you want to be with your baby?"

Helen scoffed. "Later. Once he was a little older, he was more fun. I was better at reading his needs and we meshed a little better. It also helped that we got a nanny. With her help, I got to sleep at least once in a while."

"Did you say you went back to work early?"

"I sure did," Helen said. "Part time, but the best hours of my day were at work. At least there I could understand what people were trying to communicate." She recalled walking the floor with baby Jake, willing him to tell her — just tell her! — why he was crying again.

"I really, really want a baby," Evie said dreamily, "even though you make it sound impossible."

Stephen turned to look at her. "More than a PhD?" His voice was gentle, with an audible smile.

Evie made a soft chuckle. "Can't I have both? Women can have it all, right?"

Not really, Helen thought.

Evie continued. "Look at Helen. She's a mum and a successful professional." They all turned to look at Helen.

"What? What do I look like?"

"Better than you did," James said critically. "Compared to last fall, you look rested. And I think you put on a few pounds."

She dropped the rhubarb square she'd picked up.

"You could have a few more," he added, but her hands stayed in her lap.

No more dessert. "I worked a lot of hours," she acknowledged. "I might have missed out on a lot of Jake's life. But there wasn't much choice."

Stephen chose from the dessert platter. "Sometimes it's hard to see choices when there's an obvious path right in front of you. When I became tenured at my university, I expected to stay forever. That's what people do. But I came here on sabbatical and met Evie, so I see things differently. Just because I can stay at my job doesn't mean I must. I'm trying to consider what I want instead of just what's expected." He looked at Helen with an unexpectedly warm smile. "It's not easy."

Why did she feel a kinship with this man, Evie's boyfriend, partner, whom she barely knew?

"Everybody's got an opinion when a mother wants to work hard at her career. Fathers don't get the same level of criticism. They're good providers, and ambitious. Those words never get applied to mothers."

Her voice might have been a bit sharp. There was sudden quiet around the table.

"Well, I guess I shut the conversation down," she said. "Sorry about that."

"It sounds like things have been hard in a lot of ways," Evie noted. Oh, sister, you have no idea. Helen's eyes smarted.

"Everything's better now," she said briskly. "Except the weather. And I don't know if Jake is coming for Easter."

The conversation turned to other matters. As the evening grew deeper, Stephen and Corinne took their leave. Helen and Evie finally cleared the table and tidied the kitchen. As Helen was gathering her things, James called to her from the living room.

"Don't you worry about Easter," he advised. "If Jakey can't come, it's okay. We'll go over to Rett's and hide eggs for the little ones anyway.

This is their first Easter here, and that old house has a lot of good hiding places."

"I wasn't worried, Dad," she lied. "I'm sure we'll have a good time. Good night."

Though she appreciated her new house, tonight it was lonely. When she took a moment to check her messages, the one from Reggie loomed. With a sigh, she clicked.

Jake said you invited him for Easter but he wanted me to tell you he's coming here for his holiday. I know you'll be disappointed. I asked him to call you but he said no. Sorry.

Angry tears sprang up, and she stomped into the kitchen to pour herself a drink. Damn Reggie, damn Juliet, damn them all. Damn it.

Jake. My boy. My boy who is so mad he can't bear to be around me. My baby. She tossed back the scotch.

She'd lost the threads of her life. Lawyer, wife, and now mother... She was none of these now. How had that happened?

Old Haunts

S tella Mare Regional High School sat on the hill next to the community center, an old building that had educated hundreds, probably thousands, of kids. It looked tired and old, just like her. But the energy from the kids piling into yellow buses was unmistakable and so familiar. She'd been one of them once.

Helen headed into the building as if she belonged there. She could belong, except her child didn't live with her. Thoughts about Jake made her stomach hurt, so she focused on what she could see.

The signs clearly stated visitors should check in at the office, but when she glanced in, there were no adults in sight, only a boy slumped into a plastic chair, apparently awaiting his fate. She breathed a little easier and turned toward the gym. Funny how muscles remembered, even if you hadn't been in a place for over twenty years.

Evie had painted a mural somewhere here. It was legendary in the family, but Helen had never seen it. She pushed open doors from the empty hallway. Where would a mural hide out?

Well, not at the gym, apparently, where kids played basketball, and a small cluster of noisy spectators, parents by the look of them, cheered. A spurt of longing made her heart ache. She'd once been a cheering parent at the skating rink. Barely missing a beat, she reminded herself Jake was doing what he really wanted, which apparently included being away from his mother. She stifled a sigh.

The trophy case in the hallway outside the gym, the very gym where she'd graduated, drew her. There were medals and trophies for field hockey, football, basketball, even debate. There were other debate trophies, but hers from 1997 was still displayed prominently. Gazing at the lightly tarnished silver cup, her stomach churned, chest tightened, and the hallway darkened. She leaned her forehead against the glass. There was nothing to see but that trophy. Darkness pressed in from the sides and her knees wobbled.

A sudden shout from down the hall made her jump, but also brought her back to herself. Here and now. Be here, right now. Her mantra was automatic. Recovering, she stood up straight and wrapped her coat tightly around her. Turning her back on the trophy case, she hurried away from the gym. Her breath eased with every step.

Her feet took her down the hallway toward the little theatre, probably a better guess for Evie's mural. Hadn't Evie been one of those drama kids? She had a brief memory of fake tattoos, dramatic makeup, and an asymmetrical haircut. The hallway to the theatre carried a mural, but the paint looked fresh. Yes, the artists, two girls, had signed and dated it. Last year. Clearly not Evie's work.

She peered around another corner to see a fanciful seascape, complete with mermaid and kraken. She headed toward it, eyes on the tiny signature. E.M. in a fancy script, and the date, more than fifteen years ago. Surely this was Evie's mural. Not as big a deal as everybody made it, she thought critically, but kind of cute. Evie now would surely do a better job, but of course she'd been in high school then.

Helen peered at details, so she could report and Evie would know she'd really been there. The kraken surfaced, waving threatening tentacles at a ship carrying people. At least it looked like people, tall people with long hair, blue eyes. Nordic-looking people, she decided, all women. Maybe they were girls. Frightened, certainly. Under the sea, the mermaid cavorted with the bottom half of the scary kraken. Helen bent to look closer. The mermaid, all dark curls tumbling around a big smile, was pulling on a tentacle. Was she trying to stop the kraken?

Helen rubbed her eyes for a moment. When she looked back, it made sense. The kraken was a puppet. The mermaid was manipulating the kraken to scare the people; it wasn't real at all. Those tall, lean, long-haired blue-eyed females were frightened of a puppet handled by a mermaid. Helen squinted harder. That mermaid looked a lot like her sister Evie.

"Hmph." She stood and flexed her back, lips pursed. Seemed like teenage Evie worked out her aggravation about her sisters on the high school wall. The flicker of annoyance, though, was far more comfortable than the anxious distress she'd felt at the gym. Maybe it was a good time to leave.

The feeling of unease persisted even after she got home. She rummaged for a meal, but when it came time to eat, she only picked at her plate. Scraping it into the bin, she stuck her dishes into the dishwasher, wiped down the pristine countertops, and retreated to the living room. As she scrolled her phone for music, a voice mail notification popped up.

Jean-Louis.

She fingered the tennis bracelet under her sleeve. He wasn't supposed to contact her. They'd agreed, and it had been weeks since they'd spoken. Maybe it was some kind of emergency.

Curled into the corner of the couch, she gazed at the red notification until her eyes blurred. Dear Jean-Louis. Someone who thought she was special when everyone else was done with her. A man, a man she respected, who wanted to spend time with her while Reggie, so in love with Juliet, hadn't been bothered to discuss their separation. Jean-Louis was there when she was impulsive, doing things that turned out to be mistakes.

Her partners were aghast when they learned of her connection with Jean-Louis, despite it being her business, not theirs. Things happened, though, and she had to acknowledge Sarabeth had a point. Jean-Louis was married. He and his wife, though living quite separate lives, were clients, and when the wife had called to complain, Sarabeth had been both embarrassed and incensed.

The memory tumbled in without warning, taking Helen back to the December meeting in Sarabeth's office.

Her stomach sank as she entered and walked silently across the thick oriental carpet. There was no good reason for her reaction; she was a full partner in this firm. What were they going to do, scold her? Jordan Jewett, the other senior partner, sat in the big chair, while Sarabeth sat behind her desk.

"Sit," Sarabeth ordered.

Helen nodded at her, but went to the credenza to pour herself a coffee. She'd seen Sarabeth deal with employee problems before, and she recognized the signs. Kind, easy-going Sarabeth got hard and rigid when she had to deliver bad news. Helen took her time pouring cream into her cup, stirring deliberately and setting aside the spoon. She didn't even like cream in her coffee, but she needed a moment before she faced the two of them. Carrying her cup with great care, she reached the other chair and sat down.

Sarabeth leaned her elbows on the desk. "We have a problem," she announced.

Helen leaned back in her chair. "Do you?" she asked casually, but her heart was pounding. The whole fall had been so crummy, between Reg moving out, insomnia, and her own inattention to work in the face of her life falling to pieces. What else could have gone wrong? Well, she would not assume responsibility for Sarabeth's "problem" until and unless it was firmly hers.

"You and we have a problem," Sarabeth enunciated slowly.

"Oh?" Helen forced herself to stay relaxed. Jordan was still as a mouse in the other chair.

Sarabeth got up and paced around behind the desk. "I had a call from Monique Levesque-Poirot this morning." She spun around to glare at Helen. "She is very upset."

Helen shook her head. "Who is that?"

Sarabeth heaved a dramatic sigh. She was excellent in the courtroom, Helen recalled, presenting case summarizations like a movie synopsis, so the jury couldn't help but make the decision she pointed them towards. Helen was determined not to be swayed by Sarabeth's emotional presentation. "Madame Levesque-Poirot is Jean-Louis Lamont's wife of thirty-eight years, as she reminded me. And they are both clients of this firm."

She looked over the top of her glasses at Helen, who fought an urge to giggle. Hysteria? Maybe.

"What is the problem, Sarabeth?" Helen kept her voice even and quiet, a counterpoint to Sarabeth's increasing indignation.

"She claims you are having an affair with her husband," Sarabeth declaimed.

There it was, right in the room.

"Are you?" Jordan's quiet voice cut through the silence. He looked pained as he gazed at Helen. She remembered her first day in the firm as a junior associate, and his kindness and encouragement of her ambition to make partner. Her heart sank, looking at his kind brown eyes. She shook her head slightly, then looked back at Sarabeth.

"That's ridiculous and you know it," she replied energetically. "Jean-Louis has been very kind to me over the last few months, that's true. I am not having 'an affair', as you call it." She bracketed the phrase with air quotes with her unoccupied hand, then leaned back again in the chair. Here and now, here and now, she counselled herself. She gave a brief thought to Ms. Levesque-Poirot, whom she'd never met.

Sarabeth sat back down. "She has evidence." She looked expectantly at Helen.

Helen shook her head. "What evidence? There's no affair." She fingered the diamond tennis bracelet he'd clasped around her wrist last Saturday at dinner. "He's been kind, as I said."

Jordan moved in his chair. "Helen, I'm not sure you understand the magnitude here. This couple owns three businesses that keep our corporate division solvent. They are, arguably, our most important clients. We also handle a family trust for Monique, and some real estate assets for Jean-Louis. We cannot afford to alienate them."

"There is no affair." Helen was obdurate. "Not at all."

"What then? What is she upset about?" Jordan's soft inquiry made Helen look his way. His eyes were kind; hers filled. Stuffing the feeling down, she matched his quiet tone.

"Dinner. Drives in the country. We went to an art opening together." She didn't report on the late fall weekend on Georgian Bay.

"That's a lot of time together," he remarked.

"But not an affair," Helen reiterated, her stomach squeezing all over again.

Sarabeth got up to pace again, brisk and angular. "It's all in the definition. I don't care if you've had sex with him or not, Helen. His wife doesn't like what's going on, and they are clients of this firm. You're taking something from this client."

"He's not my client," she retorted quickly, and immediately regretted the words.

Sarabeth narrowed her eyes. "This firm is a partnership. *We* have clients. You can't use that as a defence."

"I didn't realize I was on trial here." Helen lifted her chin. "Exactly what are you trying to say, Sarabeth?"

Sarabeth glanced at Jordan, who cleared his throat, then began, "Helen, we're offering you a chance to leave the practice."

"What? Leave?" She was sputtering, she couldn't help it.

Jordan sighed. "What you've done is a breach of ethics, as I see it. Everyone makes mistakes, and you've been under a lot of strain lately."

His voice was quiet and kind, and her eyes were wet again immediately. The last few months had been terrible.

His voice cut into her. "Your relationship with Jean-Louis, whatever it is, cannot continue. You are putting our practice at risk, not to mention damage to yourself," he added. "To your self-respect, Helen."

She swallowed hard but could think of nothing to say. Jordan went on. "We're prepared to buy you out of your partnership."

Helen wasn't thinking fast, but she heard the words. "You want to buy me out?"

"That's correct."

Sarabeth chimed in. "A buy-out engages your non-compete clause from your contract."

Helen looked from one to the other. "You want to buy me out, but I can't work as a lawyer in Ottawa?"

"You'll have to review your original contract, but that's the general idea," Sarabeth said. "Believe me, Helen, this is your best option. While we have no intention of filing a complaint against a member of our firm, Ms. Levesque-Poirot doesn't have that restriction."

A complaint would involve a public hearing. Helen imagined Reg in a tribunal saying, "She was a terrible wife," with Juliet at his side and Jean-Louis looking tragic. A fearsome board of women lawyers, all looking like Sarabeth, would glare at her. She almost didn't hear Sarabeth's next words.

"I think if she knows you're leaving, it will all blow over," Sarabeth said. "I assured her we would take care of things on this end."

Take care of things? "I assume you mean punish me," she said sharply.

Jordan sighed again. "Helen, we don't want to punish anyone. We're doing what we must do to preserve our business. I expect things will work out well for you, too, in the end. I've asked our accountant to value your partnership, so we can make you a fair and legitimate offer. No punishment."

She glanced at Sarabeth, whose folded arms and grim lips begged to differ. Looking away, she stood. Speaking directly to Jordan, she said, "I admit to no wrongdoing. I will need to see your proposal, consult my own counsel and after that, let you know what I decide."

He nodded. "Of course."

Sarabeth threw in a demand. "You need to stop seeing Jean-Louis. Confirm right now that you won't see him again."

Helen glared at her, but Jordan spoke before she could. "Helen will manage herself professionally, I am sure," he said to Sarabeth. "We don't need those assurances."

Slightly comforted, Helen headed toward the door when Sarabeth gave a tight nod. She walked tall, feeling them watching. As the door latched quietly behind her, she overheard Sarabeth say, "I never thought she'd ever do such a thing, Jordan. It's heartbreaking."

Her breath caught in her throat, she hurried toward her office. Thankfully, her assistant wasn't at her desk, so she didn't have to talk to anyone before reaching her haven. She pulled the heavy oak door closed, flicked the lock, and sank into a chair, head in hands.

A ping pulled her out of memory and back to her living room. Her phone lit up, highlighting again the notification from Jean-Louis. There it was, the past intruding on the present, making Helen's stomach churn. Here and now could be uncomfortable, too.

Jean-Louis understood the deal: they hadn't spoken since that day in December. Why was he calling her now?

It really didn't matter. She couldn't talk to him for any reason. Her application to practise law in New Brunswick was pending. If there was a complaint in Ontario, it would only slow things down even more. She'd put her feelings about Jean-Louis in the same box as her feelings about Reg and Juliet, losing her partnership, and some of the terrible feelings she carried about Jake. A nice, tight, waterproof box. No tears allowed. Her job was to move ahead.

She deleted the voice mail and blocked the sender.

Attempted Coup

It was Friday night again. The family expected her at Dad's house. Was this going to be every Friday night? It was April, and she'd been at her father's house for Friday night supper every week since her arrival, and every week something really stupid happened. What nonsense would happen this time?

Jaw tight, she pulled ingredients out of the refrigerator to make a salad. Dad shouldn't be eating pizza with his diabetes. With a salad, he could eat something healthy, even if everyone else was in a meat-lovers' coma. And the desserts. Why on earth they needed dessert after pizza night was beyond her.

What asinine thing would Evie say about feminism? And Rett, would she entertain with another goat story?

This was not how she wanted to spend her Friday night, listening to her sisters' silliness, eating nasty food, and watching the kids compete at leaping off the stairs until somebody got hurt and Rett shut it down.

She wasn't making a great adjustment to Stella Mare. She should have friends by now. What was keeping her from connecting? It must be her family. If she wasn't expected at this stupid Friday night ritual, everything would be so much better.

It wasn't her fault she hadn't met anybody. She always initiated contact with her sisters: they didn't know a good thing when she was right there with them. She could help them live better lives, but were they open to that?

No. They just kept on living their lives, as if she wasn't even there. She'd given up everything to be the big sister they needed, and they had no respect. And now she was stuck with Friday night family dinner. Again.

Pizza and dessert. Ugh.

But complaining didn't solve problems. Complaining wasn't productive behaviour. Instead, she could do something. She could offer something else. She sent a text to her father.

I'm not feeling it for pizza. I'll cook dinner for tonight. You expecting the regular? Dorie and Chad, Evie, Stephen, Rett and the kids, Corinne? Eleven?

Ten minutes later, while she was looking for recipes, she got a return text.

Rett's kids like pizza.

Does that mean we always eat pizza? I'll cook.

Silence.

A few minutes later, she headed to the little grocery store for supplies.

She arrived at her father's home early to set her stew to heat on the back burner, slice bread to warm later, and toss her salad. Rett and the kids swept in through the kitchen door, bringing in the crisp air, the scent of wood smoke, and their dog, Charlie.

"Hey." Helen smiled at Mason, first to hang up his coat.

"We're having pizza," he said with a bright smile. "I love pizza night at Grandpa's. I got to go see Mallow." He loped into the living room, seeking one of the big dogs. The two giant mutts looked so similar, Helen couldn't keep them straight.

The little girls fluttered by, too, waving at Helen on their way. In the next room, James greeted all the children.

"Must we have pizza night every Friday?" Helen asked. "I cooked."

"Depends," Rett said. "What did you cook?" She took the lid off the big pot and sniffed. "Beef Bourguignon? Really?" Rett's eyes were large. "Who did you think you were cooking for?"

"You. Me. Dad."

"I have kids. We eat pizza. It's everybody's comfort food."

"Well, I cooked tonight," Helen said firmly. Before Rett could reply, the back door opened to let in Dorie, Chad, and the white poodle. Stephen followed.

"How many dogs are there going to be in this house?" Helen asked irritably. "Dog hair is everywhere."

"Not Frou-Frou's," Dorie said defensively. "He's hypoallergenic. No shedding."

"Besides, dogs are always welcome here," Rett said, fixing her with a steely gaze. "Mum always told everyone to bring their dogs."

"Is Evie home?" Stephen asked. "I looked for her at the gallery, but she wasn't there."

"Not yet," Helen said. "Dad's in the living room. He might know something."

Stephen and Dorie left for the living room, white poodle dancing in attendance. Chad stepped back outside, leaving Rett and Helen in the kitchen. Helen stirred her stew.

"There will be pizza," Rett said. "Just so you know."

"Do whatever," Helen said. "You're just stuck in the same old thing."

"I have kids who like pizza. And who love the ritual of Friday night pizza with their grandfather."

"Well, I don't know why you impose it on everyone," Helen continued peevishly.

"Who is imposing on whom? You show up and decide to change the plan, the one that's been in place for, oh, maybe years. But how would you know?"

Evie and Corinne walked in, chatting. Helen glared at them. Rett was unreasonable. Pizza was just not good for you, especially not good for Dad, not all the time.

"Evie." Rett's voice was stentorian. "Helen thinks we should give up Friday night pizza."

"Really?" Evie looked from one to the other as she took off her coat. "Sounds like the middle of a conversation."

Corinne glanced at all of them, then said, "I'm going to go talk to James."

"Taste this," Helen demanded, holding out a spoon to Rett. "This is so much better than pizza."

"You are missing the point," Rett snapped. "It doesn't matter how good it is. What matters is you show up out of nowhere and start making your own rules. And that's probably fine, except you expect everybody else to follow them. No, I don't want your stew."

She stomped off toward the living room, leaving Helen holding out a spoon.

"I'll try it," Evie said mildly. "Since I'm the only one here at the moment." She took Helen's spoon. "Yum! Stephen will love that. Red wine, right?"

Helen nodded. "It was Reg's favourite. Well, back when I used to cook. Isn't that better than pizza?"

"Helen, that's a terrible question. We don't need to compare. The kids love pizza. We eat pizza with the kids on Friday, just like we watch a terrible kids' movie, and yes, your food is delicious."

"Healthier for Dad, too," Helen said self-righteously.

"Well, but really, Dad barely touches the pizza. He has one slice, usually, and he stopped drinking any alcohol at all after his diagnosis. The pizza's mostly about the kids. Well, the kids and Dorie."

"What about Dorie?" Dorie asked, returning to the kitchen. "Don't worry, Helen, I left the dog in there."

"You like pizza," Helen stated.

"I do like pizza," Dorie agreed. "It's the world's most perfect food."

"That seems unlikely," Helen argued. "I'm tired of pizza every Friday, so I cooked for tonight. But that's an unpopular position. I worked all day to make a lovely meal, but we're still going to order pizza because the children prefer it."

"What are you so mad about?" Dorie asked. "Nobody told you to cook."

Rett came around the corner from the living room. "Okay, I'm placing the pizza order. What's your pleasure? And where's Chad, anyway?"

"Chad gets uncomfortable when things get tense," Dorie said shortly. "He went to the truck after that crack about dogs and dog hair."

"What? Now I have to worry about upsetting Chad, too? Come on."

"You don't have to worry about anything," Evie said placatingly. "Thank you for cooking, and we will enjoy your food and we'll also eat pizza."

Helen slammed the lid on the stockpot. "I do not understand this. I made a gorgeous beef stew, a beautiful green salad, got fresh bread, and you want slop from the local pizzeria?"

"Helen, you're ridiculous!" Rett shouted. "Eat what you like. We'll have pizza."

"Quit yelling at me, Loretta. I don't have to listen to you!"

Dorie leaned over to Evie and whispered, "You're not the boss of me." Evie shot her a quick, scared smile.

A roar came from the living room. "Stop it, stop it!" James stomped into the kitchen. "You girls knock it off. You're giving me indigestion and you should see the expression on those children. Stop that bickering right now."

Shocked into silence, Helen stared at her father's red face. He looked at her, then at Rett, then at Evie and Dorie. "You girls have got to learn to get along. You'll kill this old man with your fighting. Now figure it out." He turned on his heel and left the kitchen.

Helen looked at Rett, who straightened her back and marched after James, speaking calmly to the children. "Okay, kids, I'm going to order the pizza. Mason, you want pepperoni?"

Evie, eyes on the floor, glided away into her office. Dorie looked at Helen, tears in her eyes. "Dad's really mad," she whispered.

"Yes, apparently," Helen snapped. "You were all fine without me." She packed up her basket of food, pulled on her coat, and headed out into the night.

Helen Takes a Hike

I t took until Sunday, but Helen, awash in regret, called her father to apologize. James was stiff, unlike himself. It made her feel little and awkward.

"I'm sorry, Dad. I didn't expect things to blow up like that." She could almost see his frown.

"Well, they did. Fix this. I will not have the four of you tearing each other apart. I can't have it."

"I know. I've been trying to get the girls to do something together, but they don't want to."

"Why would they?" he asked. "You four can't even have a pleasant pizza night." He was right.

"Yeah. I'm sorry, and I'll do better. I promise."

A day later, she called Rett. "Listen, I'm sorry about what happened at Dad's. What do you think about a spa weekend with all the sisters?"

She could imagine Rett's automatic frown. "Who has a free weekend? And extra money?" In the background, kids were squabbling. Or maybe they were just playing. Helen never knew.

"I just thought it would be nice to do something together," she said.

"Sure," Rett agreed. "Maybe. Trying to fix what's broken? Is Dad prompting this?"

"Oh, it was just an idea," Helen said breezily.

"I don't know about doing things together. Harry's away for another few weeks, the kids have a lot going on, and so do I. Plus money. It would have to be a cheap together thing. Like a walk and a coffee."

Helen sighed. "Think bigger, Rett. We can always go for a walk and have coffee."

"Yeah, but do we?" Rett asked wisely. "Besides, you can think bigger. You're the one that wants to get everyone together. I've got to go."

Helen threw her hiking boots and pack into the car, checking to be sure she had two bottles full of water. It was late April, kind of early for hiking, but she was eager to get back to Fundy National Park where she had spent a day with her sisters last fall. She stopped at the Sunshine Diner for a flat white to go, then headed east along the shore of the Bay of Fundy.

Last September, all four of them, plus Rett's three kids and at least one dog, had driven to the park to hike down the Laverty Falls trail. The kids were predictably whiny, but Helen had let Rett handle that. There was no whining amongst the adults, at least, though there were a few minutes where Helen herself felt like complaining about the steep climb back up the Moosehorn Trail. The day had been brilliantly sunny, warm enough for hiking, but not too hot, and strenuous hiking was good for her. She recalled everyone got along well that day, even though Rett was going through some big life changes, Evie had just opened a show at the art gallery, and Dorie always had some dog emergency going on. What was different now?

Her. She was the difference. Instead of being a visitor, she was trying to become part of their lives. It could be they didn't want that.

She curled her lip at the idea. Instead of thinking, she cranked up the music and stepped on the accelerator. With any luck, this trip to Fundy would be a good enough day. Good enough to have pictures to share, as well as leave her tired enough to sleep. Strenuous exercise in the wilder parts of the province was just the thing.

The trailhead was near the parking lot. She laced up her boots, ate an energy bar, and took a swig of water before shrugging into her day pack. Hat firmly on her head, she started down the trail through the yellow-green buds of hardwoods and the deep dark green of spruce and the occasional fir. Birdsong was everywhere as the sunlight filtered through skeletal branches. April, even late April, meant patches of snow in the woods, tiny green shoots poking through the cover of dead leaves, vernal pools catching light, housing tadpoles and insect life.

She snapped pictures all the way down the ravine, only occasionally dropping her gaze to the rugged trail underfoot. She was tiring when she tuned into the flowing water. Last September, the falls had been full enough, but the spring run-off meant a tremendous rush of sound, presaging a deluge tumbling over the rock precipice. Her foot slipped, and she grabbed at a sapling, realizing the spray from the cataract was dampening the ground and her, even so far away.

Exhilarated, she pressed forward, steadying herself with the small trees. As she emerged onto a platform of rock, she looked down into a curling turmoil of water and foam that engulfed the lower platform where they'd sat to have lunch last fall. Spring at the falls was a different animal entirely.

As she considered her options, she backed away from the precipice and perched on a fallen log. Her thoughts were silenced by the roar of the water. Mesmerized by the cascade and the apparently random pattern of thousands of gallons of water, she gazed below her feet.

As she watched, the repetitive parts of the pattern became clear. Even apparent chaos had patterns. You just had to take time to look.

Her pack held lunch and a thermos of tea. Chewing, she settled into the rhythm of the place, noticing more. The chickadees in the brushy tree next to her chirruped and sang. One of them came close, cocking its head toward her. She put a crust from her sandwich down on a rock and watched him peck at it. As she listened, the sound of a rap-rap-rap arose up the hill; a woodpecker, looking for lunch in a dead tree. Sunlight falling on the moss where her feet rested changed colours as a cloud passed over the sun. Ozone was strong, with all that water rushing around, but so was a deep, earthy, woodsy smell, more where her boots crushed the new moss and pushed it aside. The dirt was thin here, a light covering over the rocks, but enough to grow some twisted, gnarly evergreens. The big rock to her left held a deep crevice, and a contorted spruce sprang from the cleft, roots growing into and over the feldspar. Igneous rock, born from volcanoes a million years ago, had been brought to the surface by glaciation, then worn down and broken by the likes of a plant. Or generations of plants. There was something impressive in the life force of that convoluted ancient tree and the tiny birds twittering in and around it. Her problems receded against this ancient background.

Of course! A hike was what the sisters needed. That day last fall had been full of sisterly togetherness, along with Rett's kids and assorted dogs. That had been a great day. Hiking was better than a spa day, and cheaper, too. But it needed to be more than just a day hike. Something bigger. Thinking hard, she tucked her things back into her pack and headed back up the ravine toward the trail head.

Helen invited her sisters for coffee at the Sunshine Diner. It took three tries to find a time when they were all available, but it finally happened. Once everyone settled with their drink of choice, Helen made her pitch.

"Us hike the Fundy Footpath? Are you out of your mind?" Rett's face was red.

"They opened the road," Evie said. "You don't have to hike it. You can drive it."

Helen shook her head. "No, that's wrong. There's a parkway, but it's not the same. The footpath is still there. Still a hike. Still an icon."

"What do you mean, an icon?" Dorie wanted to know.

"An icon means normal people like us don't do it," Rett replied grimly. "It's iconic because it's hard, and nobody in their right mind wants to actually climb that much for so little gain."

"You sound unenthusiastic," Helen observed.

"Completely," Rett agreed. "And Evie, everyone makes that mistake. Once they built the parkway through, that was good enough for me. I get to see sweeping vistas of the bay, great beaches, overhanging cliffs, all that jazz. And I don't need to carry a fifty-pound hiking pack and wear stumpy boots to do it."

"Why are you so opposed?" Helen asked, jaw tight. "Dad said..."

"Dad? What did Dad say?" Evie's soft voice cut through the noise. "I bet Dad didn't recommend this trip."

"Well, he said we had to do something," Helen equivocated.

"I'm not surprised, after our last pizza night," Dorie said sotto voce.

"If you have something to say, say it!" Helen was sharp. Dorie flinched.

"Dad hates it when we fight," Evie murmured. "He's been upset for a week."

"Did he say we should go hiking? That doesn't sound like Dad." Rett wore her big frown.

Helen got annoyed just looking at her. "For Pete's sake, Loretta, fix your face. I swear I haven't seen a pleasant look from you since I moved to Stella Mare."

Rett looked grimmer. "For good reason. Every time you open your mouth, Helen, you're trying to push people around."

"I am only helping. Why do you get so worked up when I'm just helping?"

Dorie spoke up. "I'd like to hike the Fundy Footpath. Think about it. Campfires, s'mores. All those birds. Sunrises over the water."

"At four in the morning," Rett muttered.

"Did Dad really suggest we go hiking?" Evie persisted.

Helen softened. "Not really. He's bothered when we don't all get along." She glared at Rett. "It disturbs our father."

"We were doing good until you showed up, Helen," Rett warned. "So don't blame me for this mess."

"Doing good? Is that how you see the disaster that is your professional career, Rett?"

Rett stood up, nearly spilling her coffee. "That is exactly what I mean, Helen. I don't want to go backpacking with you. I don't even want to have dinner with you, but I do it for Dad's sake. This meeting is over." She grabbed her coat and marched to the diner door. Her retreat was thwarted by a need to return to the cash register to pay her bill.

The other three were quiet, watching her departure. Helen lifted her chin. "I don't know why she's so touchy."

"You really don't?" Evie asked. "Did you hear yourself? That was kind of heavy-handed."

Peering at Evie, Helen said, "Don't you agree that she's wasting herself, that graduate degree and all her experience, working part time in a little clinic?"

Evie shook her head and looked away. Helen went on. "She could do so much more. She could be an assistant professor of nursing by now. Could be in management again. She's got so much to offer. I can't see why she's wasting it."

Dorie looked like she might burst. "She's working really hard, Helen. She's been doing everything since Harry went away. Don't be so hard on her." Her tone was imploring.

Helen huffed. "I don't know why none of my sisters has any ambition. You're all smart, strong, talented women, but you're wasted here."

Evie looked at her curiously. "Wasted here in Stella Mare?"

"That's exactly what I mean," Helen stated with authority. "You could wow the art world in Toronto instead of going back to school at your age. And Dorie, you're still young enough to make an entirely new career. A real career."

Dorie's thundercloud face spoke volumes, though her voice was mild. "I'm happy with my career, thank you."

"If you think Stella Mare's such a dead-end place, why are you here?" Evie asked in her quiet, diffident way. "That's a bit inconsistent, isn't it?"

Helen sat up straight. "Not at all. I've had a successful career. I just came back to help my family."

Dorie scowled further. "You're not even forty yet. Kind of young to talk about your career in the past tense."

Helen scowled back.

"It's nice you want to help," Evie said.

"I agree." Helen softened. "But every time I offer any aid, some sister gets her back up."

"It could be the way you offer your advice," Dorie said through gritted teeth. "And besides, advice isn't really help. It's just advice. Or criticism."

Confused, Helen repeated, "Criticism." Was she being critical? "Everybody's too thin-skinned," she said. "Hearing the truth can be hard."

Dorie let out a gusty sigh. "We need to reschedule this meeting," she suggested and picked up her coffee cup. "After everybody has cooled down a little."

"You mean Rett," Helen said with aspersion.

"I mean everybody," Dorie said. "Let's go, Evie. We'll figure it out, Helen, but it won't be today."

A Visit to St. Stephen

Helen tapped at the back door. She'd invited Rett out by way of apology, but, as usual, Rett wasn't ready.

"Harry's on FaceTime with the kids," Rett said hurriedly. "I'll just be a minute. I've got to catch him before he hangs up."

She took off, leaving Helen to wander the kitchen. Rett and the children were talking upstairs, but she tuned out the chatter to poke around. This kitchen was old, decrepit, but Rett's gingham curtains, tea towels, and jars of staples made it homey if not elegant.

She peered into the old cookie jar, remembering it well from their own childhood. There were hermits in there, she noted, but firmly replaced the lid. No need for extra calories. They were going out anyway. The cookies smelled good, though.

Footsteps on the stairs alerted her to Rett's arrival.

"Okay, Harry's said goodnight and they know Dorie's coming." She blew into the kitchen. "There are cookies," she invited, nodding toward the jar.

"No, thanks. We're going out. I need to save my calories."

Rett gave her a critical glance. "Calories keep me going," she said. "Nothing fancy, right? We're just going to talk."

"We're out for a pleasant sisterly evening," Helen said. "I thought the bookstore in St. Stephen."

"Bookstore?"

"They're having a reading. An author talk."

Rett looked markedly unenthusiastic, but said, "Sure. Whatever. It's your night."

"You said not expensive and not fancy," Helen reminded her. "The bookstore seemed about right."

"Yes, you're right," Rett agreed. "Now all we need is Dorie, and look, here she is!"

Dorie slipped in through the kitchen door, patting Charlie the yellow Lab who came out of his corner to greet her.

"Hey, where was he when I arrived?" Helen asked with mock ferocity. "Don't I count?"

"He probably knows you don't like dog hair," Dorie said mildly. "Don't take it personally. He's trying to get along. Just like us."

"He's smarter than I gave him credit for," Helen said.

"Maybe," Rett tossed in. "I think Dorie gives them all too much credit. Listen, Dore, the kids are waiting for you upstairs. They're excited about having bedtime stories with Dorie, according to Mason."

"Great. I brought some new books." Dorie brandished a small pile. "You two have fun."

"Thanks. We'll be home by nine," Rett said.

Helen glanced at Dorie behind Rett's back and mouthed, "Eleven latest."

Dorie giggled and headed upstairs, while Rett found her coat, her phone and her gloves and the two headed out.

"It wasn't a bad idea to get a drink before the book talk," Rett said as she and Helen navigated the sidewalk between the bar and the bookstore. "I don't realize how tense I am until I get away and relax a little."

Helen, gratified, took her sister's arm. "It's nice to see you relax," she said.

"I'm always up to my elbows in something," Rett said. "Bread dough, homeschool projects, finding new customers for the stuff we make, plus all the usual stuff from my job."

"How do you like your job?" Helen asked, consciously exchanging criticism for interest. Feigned interest, but interest. "What's it like?"

"It's a job," Rett said. "No. Better than that. It's a job where I can do some good, but I leave the work there when I go home."

"It's a day job. No shift work."

"Right. Shift work would have been impossible with Harry away. We weren't realistic about that last fall, but of course, my job evaporated before I could find out." Rett had lost her full-time job just as her husband went out West temporarily for training.

"That was so rotten. But it's too bad your skills are wasted here," Helen said.

"Did you not hear me? I said I like the job." Rett pulled open the bookstore door. Helen followed her into the pool of yellow light.

"Sure, but it's limiting, isn't it?"

"Can't you let it go?" Rett turned to face her. They were the same height, eyeball to eyeball. "Drop it. I'm relaxed and I don't want to fight."

Helen looked away. Even when she tried to avoid it, she ended up aggravating her sister. "Yes, okay. Let's go find this book talk."

They wandered around the store to find a corner with a few chairs set up and a table with books piled on it. Finding seats near the middle, they hung their jackets over the backs of chairs and settled. Rett frowned as she gazed at a poster of a scenic vista of the Bay of Fundy. "This was a set up," Rett whispered harshly.

Helen put on her best inscrutable look.

"A hiking book! You're still trying to get me to go hiking with you."

"Let's just listen," Helen advised. "Keep an open mind, that sort of thing."

Rett heaved a giant sigh and folded her arms. "Hiking is not right for us," she whispered. "Evie doesn't do any physical work, and Dorie's never been in a tent overnight. You're expecting too much from them."

Helen was incredulous. "Dorie never slept in a tent? She's a New Brunswick kid. Everybody camps. You must be mistaken."

Rett shook her head vigorously. "We camped when we were kids, but not Dorie. Mum and Dad weren't camping then."

Helen considered. When Dorie was born, the household was full of teens. "I was sixteen when she was born," she mused. "I don't remember too much about home at that age."

"You wouldn't," Rett said. "Not being mean, but realistic. You were looking to get out of Stella Mare however you could."

All true. From the fall of her grade 12 year, she had known she was leaving and never coming back. Just thinking of it brought on the familiar clenching in her gut. "High school was a nightmare," she murmured.

Quizzical, Rett turned her way. "Really? Why?"

"The talk is about to start," Helen said and nodded toward the front of the room where a woman stood holding a microphone.

The author told enthralling stories and showed breathtaking slides of mountain vistas, sunrises, and animals and plants encountered in her travels in New Brunswick. "We might not be the 'Picture

Province,'" she said, "but we are much more than the 'Drive Through Province.' There's much more here than most people realize."

After some applause, people milled around, some approaching the speaker and others, like Rett, headed to the snacks table. Helen headed toward the podium. As the last of the autograph seekers moved away, she spoke.

"Hi, Ms. Steeves. Can I ask your opinion of something?"

The woman smiled. "Call me Andrea, please. And ask away."

"I want to hike the Fundy Footpath with my three sisters. Can you share any words of wisdom for new hikers getting ready to do that trip?"

Andrea, looking around, said, "Oh, the Fundy Footpath. That requires a chair. Let's sit down."

They sat just outside the thinning crowd, and Helen looked at her expectantly.

"My book about the Fundy Footpath is one place to begin," Andrea said. "You'll also need the guidebook by the Fundy Hiking Trail Association."

"I have both," Helen asserted. "Unfortunately, my sisters aren't as excited about this as I am."

"You're the keener," Andrea said with a smile. "Are you a hiker?"

"Yes," Helen said firmly. "I've done a lot of hiking."

"Backpacking?"

"Well, no," she admitted. "Day hikes, but some big ones."

Andrea nodded. "And you want to do this hike with your sisters. Do they have backpacking experience?"

"I don't know," she said slowly, but with a sinking feeling that she did, in fact, know. Dorie and Evie certainly had not been backpacking. Rett might have done.

"Is experience necessary? I mean, you have to get experience some-where, right?"

Andrea laughed. "That's true and no, experience isn't necessary but beneficial. Why do you want to do this?"

"It's a challenge," Helen said immediately. "I like challenges. It's a big hike, and everybody who hikes knows it's a big one."

"It is a big deal, for sure," Andrea agreed. "It might not be the most gratifying trip, though. The weather can be a bear. There can be fog when you want to see vistas. The continuous ups and downs are hard."

"But when you've done it, you've done something worthwhile."

"Yes. So that's your reason. What about your sisters? Why do you want to do it with them?"

Because my father insisted, Helen thought, but then reconsidered. "I want us to get closer. It's been a long time since I've lived here, and I want to reconnect with my sisters. I figure the great outdoors is a good way to do that."

"You could consider day hiking. Or even a spa weekend," Andrea said seriously. "If your sisters are not on board, and by that I mean genuinely enthusiastic, this hike can be a great big slog. You might not achieve the desired outcome."

She means we might end up worse than we are now. Annoyance fought with appreciation in Helen's mind. "I thought you'd be an advocate," she said.

"I can't advocate for putting people into a challenging situation without the proper tools for success," Andrea said dryly. "A desire to make the trip, to make it together, is a prerequisite. You can do a lot with less skill, as long as they have a desire."

Helen glanced across the room at Rett. "Well, I guess we'll work on finding that desire," she said. "Because we are going to do this."

"Good luck to you," Andrea said, rising. "I hope it goes well."

"Right," Helen said, absently. "Thank you," she added.

Helen made her way across the room toward Rett. No matter what the author said, there was no way she was giving up on this idea.

"You ready?" Rett asked. "This was fun, but I need to get back to the kids."

Of course she did. It was only Helen who was going home to an empty house.

Getting on Board

The Fundy Footpath.

The path to their future as sisters. The place where they would work out their differences, change their dynamics, become better than they were. Helen was sure the trip would do all this, and even more. All she had to do was get the girls on board.

To that end, she left hints: dropped the guidebook in Rett's mailbox, emailed videos to Dorie, sent notes to Evie about the spectacular photography along the Bay of Fundy. Before the next Friday dinner at Dad's, Evie called her. "Helen? We've been talking."

"We who?"

"Rett and Dorie and me," her sister said. "Maybe we should do that hike."

"Really?" Helen's heart lifted. "You want to?"

"Oh, I wouldn't say that, necessarily," Evie demurred. "But we have to do something to show Dad we're all trying. I don't want to be fighting with my sisters."

Helen sighed. "I'm less sure now about the whole idea. Dad pointed out if we can't eat pizza together, we probably can't do anything together."

"I disagree," Evie said in her soft voice. "We need practice, and we need to get better acquainted."

"I know you," she said sharply. "All of you."

Evie paused, then said, "I don't know you, though. Not really. But the news is the girls agreed to your trip. Are you pleased?"

"It can't be my trip," she said tightly. "It would have to be our trip."

Evie laughed. "That goes without saying. But are you in?"

"Yes, yes, I'm in. Of course."

Getting the sisters on board was accomplished, but how firmly were they committed? Helen was certain of Rett, mostly because Rett never said yes when she meant no. If Rett said she was in, she was. Evie was different. Helen had to check this out, but Evie brought it up before she could.

"Can we talk about the hike?" Evie asked, a little awkwardly. They'd finished an early dinner with James, who had left to walk the dogs while the girls cleaned up.

Helen's heart sank. "But you agreed."

"Of course," Evie said, sounding surprised. "I'm not trying to get out of it. I just wanted to say I'm really excited to be included."

"What do you mean? Of course you're included."

"I told you I've always felt different. This trip is a chance for me to really be one of the Madison sisters," she explained. "I can do lots of hard things. I might be a little scared of this trip, but we'll get through it and be better for it."

"Thank you. That's the nicest thing anybody's said about it." Helen was touched. "It probably will be hard, but you're right. We're Madisons and we can do it."

"You bet."

Even though Dorie had agreed to the hike, Helen heard whispers about her struggles. She was worried about leaving the dog sanctuary, afraid her pack would be too heavy, and hated the idea of sleeping on the ground. She would be the weak one. Even though her youth should make it easier for her, she had the least self-confidence.

Helen called Rett to talk about it.

"You need a job," Rett advised. "You're sitting around obsessing. Is that how you handled challenging things at your work? Get a grip."

Rett banged pots around as they talked. The noise was distracting. "What are you doing?"

"Me? Making cheese," Rett answered breezily. "The nanny goat is incredibly productive. Need some goat cheese?"

"Uh, no. But I need Dorie to feel better about this trip."

Rett heaved a sigh. "You're probably right, but I don't think telling her that is going to help."

"What do you suggest?"

"I don't," Rett said blandly, "but I can talk to her if you like. She's not mad at me, at least not at the moment."

"Is she mad at me?" Helen was shocked.

"More like she's scared of you," Rett said.

"Me? I'm not scary."

"Not to me," Rett agreed, "but things are different between you and Dorie. Four sisters. Every relationship is unique."

"That's not news. You're so annoying," she snapped.

"I might be annoying, but I'm right," Rett said clearly. "I gotta go."

Helen dropped her phone on the couch and leaned back. Rett didn't need to school her in group dynamics, though the leadership training courses she'd taken had never mentioned sisters. Dorie was not afraid of her. That was ridiculous. Silly.

She called Dorie, but the call went to voice mail. She couldn't figure out what to say. "Are you scared of me?" seemed too direct, so she clicked off and dialed the landline at the dog sanctuary. There was still no answer, but Dorie's voice on the outgoing message was reassuring. "We're busy with dogs right now, but please leave a message. I want to hear from you, and so does Frou-Frou." It ended with the sound of a bark.

"Hi, Dorie, it's Helen. I just wanted to see if you have time for lunch or coffee or something. Call me. Or text."

There. That was all she could do about that.

It was late the next afternoon when Helen got a response. Dorie's text was brief.

We're really busy right now. I can't take any time off.

That was outrageous. How on earth could she be too busy to eat? Helen tapped a reply.

Are you avoiding me?

The reply arrived immediately. *Just busy.*

How about if I visit you? Help out?

A moment passed, then the return text appeared. *I never turn down help. When should I expect you?*

As Helen's car crept down the potholed gravel driveway, the cacophony of barking grew louder. She pulled up to the old red barn beside the Best Friends Dog Sanctuary van and parked. Dogs in the fenced play yard bounced and barked to get her attention. She glanced over but headed directly for the office entrance.

Her visit last fall had been perfunctory, and she'd missed some details. The hand-carved sign over the office door drew her. In lettering like that on the van, it proclaimed the name of the place, but there was more. There was her mother's name: In memory of Agnes Madison, Agnes and some other woman, a benefactor, she figured. What a thing for Dorie to do. Her eyes watered. Dorie's dog sanctuary was a living, breathing, active memorial to their mother. Mum would most certainly have approved of Dorie's project.

Thinking of her mother brought a wave of shame, but she pushed it aside. No matter what Helen might have done in Ottawa, Mum would certainly want her girls to be getting along, doing something together. She also, Helen was certain, would want Helen to lead them in the right direction.

She pushed open the door. A tri-pawed golden retriever greeted her exuberantly. She eased him away and brushed dog hair off her pants. "Dorie?" she called, above the general racket.

"In here!" Frou-Frou looked at her from an open door, then disappeared again. Helen followed. The white poodle was familiar from his presence at family gatherings. Dorie would be near.

The space was cavernous, reminding her it was once a barn, but shelving filled the near distance. Dorie was heaving bags of dog food onto shelves, but she stopped to greet Helen.

"Hey, thanks for coming," she said, brushing her hands on her jeans. "Welcome to the back room."

"You have a lot of stock back here," Helen observed, checking out the racks of canned food, piles of old towels, and a couple of stacks of newspapers. "Will you use all this?"

"Oh, gosh, yes. This is only about eight days' worth of kibble. We have a lot of mouths to feed," Dorie explained.

"What do you want me to do?" Helen asked, looking around. "I said I'd help."

Dorie laughed. "I think I can take a break and have a cup of coffee with you."

"No," Helen objected. "You were too busy, so I said I'd help."

"Well, I might need some help in the office," Dorie said. "Hauling bags of dog food and cleaning out the kennel isn't something I'd ask you to do, but let's look at some of the paperwork stuff."

Dorie made a fresh pot of coffee in the office, and they sat together at her desk. A black pug snored prodigiously in the middle of the floor, and the white poodle leaned against Dorie's leg. The golden lay by the door.

"It's kind of peaceful here now," Helen noted.

"Yeah, there's a lot of dog energy whenever somebody shows up, but they settle pretty fast, and a lot of them are old and need sleep. Like Pomo there, the pug."

"Does he always snore like that?"

Dorie laughed. "He does. Fortunately the other dogs don't complain about their roommates."

"I really noticed your sign today," Helen remarked.

"You've seen it before," Dorie objected. "At least pictures of it."

"Yes, but today I guess I was thinking about Mum. She would have loved this place."

Dorie flushed. "I like to think that." She looked into her cup. "I still miss her."

"Me, too. It still seems weird that she's not here."

"You haven't been here much," Dorie said, then quickly added, "I know you were busy with work and Jake and everything."

"You're right, though. I was telling Dad it's almost like I have to get used to her not being here, while the rest of you probably did that the first year after she died."

"Maybe the first three years," Dorie said darkly. "It was hard."

"You were so young. We all were, but you were still a teenager."

Dorie's face grew still. "I was lost without her."

Helen waited.

"I couldn't imagine a future," Dorie said quietly. "Rett and Evie couldn't believe I couldn't get my act together, but I really couldn't."

"I'm so sorry I didn't help," Helen offered. "I should have been able to support you."

Dorie looked at her quizzically. "Why do you think that was your job?"

Helen had no answer other than it was just a fact. Her job was to lead, help her sisters through life. Especially the littlest one. "I don't know, but I still wish I could have helped."

"It sounds like you could use some help now," Dorie said sympathetically. "Experiencing life here without Mum, for the first time really, right after losing your family."

Helen felt a shock up her back. "I haven't lost my family," she snapped. "Everything's managed there."

"Sorry!" Dorie held up her palm. "I didn't mean to upset you."

"Well, you did," she retorted. The golden clambered to his feet to hop over and push his nose into her hands, clasped tightly together. With a sigh, she gave in and scratched his ears, glancing sideways at Dorie. "I'm doing fine. You don't need to worry about me. My job is to worry about you."

"Hardly. Besides, there's nothing to worry about. I'm good. My life is good."

"Are you sure? I know this dog thing is important to you, but what about benefits? Paid holidays, health plans, retirement?"

"What you're calling 'this dog thing' is a funded not-for-profit with ongoing grant support. There are a lot worse ways to make a living than running a non-profit and doing real, measurable good in the community." Dorie's eyes were like flints.

"Somebody has to watch out for you," Helen insisted.

Dorie was silent then sighed. "Forget it. You're determined to be right."

"Come on, Dorie. You have to admit this is a dead end. Your boyfriend's kind of a dead end, too, isn't he? No job?"

Dorie stood, her back very straight. "Chad is a well-respected free-lance videographer. He's my fiancé, and no, he's not a dead end. Neither am I, and I don't think I need any help after all."

"Free-lance means no job, Dorie. Don't be a child about this," Helen insisted. "Be reasonable."

Dorie's eyes glittered, but her voice remained firm. "It's time for you to go." She turned on her heel, moving fast toward the door to the back room, white poodle at her heels. She closed it behind her with an audible click, leaving Helen alone in the office.

Immobile, Helen tried to breathe. What just happened? She came to help Dorie out and to convince her the hiking trip was going to be great. What now?

Making Plans

She wouldn't have known about the planning meeting if Rett hadn't mentioned it on video-chat about something else.

"Dorie's planning to go on the trip?" she asked her sister.

"Yeah. Why wouldn't she?" Rett asked. "Did something happen?"

Helen sighed. She could not understand these sisters. "She was pretty mad at me last time I saw her."

"Well, she didn't mention it when she called for a meeting," Rett said with a smirk, "but apparently she didn't invite you."

"This trip is my idea. I'll be there."

She ran late though.

"What do we need for a backpacking trip?" Dorie asked, just as Helen came through the kitchen door at her father's house. Her three sisters sat at the kitchen table and barely looked up at her arrival.

"Hi, guys," she said, but nobody responded.

"I looked it up online," Evie said. "There's a pretty long list. I printed it out for each of us." She handed sheets of paper around.

Rett left the table to fill her coffee mug. "I'm not buying a bunch of new equipment because Helen's got a bee in her bonnet."

"I'm right here, in case nobody noticed," Helen said grimly.

"Hi, Helen," Evie said quietly.

"Bee in her bonnet?" Dorie grinned at Rett. "Who are you, Dad?"

Rett gave a short laugh. "Maybe Mum. Anyway, I'm not exactly awash in cash and I bet I'm not the only one."

Evie shook her head. "Saving every dollar for grad school, and there aren't a lot of them to save."

"Same," Dorie said, "only not for school. It's been great to get a salary since the big grant came through, but it's a pretty small salary."

"This doesn't have to be expensive," Helen said. "That's one reason it's a good choice for us."

She glanced toward Dorie. Catching her eye, she mouthed, "I'm sorry." Dorie gave a tight nod.

"No outfitters, right?" Evie checked.

"No outfitter. Dad says he can drop us off at the start," Helen said.

"We'll take my van to where we'll be finishing the hike," Rett said. "Then we need a ride to the start."

"Dad said he'd drive that shuttle from the end to the trailhead. Chad's available later that week if we need him." Dorie offered. "The sanctuary van is big enough for all of us and our stuff."

"That's good, but I don't think we're going to need another car." Helen praised. Maybe there was some benefit to the unemployed boyfriend. Fiancé. "We have drop off and pick up managed. Now we just have to figure out the least amount of stuff we need, and the food."

"Food," Evie echoed. "Do we have to eat that dehydrated stuff?"

"It's lightweight," Helen explained. "It's not terrible once you re-hydrate."

Rett shook her head. "We can eat real food. We just have to be willing to carry it."

"We don't all eat the same things," Dorie pointed out. "That could get complicated."

"We'll figure it out," Rett said. "It can't be that hard. People take trips like this all the time."

"I don't," Evie murmured darkly, but the sisters laughed.

Dorie got up to light the lamp on the sideboard as the dusk crept in. She picked up one of the multitude of family photos and brought it back to the table.

"Look at us," she said, laying the framed picture flat on the table. The kitchen was quiet as they all gazed at the photo. "Everyone has a copy of this one, right?"

Helen shook her head. "I don't." She looked at the composition: four daughters and their mother. "This was my graduation from Dalhousie, based on my oh-so-attractive cap and gown."

"Right," Rett said. "Helen's big day. I wasn't my best self, since you were in the spotlight once again." She snickered. "Look at that pucker in my mouth."

"Really?" Evie peered more closely. "You all look so much alike, even Dorie, little as she was. Whenever I see this picture, I just notice how absent I looked, like I didn't belong."

"You were gazing off into the sunset, I think," Helen said with a smile. "How old were you?"

"Well, you were twenty-one, Rett nineteen, so I must have been seventeen. Getting ready for my 12th grade year," Evie mused. "Space cadet."

Twelfth grade, Helen thought, and a chill swept through her. Darkness shrank her field of vision, so she focused on the photograph. Here and now. "Dorie, you were practically a baby."

Dorie scoffed. "Yeah, that's me, baby Dorie. Hiding behind Mum's skirt there, wasn't I?" She leaned on the table to see. "I guess I was little. I don't even remember this picture being taken, even though I've looked at it a million times since Mum died."

Helen's body returned to normal in the silence around the table. "Funny how we each see something different," she noted.

"We all look at ourselves," Rett agreed, "in some critical way. But look at Mum here." All four of them leaned closer. "What do you think she was thinking?"

"She looks pretty happy," Dorie observed.

"Yeah," Evie agreed. "But she could have just been scolding somebody. She was good at smiling for the camera. You all were."

"Not you?" Helen peered into her face.

"I never wanted to be seen. You all were the pretty ones. I was the different one."

Dorie hooted with laughter. "Evie Madison, you have no idea what I had to live up to when I followed you in school. 'I hope you're creative, like your sister.'"

"No. When I was in school, it was all about 'your smart sister Helen' and 'your athletic sister Rett' and why don't you do anything?" Evie spluttered a little.

Helen tutted. "That's terrible. Kids shouldn't have to live up to their relatives." But Jake, he had to live up to his father, she thought. Or his father's expectations. Or maybe even mine.

Rett laughed outright. "Following the smart sister wasn't a lot of fun, either. It was okay at the beginning of high school, but by grade twelve you were driven, Helen. Like no fun at all. Just work, work, work."

"Is that why you guys fought so much?" Dorie asked, eyes wide. "Comparisons?"

Helen shrugged. She ignored the frisson of fear in her belly. Twelfth grade. Why did those words chill her so? This conversation was getting uncomfortable. "High school was a long time ago. We're all different people now."

"I don't know about that," Rett said. "We're still us, just with more miles on."

Dorie giggled. "Some of you have more miles than others."

Evie elbowed her. "Watch yourself. Mum's not here to protect the baby sister from her siblings."

Scowling, Dorie said, "Did that really happen? I remember you guys being fairly mean."

"Why do you think you were hiding behind Mum's skirt in this picture?" Rett asked, waving the photograph. "You were a pain in the butt, and whenever we called you on it, you hid behind Mum."

"Me? A pain in the butt?"

Helen laughed. "Dorie, you were a little girl in a house full of teenagers. It wasn't anything you did in particular. It was just a difficult dynamic." Oh, she liked that phrase. Maybe that's what happened with her and Reg, too, a difficult dynamic. Keeper!

"You guys fought so much," Dorie recalled. "I remember Mum talking to Corinne about it."

"In front of you?" Evie asked.

"I was always with her," Dorie explained. "I heard a lot of things I probably shouldn't have. I think she felt like I was part of the woodwork or something."

"Really?" Helen felt weird, suddenly. "Like what did you hear?"

Dorie shrugged. "Oh, like if Corinne was dating, and about some friend of Mum's having another miscarriage. That's how I learned what that word meant. Stuff about Grandma Sarah. I didn't pay much attention."

"What did you hear about me?" Helen asked, throat tight.

Dorie looked up at her. "Nothing much. Hey, you look like I was going to say something terrible. Nah, it was always how wonderful Helen is, how well she's doing. After you moved away, it was always about your great life, your law practice, Reg. And you'd have thought you gave her a present when you had Jake! She was ridiculous."

"What's ridiculous about being infatuated with your first grand-child?" Helen asked defensively.

Dorie scoffed. "I was what, seven, when you had Jake? I felt up-staged by a baby in Ontario. Mum was all excited about him."

"She almost missed my graduation," Evie said.

"Helen did miss your graduation, both of you," Rett said grimly. "Along with everything else that happened here after she moved."

"What? What a nasty...." Helen was sharp. "I was having a baby, thank you."

"Jake was born in February and Evie's graduation was in June. You could have come," Rett pointed out. "Just like so many other things you missed."

"Do we have to do this now?" Evie asked. "We were just planning this trip. Let's get back to that, okay?"

Helen shook her hair back over her shoulders. "Evie's right," she said evenly. "Let's look at this trip." The further they got from dangerous topics the better.

Rett glared at her, but picked up Evie's checklist, while Dorie replaced the photograph on the sideboard. "That's what we do," she said, but quietly. "Set it all aside."

Helen's hand smacked the table. "You guys didn't visit me, either."

Evie looked at the table, but Rett stood up. "Right, Helen, like I could leave my job and my family and just flit off to Ontario. Not realistic for somebody with a job and a family."

"Exactly!" Helen said with finality. "That works both ways."

"Guys," Evie said tiredly. "Let it go. Let's plan this trip."

Helen narrowed her eyes. "You're angry I was away. But I'm here now. So yes, let's work on what we can change."

Rett scoffed. "Psychobabble. But okay. What can we accomplish?"

Evie put a calendar page on the table. "We have five lunches, four dinners and four breakfasts to figure out. Who wants to be responsible for what?"

Rett pulled the page toward her. "Look at this. We get back right before Mum's picnic. How are we going to manage that?"

Helen sighed. Was there no end to the obstacles her sisters could find? "Can't we change the day of the picnic?"

All three of them looked at her in shock. "Uh, no, Helen," Dorie said. "It's the day. It's always summer solstice."

Rett shook her head. "If you'd ever been here for one of them, you'd know the event has to happen on the solstice. We only changed that once when there was a weird post-tropical storm that came early, and even then it probably wasn't a good idea."

"What, you think Mum's going to care?" As soon as the words were out, she regretted them.

"Dad does," Evie said firmly. "I care, too."

"Okay, sorry," Helen held up her hands. "I didn't mean to offend."

Rett was still glaring. "You'll get to see what goes on," she said. "Not just get away with sending a letter."

"It is kind of a big deal," Evie offered. "There's a fair bit of work to organize all the things, but I'm pretty sure Stephen would pitch in while I'm off in the woods getting devoured by mosquitoes."

"Not mosquitoes, black flies," Dorie advised. "That's great of Stephen. He's a terrific cook."

"He loves potluck anything, he's great at talking to people, and he can keep a decent spreadsheet."

"Great," Helen said. "He's hired. But what else do we need to organize?"

"Invitations. Firewood," offered Evie.

"Drivers to pick up Mum's friends and take them home," Rett added.

Dorie chimed in: "Music. Whatever Dad thinks of at the last minute."

"Let's remember it's Dad who wants us to take this trip," Helen warned.

Rett scoffed. "Not exactly. I think you want the trip. Dad just wants us to get along."

"You guys!" Evie burst out. "Can you not fight over every detail? We have this trip to plan, Mum's picnic is right afterward, and we have a lot to do. You're giving me a headache."

Helen gazed at her then caught Rett's eye. Evie had always been a little sensitive. "Okay, sure," she agreed easily. "Rett?"

Rett nodded.

Dorie was gazing thoughtfully at the paperwork on the table. "Four nights, four dinners. We can each take one, and then just do our own lunches and stuff."

"What about breakfast? I'm not hiking anywhere without coffee," Rett pointed out. "I bet I'm not the only one."

"How do you even make coffee out in the woods?" Dorie wondered. "Campfire coffee?"

"Campstove coffee," Helen corrected. "I've seen some backpacking stoves that work."

"No lasagna, I guess, "Evie said. "All sandwiches, all the time. Ugh."

Helen shook her head. "You're not thinking creatively, sisters. We can have lots of good meals with a little stove or a campfire. Let me come up with some ideas, and you can pick which ones you want to do."

Rett's eyes narrowed again, but Helen tipped her head toward Evie in a silent reminder, and added, "Or you can just google it. That's what I was going to do."

They pondered the equipment list for a while longer, until Rett looked at her watch and jumped up. "Kids to bed," she said. "This will have to do. How long until this trip happens?"

"More than a month," Dorie announced. "Many weeks. It'll be fine."

Helen rose, too. "It'll be grand. Like Mum used to say."

"Right," Rett said dryly, but they all laughed.

<h1 style="text-align:center">Consultation</h1>

Helen picked up Rett's call the next morning.

"I've decided your caution is probably correct. We are not ready for this trip," Rett said. "We don't have the equipment, the knowledge, the physical stamina or the will to do this."

Helen sank into a chair in her living room. "I think we can do it."

"I know you think we can," Rett said, "but did you hear those girls last night? Dorie thinks she can backpack in sneakers, and Evie can't really imagine not having a hot shower for four days. Nobody is used to carrying heavy weight, and honestly, Dorie's never slept in a tent. Remember what that author said at the book talk?"

"Which part? About how the Fundy Footpath was a challenge worth doing?"

"The part about you're only as strong as your weakest link, and everyone has to work together to get through it."

"So what?"

"I don't think you realize how weak our weakest link might be." Rett sounded grim. "You know, once we're out there, we are all we've got. Dorie can't call Chad to bail her out, and Evie can't take a nap when we have to get to the next campsite."

"They're preparing," Helen said, but her stomach was sinking. "Rett, I really want to do this trip with my sisters."

"I know you do. I don't really get it, but I know it's important to you. But don't let your desire cloud your judgment. We all need to be on board, fully prepared."

"That's what I've been saying," Helen argued.

"They don't know how to prepare. I don't know how to prepare, not really. None of us has ever carried all our own stuff for four days and nights."

Helen sighed. "It pains me to say it, but you could be right." She started rummaging through a drawer. "We could consult Andrea, the book author. She's done this hike about twelve times, leading groups of teens and women, and she's available to lead small groups."

"We can't afford a leader," Rett objected. "Like the outfitter. Just not reasonable for us."

"I know," Helen agreed, "but she'll give us a consultation. Tell us what we need, instead of relying on Evie's Google expertise."

"Okay. Why not? Just not if it's too expensive."

"I'll let you know," Helen promised. "Thanks."

"Oh, I love to talk about the Footpath," Andrea said. "It's one of my favourite places."

"See?" Helen looked around the table at her sisters. "It's a great hike."

The five women sat around a table at the Sunshine Diner. Evie had her clipboard. Dorie was peering into her coffee cup, but Rett and Helen were rapt.

"Great, yes, but you want to be prepared so you can enjoy it," Andrea said. "Have you guys done much hiking?"

Evie looked at Dorie, who continued her morose gaze into her coffee. "We did Laverty Falls last September," she said. "All of us and the kids."

"Good!" Andrea said briskly. "How about under a pack? Ever carried all your own stuff?"

"Into the airport once," Rett said. "What? Nobody thinks that's funny?"

Andrea went on. "Okay, no backpacking experience. What do you have for equipment? Tents? Sleeping bags?"

"Yeah, I think so," Rett said. "We can scrounge around."

"There are some outdoor clubs that might loan you equipment," Andrea said. "Remember you'll be carrying everything, so light gear is best. You'll need tents, sleeping bags and a mat, cooking gear, a way to make your water safe."

Evie was scribbling frantically, but she looked up at that. "Safe?"

"You can't drink straight from the streams. You'll have to filter or otherwise process your water. Everybody needs good footwear that fits just right, that you've hiked in before. Extra socks, warm layers, and rain gear, food."

Helen was reeling but tried not to let it show. "Anything else?"

Andrea laughed. "Oh, probably. Poles! Hiking poles for everyone."

"Like a little old lady?" Dorie protested. "I don't need poles."

Andrea went on. "Do you have your map? I want to see what you're planning."

Helen laid the map out on the table, and they crowded around one side so they could see it. "I thought we'd travel east to west," Helen said, pointing out the start. "I like the idea of ending at Big Salmon."

"That's fine," Andrea said, "and you could also consider making it a shorter trip. You can pick up the trail in several places. It's a good hike even if you don't travel end-to-end."

Rett looked at Helen as she slowly said, "I think we want to do the whole thing."

Dorie scoffed audibly, and Rett's eyebrows lifted.

"Okay," Andrea went on, oblivious to the sister signals flying around the table. "You should plan for five days and maybe you'll finish in four."

"What makes the difference?" Rett asked.

"A lot of things. Fitness, fatigue, weather," she said. "If you want to have more time to relax and enjoy your campsites, or if you are more interested in just completing the hike."

"Bugs," Dorie said gloomily.

"When are you going?" Andrea turned back to Helen, who confirmed dates. "It's not the worst time for bugs. You should be okay, but of course you'll take bug dope."

The conversation continued for nearly an hour. Before Andrea took her leave, she looked at the little group. "If you do this, it'll be an adventure. It might even be a big adventure. You have to remember, though, it's the adversity that makes adventure."

"What do you mean?" Rett inquired.

"Going on a roller-coaster is fun, but it's not an adventure, because you know you're perfectly safe and taken care of," the consultant explained. "When you hike, you don't have those safeguards. You only have yourselves to rely on. The more adversity you encounter, the more adventure you'll have. To a point, of course."

"Of course," Helen said, trying not to see Dorie's worried face. "Well, thanks for all your wisdom. I'll be in touch."

Andrea left, and the sisters slowly collected their things. "It's a lot to consider," Rett said to Helen as they prepared to leave the diner. "We don't have the right equipment, and I know we don't have the required level of fitness."

"We have motivation," Helen said urgently. "I think this is going to be the making of the Madison sisters. Bring us together, stronger, better."

Dorie's face was full of misery. "I don't think this is for me," she said. "I know I'm the youngest, not middle-aged like you guys, but I don't know if I can do it."

"Who's middle-aged?" Evie spluttered. "We're not old. And besides, you can do it if you want to."

"Wow, Evie, good attitude," Helen said cheerfully. "Let's just take some time to look into the details. I think we can probably borrow equipment, practice a little, and we'll be great. You, too, Dorie."

Rett patted Dorie's shoulder. "It'll be good. We'll help."

Helen pushed the diner door open with her shoulder. "Can you guys come for supper on Thursday? We can talk more then."

(More) Second Thoughts

On Thursday, Helen's phone blew up with excuses. Dorie had a meeting with her grant funder. Evie went out of town to look at some old artworks in Saint Jacques. Rett couldn't find anyone to stay with the children.

"I'll come to you," Helen said to her next-oldest sister. "We've got to get this project moving."

"I guess so," Rett said, distractedly. "Mason, do not hit your sister. Did you hear me?"

"Do you want me to bring food?" Helen asked. "Or do you have something?"

"Come on. Of course I have food. I feed children. Come over by five thirty, though. We eat early."

After a meal of soup and sandwiches, the kids left to play, and Helen and Rett sat at the table to talk.

"Andrea put me in touch with the Outdoorswomen Club," Helen said. "They have some equipment to loan us, and what we can't borrow, the Fundy Outfitters can rent to us."

"Money," Rett said. "I don't have any extra, and I'm going to have to spring for hiking boots."

"I'll do equipment," Helen snapped. "We just keep coming up with obstacles, and I don't understand why."

"You really don't?" Rett looked at her curiously.

"I don't. This is a great idea to strengthen our family, and everybody's got some reason to pull back."

Rett said nothing. "Except you," Helen continued. "I appreciate your support."

"You're making this about you, Helen," Rett said suddenly. "Like it's your project and everybody has to do what you say, what you want."

Shocked, Helen leaned back. "It's for all of us," she stammered. "Not just me."

Rett shook her head. "You don't get it. It's always about what you want, the way you see it. The other girls aren't into this trip at all, but you can't see it because you're so sure you're right."

Stung, Helen got up and took her teacup to the sink. Leaning on the counter, she rinsed it out. When she turned back to Rett, her voice was steady. "I am right. This trip is good for us."

"Maybe," Rett temporized, "but it has to be our trip, not yours. That's the only way this is going to work. Dorie's frankly terrified, and Evie is trying to cope by being super organized and keeping spreadsheets, as if that's going to help her on the trail."

Helen sat back down. "What about you?"

Rett shrugged. "At first, I had reservations, and I still do about Evie and Dorie, but I'd like to do the Fundy Footpath. I do like a challenge, and I wouldn't mind a few days off from home, either. But I don't expect it to become the big bonding experience you hope for." She toyed with her cup. "In fact, it could tear us apart even worse than we are right now."

Helen's belly knotted up. "That's hardly optimistic."

"It might be realistic. Andrea was very clear about the work involved, the fitness, the preparation. Especially the teamwork. That's where we'll fail. We are so not a team."

"What do I do about that?"

Rett laughed. "You don't do anything about that. You can't fix people. It's not how things work."

She was wrong, of course. Helen helped fix Rett last fall. She'd fixed things with Evie by coming to her show last September. "Dad told me I had to fix our sister relationship. He told me to fix it."

Rett headed to the sink. "Consider what went wrong," she tossed over her shoulder. An uproar from the living room sent her out to referee, and Helen slowly stood, pushing in her chair.

The only thing that had gone wrong was people couldn't receive constructive criticism. She'd never had that problem professionally; she had successfully built a team of associates who thrived under her leadership. Sure, a few hires hadn't been a good fit and had to leave, but mostly the team had been tight. Until last year, anyway, when she'd needed to hand off work to Sarabeth's juniors. She gave her shoulders a shake.

Her sisters needed to respect her greater experience and authority. She had demonstrated the ability to make a good life away from home, a successful professional career and family life... She pivoted abruptly to follow Rett into the living room where chaos reigned.

Narrowing her eyes, Helen entered. Rett's kids were wild. She should have better control. "Oh!" She jumped when a throw pillow flew past her face to smack the wall behind her.

"Get it, Aunt Helen," Mason shouted. The air was full of laughter and flying pillows. Helen's jaw tightened. This was exactly the problem.

"Mason! What's wrong with you?" She wheeled to grab the pillow from the floor and glanced back at his grinning face. She wanted to be outraged, but the room was full of giggles, and there was Mason with a gigantic grin. "Auntie Helen! I'll get you!"

Her face softened, and she heaved the pillow with all her might right at her nephew.

"I got it!" he shouted, then pitched it directly at her, this time hitting her in the chest. "Gotcha!"

"Oh, I'll get you back, Mason," Helen said, grinning, holding the pillow like a weapon as she approached. He giggled, and hid behind the couch, but she was there in a moment, lightly whacking him on the shins with her pillow. "Be nice to your Auntie Helen," she said, mock-fiercely, while Mason held up his hands for mercy, still giggling.

In the meantime, the twins tossed pillows at their mother, who caught one and flung it back, then dove in to grab Maggie around the waist. Tossing the little girl over her shoulder, Rett paraded around the living room. "Look at what happens to little girls who throw pillows at their mothers. Ooh, you are in trouble!" She tossed Maggie on the squishy couch and tickled her.

"Me, too!" squealed Callie, jumping into the fray. Helen reached for Mason, but he ran around the couch to jump on with his sisters.

"Mum, mum! Save me from Aunt Helen!" he shrieked. The dog barked, the kids giggled, and Rett threw herself off the puppy pile of children.

"You guys," she said, breathless. "You're wearing your old mother out."

Helen dropped into the chair across from them. "You sound like Mum," she said to her sister.

"Who?" Mason asked.

"My mother. Your grandmother. Do you remember her, Mason?"

He turned to his mother. "Do I?"

Rett made a little sad face. "Maybe not. She died when you were three. We spent a lot of time with her and Grandpa though."

Mason squinched up his face. "I remember. She was in a bed."

"She could be lots of fun," Rett told him. "She was sick when you were little, but when we were kids, she was so fun."

"You were a kid?" Maggie asked seriously. "Like, I know you were, but I can't remember it."

"You weren't born then," Mason said scathingly. "Kids can't have kids."

"That's true, Mason," Rett said slowly. "I had to grow up before I could have children. Mags, you've seen pictures of me and my sisters when we were kids. Over at Grandpa's house, all the time."

"I know," Maggie confirmed, "but it's like it's not real. It's like a story."

Helen chuckled. "Sometimes it feels like a story to me, too, Maggie, and I was there. Like a fairy-tale childhood."

"Princesses?" Callie asked.

"Auntie Helen was a princess," Rett said, grinning at her sister. "I had to do all the work."

"Cinderella?" Maggie said. "Like that?"

"Ha," Helen retorted. "Kids, you don't have to believe everything your mother says. I was never a princess."

"Oh, yes," Rett went on, "Princess Know-It-All, the one who led the rest of the ragtag Madisons out of the darkness."

"For cripes' sake, Loretta. What a thing to say."

"This is boring," Callie said to Maggie. "Wanna play?"

"We can play princesses," Maggie agreed, and the girls headed for the stairs.

Mason sat quietly. Rett ruffled his hair. "You want to stick around with the old folks? Listening to us talk about the old days?"

"Grandpa was there," he said firmly. "So I want to hear about it."

Helen was still stuck on what Rett had said about her. "That was a little over the top, Rett."

Rett shrugged. "Just the way I see it. You got a lot of attention. And why not? You were smart, pretty, outgoing. All the right stuff."

"Was I really that bossy?"

"Helen, you're still bossy. That's what this whole problem is about."

Helen clicked her tongue and sighed. That old thing.

"Tell about when you were kids," Mason begged. "I like that part."

Rett gazed at him fondly. "Okay. Aunt Helen calls it a fairy-tale childhood, which means it was really good. I wouldn't use that term. There was too much fighting. Holy cow, could we ever fight. Do you remember the time you nearly pushed me down the stairs?"

"No," Helen retorted. "That was you trying to push me. I never did that."

"Ha," Rett said, smiling. "You taped a line down the middle of our room. You got the door and the closet, and you got mad every time I crossed the line. Once time you pushed me out the door and almost down the stairs."

Mason was wide-eyed.

Helen had to laugh. "Yes, I remember. I needed privacy, but that was extreme. It was pretty bad."

Rett gave her the side-eye. "Yes, it was." She turned to Mason. "Don't be like your Auntie Helen and me. It's your job to get along with your sisters."

He nodded, big-eyed. "They're so annoying."

"Of course. Whenever you live with somebody, they'll annoy you. You've been doing pretty well lately, though." A tiny smile crossed his face.

"Mum used to tell us it was our job to get along," Helen recalled. "That made things harder when we fought."

"Right, because we were letting her down."

She could be letting Mum down now, in the middle of this fracas with her sisters. She hadn't considered it, but since Mum was probably keeping a laundry list of all of Helen's faults, why not add that one? She imagined Mum in heaven, long scroll in hand.

"I wish you knew your grandmother," Rett said to Mason, absently stroking his hair. "She was the most fun mother, and the most strict. You had to behave in the Madison house, had to do your chores, be a good human, but then we could all have fun together."

"That's a fair assessment," Helen agreed. Her mind leaped to childhood memories, the good ones. Mum had made a lot of kid things fun. They had family picnics, camped regularly, had Mum's annual summer solstice bonfire on the beach, had fun with dogs, cats and whatever animal needed a home. Even chores weren't horrible. She, Rett and Evie could bake, sew, fillet a fish, throw a baseball, and ride a bike. Birthdays were legendary in Mum's household, and the legend included everybody's birthday — the dogs, the cats, Corinne, Grandma Sarah, Aunt Hannah, everyone who entered the Madison family circle.

Things changed when Dorie came. Helen remembered sharing her room with Rett, so long ago. Dorie had been so little, even younger than Rett's twins. In a flash, Helen felt Evie's truth: we don't know each other. Dorie had been tiny, and Evie a cipher the last time they lived together. They were barely in my consciousness as a teenager, Helen realized, with a wash of shame.

She glanced across the room. Rett was curled up on her ancient squishy sofa, her boy cradled against her body, the sounds of the twins upstairs playing, the woodstove crackling and the scent of yeast bread still in the air. What kind of childhood were these kids having? Dad was away, mother was busy, but still at home, feeding them, even homeschooling. Rett might throw her professional career away, but perhaps her work at home was important.

She had a momentary image of Jake's childhood; hockey even at age three, his joy in zipping around the rink in warm-ups, the quiet of a home with a single child, parents at work. She remembered tiptoeing into his bedroom to brush a kiss on his sleeping cheek when she got home late more nights than not. What was childhood like for him? Probably no fairy-tale there, unless she was the wicked witch. She sighed prodigiously.

"Tired?" Rett asked solicitously.

"Just thinking," she said. "My mind can be a hard place to be."

"Mmmm," Rett agreed. "I get that. Mason, it's probably time for a bath and story, but if you can play nicely with your sisters, we can push bedtime back an hour. I need to talk to Aunt Helen."

"Deal," he said, and headed for the stairs.

"Is that going to work?" Helen asked curiously.

"Until it doesn't," Rett said casually. "If there's no blood, it's working."

"You really sound like Mum," Helen noted.

"This hiking trip," Rett began. "You want us to get closer, learn to work together, right?"

She nodded.

"We've been working together pretty well since Mum died," Rett went on. "Dorie moved out, Evie moved back in, Dad had that health scare, and of course here I am, much to my surprise, but we are doing well, sharing responsibilities, and not taking each other too personally."

"Until I came along," Helen added.

"Well, yes," Rett said firmly. "That's not a criticism, just an observation. That's why I think you could look at the dynamics before you push us all out into the wilderness that none of us is prepared for."

"Dynamics?"

"Trust. Leadership. Respect."

"Wait, what are you saying?"

A series of shouts from upstairs brought Rett to her feet. "Just thoughts," she said. "Listen, I think I have to get these animals to bed. Have another cup of tea or something."

"No, I'll head home," Helen said. "Thanks for tonight."

"Your call," Rett said, turning toward the stairs.

"Rett?" She had no idea why, but she reached out for a hug. As she clung for a moment, tears rose. She pulled off and turned away. "Thanks."

$$Jake$$

When Easter finally came, she sat in her living room to initiate a video call to Jake. "Happy Easter!" She hoped she sounded cheery, despite her mood.

"Hi, Mum," Jake said. "Happy Easter to you."

"So, what are you doing?" She didn't recognize the room he was in.

"Not much. I helped Juliet hide the eggs for Sasha and Vicky, and they found them all. Juliet even made me an Easter basket."

Helen's gut churned. "Did she? That sounds so nice. What was in it?" Maybe Juliet treated Jake like a little kid. He'd hate that.

"It was pretty good, really. A couple of gift cards and that new game I wanted. And some really good chocolate, organic and fair trade and all of that."

"Oh." It was all she could say.

"Uh, thanks for the sweater," he added. "I left it up at school, but it's a nice one."

"Did it fit?" she asked.

"Uh, I didn't try it on yet. I'll do it when I get back."

"Okay."

There was a silence.

"Do you like the house? Your father's house?"

"Juliet's house? Yeah, it's nice. My room is big. Juliet has a dog, too."

A dog. All the ways she had fallen short as a parent.

He continued. "Dad took me over to our old house just to see it."

She wondered what that had been like. "How did it look?"

"It seems like a long time ago we lived there. Really long."

"Hmm. Maybe because of being at school? If you feel at home there, then it might ..."

"School feels like home, mostly because otherwise, I don't really have one. I mean, I have this room at Dad's house, but I haven't been here much."

"You have a room in my house, too, Jacob." She regretted her sharp tone.

"Well, I haven't ever seen it. You can't expect me to feel like your house in no place New Brunswick is my home."

"Excuse me? Half of your family comes from Stella Mare, and why would you say such a crass thing?"

"It's just a thing. People say it."

"What people? Maybe you shouldn't be associating with crass people." Now she was annoyed. Who did he think he was?

"I'm from Ottawa. Frankly, Mum, it's not all that easy to be an anglo from Ontario and go to a Quebec boarding school. I don't need to add New Brunswick to my resume."

Chagrin washed through her. "Are you having a hard time at school? Have you been putting your best foot forward?"

"School's okay. I might not meet your standards for grades, but the game is going well."

"My standards? Am I the one holding up standards?"

"Mum, you always hold up the standards. Work harder, dress nicer, be a go-getter. Aggressive on the ice and in the classroom."

She felt a mix of shame and satisfaction as she recognized her words coming back to her. "What's wrong with that?" she asked, even as her stomach sank. "Don't you appreciate encouragement?"

"This is why I begged Dad to let me stay here for Easter," he said grimly. "I have to go. Bye."

She redialed, but he didn't answer, so she switched to Reggie's phone. She could easily imagine his eye roll as he picked up his phone, but at least he answered.

"Have you heard of parental alienation?" she demanded as soon as she heard his voice.

"Happy Easter, Helen," Reg said smoothly. "How's your day going?"

"Reggie, Jake said you encouraged him to stay with you for this holiday." The background noise quieted, and she heard a door close.

"I think you might have that wrong," he said mildly. "Jake asked to stay, and I agreed."

"You undermined me."

"No," he corrected. "Jake was adamant that he didn't want to go to Stella Mare. He wanted to be here, to see his friends, and to hang out for a while with us."

His friends. Well, that made some sense. What teenager wouldn't prefer his friends to his mother and her sisters? "I want him to come see me," she said. "I don't have his friends here, though."

"You have family. He'll come around, Helen. He's still upset about the divorce. We had a long talk about things last night. We thought going to boarding school would make it easy on him, but I think it might be harder. He doesn't have to face it every day, that his parents have split."

Just like I didn't have to really grieve my mother until seeing her missing from my family home, over and over, she thought. "I want him to come in June, friends or not," she said firmly. "Can you agree to support me in that?"

"Of course," he said warmly. "You're his mother. He won't have the entire summer off, but we three can figure out a schedule."

"Okay," she said dubiously. "It would be really great if he could be here in June for my mother's picnic. Everyone comes out for that."

"I don't know if that's possible," he said, "but I'm sure you'll let us know the dates."

"I certainly will," she said, regaining her certainty. June was a nicer time for a visit, anyway.

Reggie

It was mid-May already, and the trip loomed. Four days of hiking wasn't much, not really, when it could have been a really long trip. We could have done something special, she thought, like hike the Camino or something. I don't know why I can't get cooperation.

At least the sisters were willing to try this, and Dad was over the moon that they were doing a big activity together. It really wasn't a big deal, not like hiking the east coast trail in Newfoundland, or even climbing up Katahdin, that tall mountain in Maine. But it was the best she could get them to agree to.

Well, was that true? If the consultant was correct, it wasn't an easy hike. But how hard could it really be? You just put one foot in front of the other. That's how you get it done.

Her phone pinged with a message. Evie sent her a link to a news item. What was this? Oh, some dumb hikers who put their tents up too close to the tide line and woke up wet. She went in search of her guidebook. They wouldn't make such a newbie mistake, not on her watch. It was not allowed.

Well, if the Fundy Footpath was the biggest challenge they could take on, they would make the best of it. She poked around on her laptop for the spreadsheet Evie had made to help them organize food.

Oh, this wouldn't do. Pasta three nights out of four. The carbs! Yes, they'd be hiking, but they could eat better. She sent a quick text to her sisters.

Her phone rang almost immediately.

"Hi, Rett."

"Let it go, Helen," Rett said peremptorily. "It's like a potluck. You might not get to eat exactly what you like, but you don't have to cook it, either."

"All that pasta," she started, but Rett cut her off.

"Is that the hill you're going to die on? You got everybody to go, so don't criticize what we're bringing. Really. Just don't."

Where had she heard that phrase before? The hill to die on... She was lost for a moment in memory but brought herself right back. Suddenly pasta didn't seem like an issue. "Okay, Rett, okay. Thanks." She clicked off and quickly sent a follow up text. *I'm sure everyone's meals will be great. Just happy I'm not cooking all of them!* She could pack extra protein for herself. She didn't have to rely on her sisters.

She set the phone down and wandered toward the stairs, lost in thought. The hill to die on. What a weird turn of the phrase. Nobody was at war. Not now, anyway, she thought, recalling a late fall night in the glass-and-wood house, maybe the last time she saw Reggie without other people to buffer them.

Helen sank onto the top step in her shiny new townhouse, sunlight spilling across her lap from the second-story foyer window, and lost the moment to that memory.

"Helen," Reg said, face crumpling. "I never wanted it to come to this."

"You've got things just the way you want them," she snarled. "The girlfriend, the happy home."

He sat heavily on the modern sofa. "I didn't want this to happen."

"Then you should have left little Juliet alone." She hated the sound of her voice, but she couldn't stop herself. "You caused this mess."

He shook his head slowly. "That's easy to say, and I'm sure many people are thinking it. The end of our marriage was a long time coming, long before I met Juliet. You changed. I changed."

Her shoulders sagged at the kindness in his voice, but she straightened them and lifted her chin. "You certainly did. We used to want the same things. We both worked hard, pushed the limits of what we could do, reached for success a hundred percent every day. But you lost your drive."

He gazed at his hands, dangling between his knees as he sat on the hard upholstery. "I did. Other things became important. I think it was your mother dying that made the difference for me."

"My mother? What are you talking about?" Heat filled Helen's head.

"We were racing all the time. Running to work, running home, rushing to hockey, rushing to grab a takeout meal, and having no time to just enjoy life."

"My mother died, not yours," she snapped. "I'm the bereaved party."

He looked at her curiously. "We both lost her. I've always loved both of your parents, and wanted what James and Aggie had, only a contemporary version. Having that, plus career success, would have required slowing down a little. Only you couldn't slow down."

The truth of it felt like a knife. She remembered his invitations to take a weekend off, to go to the lake, to hike and camp with him and Jake, but building a practice, especially in a big city, meant commitment. She knew at the time she might miss out, but she couldn't let work go. What would happen to her if she didn't work?

"I thought it was just Jake getting older that made you want to hang out at home more."

Reg had left their shared law practice for another job a few years ago, one where the company had "family friendly" policies. She thought it was just a ploy to get employees, but Reg didn't. It worked for Helen, too, because then Reg took Jake to the doctor, could work from home when the child was sick, and had flex time to travel for all those hockey tournaments. It wasn't for Helen, that's all. But that didn't mean her husband had to have an affair.

Her ire rose again. "I didn't change. You used to appreciate my focus. Called it my fast-track to success."

"How's that working for you?" He wasn't even sarcastic.

"It's great. Things are great. The practice is breaking our own records, and I've taken on another associate. It's fine." Her head ached.

"What about home, though, and family? Jake is growing up so fast."

"That's what happens if you're lucky," she said grimly. "Your kids grow up. Become adults. Take care of themselves."

"I suppose you want this house," he said, looking around. "It's big."

"It's a family home. Our family. Not yours and Juliet's." She'd designed that house and no, he wasn't getting it.

"Jake's probably going to Quebec. What will you do then with your 'family home?'"

Jake was young, but hockey schools took them young. When she had left Stella Mare for university, she was certain she would never live in the village again. She could not leave soon enough, nor get far enough away. What if Jake felt like that?

"Keeping this house doesn't make sense," Reggie said. "We should sell it and divide the proceeds, tucking a chunk away for Jake."

There was steel in her eyes and backbone. "I built this house. We are not selling it."

"You'd rather keep a monument to overwork and toxic stress than have us both okay financially? You want a court battle over this house?" There it was. The hill to die on.

"I might have to buy you out, but I am keeping this house. You've taken enough from me."

"You keep telling yourself you're a victim here. I'm sorry that Juliet arrived in the picture before I got the courage to leave. But really, Helen, you're not a victim. You got hard," he said. "You won't let anything touch you anymore. There's no softness left."

That certainly wasn't true. "I suppose Juliet is all softness. All sweetness and light." She could almost taste her bitterness.

Reg shrugged. "We're not talking about Juliet. We're talking about us. I really thought we'd be together forever, and I wish it had worked out that way."

Her anger dissolved into numbness. "Well, it didn't. Neither of us planned for this."

"I just hope we can do this next part kindly," he said. "I don't want to see you suffer."

She might like to see him suffer a little, but she didn't put that in words. "I appreciate that. I suggest you write up a separation proposal. Your lawyer can send it to Alicia at my firm. The house is mine."

"You want me to initiate this?"

Anger flared again. "You want to go live with lovely Juliet, so yes, you start the proceedings. I'm not doing the heavy lifting."

The doorbell rang, startling her out of her reverie to run down the stairs. She signed for an envelope of documents, then took them to the kitchen. The return address made her swallow hard; her former firm. It could just be divorce papers. Tossing the envelope on the counter, she headed back upstairs, pausing briefly at that top step. How long until her mind stopped chewing over her separation? Did she miss Reggie? She considered that. Well, not really. He'd become almost unrecognizable, taking up cooking, of all things, and skiing with Juliet and her kids, and taking Jake along with them. Her stomach clenched at that thought. She might not miss Reg, but Jake was another matter.

She found her phone where she'd dropped it and sent her son a text, even though he should be in classes. Clicking off, she felt marginally better.

A Good Team at Home

The Madisons gathered at James' house for Friday night pizza the week Harry, Rett's husband, returned from his final semester out west. Helen might hate pizza every Friday, but she liked Harry and besides, she didn't need to eat pizza. She carried her big wooden salad bowl in from the car, noting the daylight even at seven pm. Early June was good for sunlight if not for warm weather.

Rett's family emerged from the forest behind the house, streaming across the big back lawn. Helen waited on the porch, holding her bowl and greeting each as they arrived: Mason, carrying a bag of bread, the twins with some toys, Charlie the yellow Labrador with a wagging tail and perpetual doggie grin, then Harry, holding a cake carrier in one hand and Rett's hand in the other.

"Helen!" Harry broke away to give her a one-armed hug. "It's been a long time."

She nodded. "It has. Welcome home."

Rett said, "He's been welcomed by the professionals. You should see the banner and decorations the kids made."

"They must have missed you," Helen said to Harry.

"So it would appear," he said, pushing the door open.

Stephen was pouring drinks and Evie delivering them, while the kids were regaling James with tales of animals, their trip to get their daddy from the airport, and other trivia in the living room. There was the usual kerfuffle of greetings between large dogs and various people. Evie, looking flushed, said, "I'm glad I'm not cooking. Pizza is due in thirty minutes. Want to sit in the living room?"

"Sure." Helen deposited her salad on the counter and accepted a glass of wine on her way out of the kitchen. The chaos was settling, kids heading upstairs, dogs easing back to the floor in the sunporch, and James rocking slightly in his recliner.

"What are they doing upstairs?" Helen was curious. "I've always wondered about that."

"We lived here for a while last fall," Rett reminded her. "Evie found them some of our old toys, and the TV that only plays kid shows is up there, too."

"Only kid shows?" Evie plunked down beside Helen. "Really?"

Rett shrugged. "As far as they know. It works."

Another wave of noise from the kitchen brought Corinne, Dorie, Chad, and the white poodle. Soon enough, the adults were all in the living room and the dogs settled back around the recent addition. A scream from upstairs was followed by a plaintive, "Mum!" Rett sighed and headed for the stairs.

"Helen, tell us about this hiking trip," Harry invited. "I'm interested to hear about it."

"I'm sure Rett told you all about it," Helen demurred.

"I'm interested in hearing everybody's take on it," Harry insisted.

Stephen leaned forward, elbows on knees. "So am I," he added. "I can't quite imagine taking it on, but obviously you can, and so can all the sisters."

Imagine it? Helen didn't know if she could imagine it, but she knew she could do it. "I think hard work is good for a team. Helps them grow stronger together."

Dorie had been staring at her hands. Now she looked up, and her gaze was hard, but she said nothing.

"I think I'd like to be stronger," Evie said, "but mostly I want to do something fun with my sisters." She looked around the room. "All of my sisters."

Rett, coming down the stairs, put in, "I can think of a lot of fun things that aren't as challenging as hiking the Fundy Footpath. The consultant suggested a spa day, remember?"

"We're going to build character. You know, dig deep, all of that." Helen remembered words from her leadership training.

"I'm pretty sure my character is already built," Rett said, "but I think this hike will be both challenging and fun. Besides, there's no place more beautiful than the Fundy coast."

"In the fog, the rain and through clouds of black flies," muttered Dorie.

"What?" Helen hadn't heard. Was Dorie being negative?

"Never mind," Evie interjected. "It wasn't helpful." She threw a frown in Dorie's direction, confirming Helen's guess. Maybe Dorie was still mad. Time to patch things up.

"Dad, I went out to the dog sanctuary the other day," she said conversationally. "I hadn't been for a while. It looked great. Very systematic and organized."

"Oh, yes," James said, looking puzzled. "Dorie's a good organizer. But you already knew that."

Dad probably wondered what she was doing, but she plowed on. "It was good to see it for myself. They have a big operation going on there." She glanced at Dorie, who looked a bit more relaxed. "I'm happy Dorie can take the time off to do our trip."

"Everyone is pitching in so we can do this thing," Rett said, coming to sit beside Harry. "Thank goodness Harry's home. He's got a little time to learn the routine before I take off."

The way Rett looked at Harry made Helen's throat feel tight, so she jumped into the conversation. "I imagine there's a lot of kid stuff to do."

"Kids, goats, chickens, and keeping my customers happy," Rett said. "You're up to it, right?" Harry gave her a silly grin. Helen turned away, annoyed. It wasn't that big a deal. They were only going to be away four days. Maybe five.

"We hired somebody to come clean the kennels that week," Dorie offered. "Chad's got a project due at the end of June, and he'll be shooting video out of town when we leave, so we had to hire help. Alice and Dad are going to handle the morning and evening feeds and documentation, and some kids from civics class are doing their good turn in the community by helping us that week. We need a team when we're both out of town."

"I only have to get Cassandra to cover my shifts at the gallery," Evie said.

"Or I will," Stephen put in. "I'm already there, anyway." Stephen lived over the gallery where Evie had a part-time job.

"You're going to be busy organizing Mum's picnic, remember?"

"No worries! I can organize and cover shifts. I can even cook with one hand tied behind my back." Everyone laughed. "Besides, I've got Chad and Harry as backup."

Dorie's fiancé, Chad, smiled in response. He'd been quiet during this discussion, but Chad was often quiet.

"Sounds like you girls have a good team at home," James noted. "You've got a good team going on the hike, too."

There was silence. "Well, we'll be a good team by the end," Helen said. "I can't wait to see us cross that suspension bridge at Big Salmon. Go Team Madison!"

Dorie sighed and left the room, Evie's eyes following her. Rett snorted and shook her head.

Fortunately, the doorbell signaled the arrival of pizza.

Before the Beginning

It was the third week of June. Now or never, Helen thought, as they loaded backpacks for a dry run in Dorie's barn. Evie had her clipboard, but Helen kept her list on her phone. Three hiking packs stood like soldiers, but a mass of additional items cluttered the floor.

"I don't understand why we have to unpack what I already packed," Dorie complained. "It was hard enough getting this stuff in there."

"We need to share the weight," Helen explained again. "So we're only taking what we need, and nobody is disproportionately burdened."

"Like I don't have to carry the stove, the pots, *and* the tent," Rett said, heaving her backpack onto the floor. "Help me get this stuff out."

They set to, and soon the entire floor of the Best Friends' Dog Sanctuary office was full of camping items, each subject to scrutiny.

"Where's your water bottle, Dorie?" Helen asked.

"Oh, right here." She brandished a plastic bottle and took a swig.

"No."

"What do you mean, no? It's lighter than those Nalgene things, and I don't want to carry a canteen like some misguided Boy Scout."

"It won't last," Evie said. "Come on, Dorie, you know better."

"I don't have one. Does anybody have an extra?" Evie tossed her a purple liter bottle. "Okay, mine is purple," Dorie announced.

"The consultant said everybody needs three litres a day," Evie said, concerned. "We can't possibly carry that much water."

"No, we'll filter it twice a day. Where's that water filter?" Helen looked around, and Rett held it up. "Okay, put that in the group equipment pile. Everybody's going to have personal stuff and we'll all help carry the group stuff."

A lot of good-natured arguing followed about the group equipment, but ultimately, two tents, the tiny cooking kit, the water filter and the first aid kit were all allocated. Helen squatted to slide her arms through the straps of her pack, fastened the belt around her waist, and tugged at the straps to adjust them. "There."

"Are you kidding?" Dorie gasped as she hoisted her pack. "That's heavy." She tried to pull it on, one side at a time.

"Hold on," Helen said. "Rett and I'll help you." They lifted the pack so she could get it on.

"Are we supposed to be able to hike like this?"

Helen gave her a look. "If it's too heavy, leave something behind. Just not any of the group gear. We need that."

"I need everything I have."

"Sleeping bag and mat, rain gear, water shoes, a warm layer, and extra socks. That's it."

Evie chimed in. "Maybe the body wash isn't necessary, Dorie."

"But what about clean underwear?" she wailed. "Four days, girls. We'll stink."

Helen laughed. "We're camping. Everything will smell like wood smoke and forest. Besides, we'll all stink together."

Dorie scoffed. "Great."

"You must have done this before," Helen remarked. "We camped all the time when I was small."

Rett shook her head. "Remember, Dorie didn't have the same childhood we had."

Dorie lifted her chin. "It's not my fault I'm the youngest, you know."

Evie giggled. "You sound like you did when you were little."

"I'm disadvantaged because I don't have your experience."

"Don't fret," Rett advised. "You're also a lot younger than the rest of us. More resilient. Flexible. Stronger."

"Right. Like Helen hasn't been at the gym every day since she got here in January."

"Listen, it'll all be fine. We'll be grand, as Grandmother Sarah used to say, but really, lighten your load however you can. You'll appreciate it later."

The last night at home, Helen fretted over the forecast from Environment Canada. Uncertainty in the weather was not helpful. The weather app showed a cute little pile of clouds with a few splattery raindrops for the day after tomorrow. At least tomorrow looked clear. Once she got them out there, they'd love it. Even if they didn't, once Dad dropped them off, they were committed.

A ping alerted her to a text. Jake. *Good luck on the big hike, Mum. I hope you have fun. See you Friday.*

She felt her face smooth and soften into a smile. *Thanks! I'll tell you all about it when I see you.*

She settled into her king-sized bed, moonlight streaming in from the windows overlooking the cove. Tomorrow she'd be sharing a tent with Rett, sleeping on the ground with sounds of the forest and the water as her lullaby. After they got home, Jake was coming for a visit. She couldn't wait.

She woke with a luxurious feeling of having slept deeply and well. Yawning and stretching, she took in the sunlight pouring through the windows. When she turned to her phone to check the time, she was shocked to find it was nearly six am. She flew out of bed, grabbing up the clothes she'd prepared the night before. With the girls still iffy about this trip, she wanted everything to go as planned.

She was prepared by six-thirty when James' truck pulled into her little driveway. Evie was in the cab already, so Helen heaved her backpack into the cargo area and climbed in, too, brandishing her travel mug.

"Good morning," she said, settling her weight into the familiar leather seat. Evie, also carrying coffee, smiled weakly.

"Good day for it," James said. "You girls look like you belong in the woods." He chuckled as he looked them over.

"That's us, Dad," Helen said heartily. "Woodsy."

"I am hardly woodsy," Evie retorted, "but I'm willing to try."

"That's the part that counts," their father asserted. "Now Rett, then Dorie, and we're off to the trailhead."

"Why didn't you get Rett on the way?" Helen asked. "Her house is closer than mine."

"She wasn't ready," Evie said. "Kid stuff."

"Hmm," Helen said. This trip would do Rett good. She was far too caught up in all the kids' stuff. Maybe it was inevitable as a homeschooler, but it wasn't good for Rett. This trip was a good idea.

It didn't look like any crisis was happening at Rett's house, but Helen jumped out of the truck to help her anyway. Harry stood on the porch, alongside the twins and Charlie, the yellow Labrador retriever. Helen waved to them, and Maggie flew down the walkway toward her.

"Auntie Helen! Are you going to see a bear?"

A bear. What was this child thinking? Maggie liked to scare herself, so Helen said, "Probably not. Why?"

"Because if you see a baby bear, please bring him home," she pleaded. "See my book? I want a baby bear just like this one."

Helen considered. "It's very cute, isn't it?"

Maggie nodded seriously. "Very cute. And I would take good care of it."

Rett arrived, panting slightly, laden backpack in her arms. "Mags, we go over this all the time. Animals that live in the woods need to stay there. Daddy told you, I told you, even Mason told you. Remember why?"

Maggie scowled. "I just thought Auntie Helen might bring me one."

"Helen's no different from the rest of the family, kiddo. Nobody is bringing home any bears."

Maggie heaved a giant sigh. "I'm going to go pat the goats," she said with six-year-old dignity.

"You can do that," Rett said, "but give me a kiss goodbye first. I'm going camping with your aunts. I'll be back in - "

"Four days," Maggie rushed to fill in. "Bye, Mum. We'll have fun and you'll have fun."

"You bet," Rett said, squeezing the little girl. Callie and Mason ran up to get their hugs, too.

Helen jumped into the back seat of the truck to avoid watching Rett bid her children goodbye. They were pretty grown up about it, but Rett's eyes looked a little watery. No reason to get all emotional, Helen thought. It's just a little hiking trip. But of course the kids' father had been away for months, and they were used to having Rett at home. Meeting their every need. This trip will be good for Rett's kids, too.

Rett climbed into her vehicle, and James backed down the driveway. Everyone waved and shouted goodbye.

Dorie was ready and waiting with Chad's grandmother Alice at the entrance to the dog sanctuary.

"Got everything?" James asked. She nodded, uncharacteristically quiet. She hugged Alice, and lifted her backpack into Rett's vehicle before clambering into the passenger seat.

James said, "Time's a-wasting, girls. Everybody all set?"

Amid a chorus of agreement, James manoeuvred the truck around the grassy circle in front of the barn. They trundled down the driveway and turned right on the secondary road, Rett following.

"Settle in, girls, for the start of your big adventure. Next stop, the Fundy Footpath!" James declared.

"Probably not," Evie reminded him. "I'm sure I'll need a coffee refill in an hour or so."

Helen sighed. If they ever got started, it would be a memorable trip.

Finally, the Beginning

The trip was punctuated by dropping off Rett's SUV at the end point. To get there, they drove along the scenic Fundy Parkway. The fog prevented spectacular views, despite being on cliffs high above the Bay of Fundy. James followed signs for the Big Salmon Interpretive Centre, and Rett's SUV followed him.

They parked at the far end of the lot, transferring Rett and Dorie's backpacks into James's truck, then the girls piled in.

"Get comfortable," James advised. "It's a bit of a drive to the drop-off."

Evie checked her notes. "You're right. We'll be sitting here for a while longer. Everybody good to go?"

Helen could barely contain her impatience. Why did every little thing have to take so long? Finally, they were backing out and heading east again on the Parkway, to drive over Big Salmon river, a deep ravine that led to the ocean. She looked up and down the river as they crossed.

"Oh, look! There it is!"

"The suspension bridge!" Dorie sounded as excited as Helen felt.

"Next time we see it, we'll be crossing it," she said with satisfaction. "Evie, you can plan to take a picture of us there, to mark the spot."

"I'll be ready!"

Rett gazed out the window, saying nothing, but she smiled.

Helen leaned back in her seat. Finally, the trip was getting underway. James had the radio on Maritime News Network, playing local news and the morning show, talk about local politics and the arts. When the weather forecast came on, Evie turned up the volume.

"Today is going to be gorgeous throughout most of New Brunswick, the best day of the week to get outside to catch up on that yard work. Sunny and clear, except for fog blanketing the Fundy Coast. We're watching tropical storm Clayton, currently off the coast of North Carolina. If Clayton keeps gaining energy on its trip north, it could present a few soggy days for much of the Maritimes and a lot of wind for Nova Scotia. Other modeling suggests Clayton will head further east and just tap the coast of Newfoundland but stay tuned to the MNN for updates."

Evie turned around to look at Helen. "Did you hear that?"

Helen, busy looking at her phone, answered, "What?"

"The forecast, Helen. There's a tropical storm coming."

Helen scoffed. "That's the radio being sensationalist. Other forecasts say we'll have decent enough weather, with some drizzle, maybe on Thursday. Don't worry."

"Yeah, weather," Dorie said. "Bugs, heavy backpacks and now weather."

James chuckled. "You girls. You used to love camping."

"I love camping," Helen said. "You and Mum got me hooked at a young age."

Rett shook her head. "My life at home feels pretty close to camping sometimes. I don't really have to go into the woods for it."

"Oh, I think it will be fun," Evie said. "How often do I get to see things that other people have never seen? It's like an artist's dream come true."

"But you have to risk life and limb to do it," Dorie retorted.

Rett laughed aloud. "I never thought you'd be the worried one. Dorie, the family adventurer."

Dorie gazed silently out the window of the truck. Rett, too, fell quiet, and the radio chatted about events in Saint John as the truck moved ever closer to the start of their hike.

When they got to Fundy National Park, Helen's excitement rose. Or maybe that was anxiety. Well, it didn't matter, anyway. They were here. Or almost.

Helen jumped out to check in with the ranger and get a map of the park. Finding the trailhead was supposed to be tricky, and she didn't mind asking the professionals for help.

"Hello, bonjour," the young ranger said. "What are you up to today?"

"We're starting the Fundy Footpath," Helen announced. The door opened behind her and Dorie entered the little kiosk. Helen noted her pale face. Maybe she really was afraid. "Where do we start?"

"Okay, let's look at your plan," the young ranger said. "Most people start at the other end, you know."

"Yes. We want to finish there, though. It just makes more sense for us." Helen didn't want to go through a long explanation about how doing the hardest thing first was the best strategy.

"As I'm sure you know, it's a tough hike," the ranger said. "Did you bring a tide chart?"

"No," Helen said slowly. "I just took a screenshot."

"That's okay as long as your phone works," the ranger said. "Battery back up?"

"Of course," Helen said.

"Oh, for Pete's sake," Dorie snapped. "Thanks. I'll take it." She took the paper chart from the ranger's hand. "What else do we need that we didn't think of?" she asked her.

The ranger laughed. "You've got that guidebook," she said, gesturing to the book in Helen's hand. "But people make the mistake of relying on their electronics."

"I expected unreliable coverage," Helen said. "I just figured I could use it for information storage. Not like paper."

"You can," the ranger agreed. "But most phone batteries don't last five days."

They listened to a few more bits of information, then Dorie and Helen piled back into the truck. "Wolfe Pointe parking area, Dad," Helen announced. "Down the big hill."

The truck headed back onto the park roadway and pointed south toward the Bay. The view opened up, and a beam of sunshine pierced the bank of fog, highlighting the vast water and sky of the Bay of Fundy. "Look at that," James said with satisfaction. "You're going to have a nice day after all."

At the far reaches of the Wolfe Pointe parking lot, they unloaded packs and hoisted them on. James helped Evie tighten a dangling strap, then gave her a hug. "Okay, you four, take care of each other. We'll see you on Thursday."

"Right," Helen said. "We'll be fine. It's going to be great." She turned toward the woods where the Goose River trail began.

"Help Harry with the kids, Dad," Rett said. "Don't let them get away with anything."

"Oh, right, Grandpa's on it," he assured her. "No spoiling on my watch."

"Yeah," she scoffed. "Here, give me a hug." She grabbed at him, made awkward by the big backpack.

"Right, me, too," Helen said, turning back. Evie and Dorie each said goodbye, and Helen shepherded them toward the trailhead. "Come on, girls. Time and tide wait for no man."

Evie grinned. "It's a good thing there are no men here."

"Bye, girls," James said, and stumped back toward his truck.

Dorie's face in profile looked resolute, though still pale, Helen thought. Evie and Rett were ribbing each other about something, but they set off together and Helen checked her watch. Nine-thirty on the dot. Not too bad.

As they walked along the path, the sounds of vehicles and people grew distant, and the sounds of the forest predominated. Helen heard her sisters chatting ahead of her, the twitter of some little birds, and the bright, scolding sound of a squirrel, startled by their presence. The scent of spruce was everywhere, along with an earthy smell of soil and old, decaying leaves, intensified by the recent rain. Her boots stepped down on a needle-strewn path, and she could feel tension dropping away, even as her backpack seemed to weigh more. They finally made it; they were out on the trail. Doing the big adventure together. This might be okay.

The way was wide enough for conversation, but Helen was soaking in the feeling of the place, the openness of the path, the dark woods to right and left. She caught Evie's glance back toward her and they shared a smile.

A rattle and shout behind her alerted her to look. A pair of mountain bikes were heading their way. "Bike!" she shouted to her sisters, and everyone moved to the side of the trail. The bikers went by, waving, and the girls regrouped for hiking. Helen moved up beside Evie.

"So, what do you think?"

Evie smiled. "This is pretty nice. Even with a heavy pack. I forgot how much I love being out in the woods."

"It's easy to forget when you haven't done it in a while." They walked on, steps matching. After a bit, Helen asked quietly, "Is Dorie okay?"

Evie looked puzzled. "Sure, why not?"

"She just seemed a little out of sorts," Helen replied. And pale, she added to herself. But no point in giving Evie something to worry about. That girl did enough worrying on her own.

"I think the backpack part surprised her," Evie explained. "I never think about how much weight the snail has on his back, you know. Relative to the snail."

Helen giggled. "That's us. A bunch of snails, carrying our homes and everything else on our backs. Maybe we should have planned five weeks instead of five days."

The trail narrowed and became twisty as it wove uphill. The hikers settled into a rhythm climbing the easy ascent single-file and Helen took up the rear again. A drop of sweat trickled down her back, and she gave a thought to taking off her outer layer, but that would require unbelting, unhooking, and sliding out of the heavy pack. Maybe better to wait until everyone was ready for a break.

Before she could get much more uncomfortable, Dorie called it. "We've been at this for hours," she complained. "When is it break time? I need to eat. And pee."

Rett looked at her watch. "It's been forty-five minutes, Dorie."

"I need to stop," Dorie reiterated.

"Come on," Rett insisted. "You can do this."

"No, if somebody needs to stop, I think we should stop," Evie said in her quiet, diffident way. "We're not all the same."

Helen caught up to the three of them. "The top of this hill is right there. Can we get up there to find space to sit? Just up there?" She nodded at the trail ahead. Sunlight sure made it look like there was an open space close to the top of this ascent.

"Okay," Dorie agreed. "Let's get up there." She leaned into the incline, and Rett and Evie followed. By the time Helen arrived at the clearing, Dorie's pack was leaning against a tree and she was crashing around in the underbrush.

"Good call," Rett said. "There are logs to sit on. Here, I'll help you get that pack off."

"Thanks," Helen said, a little breathless. "That last bit was steeper than I realized."

Dorie returned to the group, tucking in her shirt. "Close call," she said with a giggle. "It's like being a toddler, with having to get all that gear off just to follow a call of nature."

"You probably can do it with your pack on," Helen said.

"You can," Rett retorted. "I'd be like a turtle turned on his back, rolling around trying to get up." Evie giggled.

"Yeah, this is better," Dorie said.

Helen spread out her jacket, lay back on the rock, and turned her face to the sun. The sounds of her sisters getting snacks and water faded as she slowed her breathing and soaked in the rays.

This was what she'd hoped for, the four of them having fun together. She sat up to dig around in her pack for a snack, glancing around at her sisters.

"Hey, where's the first aid kit?" Evie asked. "Rett, you have it, right?"

"The nurse gets the first aid kit? That's such a cliche." Rett snickered. "I think Dorie ended up with it. Do you need something?"

"I think so," Evie said, eyeing her foot. Her boot lay on the ground, laces trailing. "My big toe is kind of hot."

Rett got up to look. "Yeah, it's red. You need to get something on it. Dorie, we need the first aid kit."

Dorie, who had been blissfully leaning against her backpack, groaned. "It's in there somewhere. Probably in the bottom."

"Somewhere? You didn't think we might need it? Come on," Rett was scathing.

"I never did this before," Dorie whined. She pulled the pack toward her and started opening it. "How would I know what to prioritize?" She pulled items out, dumping them on the ground. "Now I'm going to have to pack this back up, and I don't even know how I did it the first time." She hauled the box marked with a red cross from the depths of the pack and handed it to Rett.

"We'll find a place," Rett said. "We'll figure it out." She sat on the ground near Evie and poked around in the box. "Here's some moleskin, Evie. Cover that hotspot and then check to see how your boots are fitting. Nobody wants to carry you out."

"Believe me, that's not my plan," Evie assured. "I hate blisters."

"Yup," Helen said. "Dry socks, boots that fit."

Evie fussed with her foot and finally got her boot back on, snugly tied.

Dorie looked at her belongings spread out in the little clearing. "Can somebody help me? I don't think I did this right the first time."

Helen moved in to help reload Dorie's pack. When they were finished, Dorie commented, "We've had our first first aid call of the trip already, and we've barely been out here an hour."

Helen nodded. "We've got some distance to cover before nightfall. Get that pack on."

Pulling her own pack over her shoulders, she tugged at the straps. It felt heavier now, but she was strong. At least she knew she was strong. She was less sure about Dorie, who was groaning a little as she stood up with the pack on her back.

"Wait," Rett said. "Let me put this box back in." She fussed with the top of Dorie's pack. "Were you hoping I'd forget? It's at least six more ounces." She waggled her eyebrows at Dorie.

"I just need to get used to this," Dorie reminded her. "I carry big bags of dog food, but not on my back."

"Fair enough," Rett agreed. "Like I carry kids and bales of hay and straw, but it's not exactly the same."

Evie eyed them as she pulled her pack on, too. "I carry groceries and that's it," she said shortly. "You badass sisters better be prepared to help this weakling out."

Dorie snickered. "Weakling my butt."

Helen, quiet, listened to the banter. Her stomach settled a bit. "Okay, badass sisters, let's hit the trail."

The First Day

The first kilometres were easy, the trail wide and accommodating, but as the elevation increased and the trail grew narrow, the work of moving themselves and their packs was harder. Even with the work, Helen relished the relative quiet; the sounds of her feet, her sisters' muted voices, and the gentle noises of the forest. They were far enough from the coastline to almost forget the Bay of Fundy was off to the left, but the overall feeling was timelessness. Wilderness.

Wild was the first part of that word, she thought. *This place is wild, even though people travel these paths. Wild in the sense of not caring about me and my insignificant life.* Her throat tightened at that idea, *her insignificant life*, and in her imagination, she saw Jean-Louis gazing across the candlelit restaurant table, then Jake's shuttered face.

A burst of squirrel chatter drew her back to the here-and-now of the wild, and she sighed. *Here and now. This is how we get through things that are hard,* she reminded herself.

After their snack break, they left the part of the trail that was in Fundy National Park and the terrain abruptly grew steep. Along with the incline, the trail itself changed character, becoming more of a single track and the sisters settled into single file, Dorie in the lead. The path was littered with rocks up to boulder size, and full of tree roots. Footing was precarious, requiring attention.

"How's that toe?" Helen asked Evie, who hiked just ahead of her.

"Must be okay," Evie replied. "It's not complaining. Moleskin to the rescue."

"Right. We all need to be vigilant about feet." Her foot slipped against a tree root as she spoke, and she stabilized herself by grabbing at a sapling.

"Might be time for those poles," Rett observed, having looked back. "This isn't easy going."

"Good point," Helen agreed, and reached behind her to locate the telescoping hiking poles attached to her pack. Evie and Rett also deployed their poles. Dorie, ahead of her sisters, continued, seemingly unaware of their movements. The four continued the clamber, climbing up and up through the woods.

"When do we get there?" Dorie asked plaintively, looking back over her shoulder at her sisters.

"Depends on what you mean," Rett said. "Nirvana?"

"No, I just mean the top," Dorie moaned. "This is hard work."

"There is no top," Rett intoned. "There is only the climb. You didn't know you were becoming Sisyphus, sister. Welcome to the afterworld of backpacking, where you only hike uphill."

A laugh burst from Helen. "Did you read the guidebook? We go up and up and up and then we go down and down and down and we do that for four or five days and we get to the end. That's the trip."

"You make it sound very inviting, Helen," Evie said. "Why didn't you describe it that way when we still could get out of it?"

"I'm teasing," Helen insisted. "Listen to the woods. Isn't that quiet the most beautiful thing? Isn't this already worth it?"

"It's not worth it if we don't get home," Dorie said grimly.

Rett gave her a poke with her hiking pole. "You in the front, get going. This is not the complaint department. Besides, we have to land somewhere to eat lunch. You keep a watch out for a good place."

Dorie heaved a sigh, but she turned back to hike uphill some more. Each sister followed, Helen at the rear. At least she was enjoying the peacefulness of the woods, despite her sisters' complaints.

It was a slog, though. Even Helen had to agree.

Lunch was a welcome break, but short, and then they were at it again. Step after step, poling for support, step after ever-loving step.

"Listen, I don't want to sound like a kid, but does anybody know how much farther? It feels like I've been pointed downhill for hours."

"You have, Dorie," Rett said. "We all have. But there's got to be a bottom, and that's where we'll camp, right, Helen?"

Helen had the trail map in her hand. "That's right. I think this should be the last downhill to Goose River, and that's where we'll spend tonight."

"Wait. Didn't we already head downhill forever?"

"We did. We crossed the creek, and now we're heading toward Goose River, also a tidal crossing. We'll cross at morning low tide. Tonight we'll camp there."

"In a river?" Dorie's voice was high.

"Don't ask," Evie advised. "If the guidebook says camp at Goose River, then that's where we're camping."

"It's a legit place," Helen reassured. "Andrea told us to make that our first night. We signed in with the ranger, remember?"

Dorie swigged water out of the purple bottle. "We'll get more water there, right?"

"That's right," Evie said. "There's plenty of fresh water this time of year."

The four followed a switchback trail down the steep hillside. Dorie grabbed at saplings for support, while the others used their poles.

Dorie was the first to land on a level surface, and she gave a shout of jubilation. "Made it!" Helen scrambled down the last of the hillside and through the thinning trees to find the wide creek bed spread out before them. She looked left, downstream, to where the watercourse emptied into the Bay of Fundy and caught her breath. The clear blue sky stretched out forever, and dark cliffs climbed up either side of the creek bed. She walked toward the open sky, gazing upward.

"Helen!" Rett's voice brought her back. "Do we need to cross now? Check the tide chart."

"Oh, right," she said, turning back. "This is the other tidal crossing, isn't it?" The two of them huddled over the map and the tide chart. Evie and Dorie drew near.

"It looks like we're at low tide now, and the next one is earlier in the morning than I want to be hiking," Rett announced. "Let's get across this river and camp on the other side."

"Are you sure?" Dorie demanded. "I just took that pack off and I don't want to put it back on for a long time."

"Sorry, not sorry," Rett said, then laughed at Dorie's glare. "Oh, did I sound like my kids there? Just a little more, and we'll make camp and rest up."

"And eat, right?" Dorie asked, shouldering her pack again.

"You bet we'll eat," Rett agreed. "I'm ready for food."

Helen looked at the river crossing. "What do you think about footwear?" she asked. "I think I'd rather do this in water shoes. I don't want to risk wet boots."

Evie wrinkled her nose. "Wet boots are awful. Okay. Dorie, you can take that pack off again. We're changing footwear."

Dorie sighed audibly. "Okay, but my shoulders are going to rebel at some point."

The sun poured into the wide canyon formed by the riverbed. When Helen took off her boots and socks, she warmed her feet in the sunshine. "Oh, that feels delicious," she noted.

"Get ready for cold water," Rett said with a laugh, and they picked their way across the wide tidal plane. "Ooh, that is some cold!"

Between laughing and chatter, they walked cautiously across the slippery pebbles toward the western shore. Helen looked ahead, trying to assess the location for camping. Where was the high water mark? This was where people sometimes got caught by unexpectedly high tides; she didn't want that to happen to them. She conferred with Rett.

"Upriver?" Rett suggested. "Where the land rises a bit?"

"I guess," Helen said reluctantly. "This flat seems easy for putting up tents."

"Tides. Bathroom. Remember what Andrea said."

Helen stifled a sigh. The leader needed to stay strong. "Okay, girls, let's head up here to find a good place to camp."

They parked packs and shook off the day. Evie stripped off her outer layers and walked into the riverbed. "Oh, I can feel the tide turning," she called back to her sisters, then headed downstream again. The next time Helen looked up, Evie lay on her back in a pool of sun-dappled water.

"That looks good," Dorie said, "but I bet we have work to do, right?"

"Are you on tent duty?" Helen asked.

"Yes, but I'm going to need her to help," Dorie replied. "So maybe I'll just stand here and eat a snack."

In the meantime, Rett had laid out the ground cloth for her tent and linked poles together. Helen went to help, and soon went inside to inflate their pads and unroll sleeping bags.

Rett stuck her head in the tent. "Nice! That's going to feel good in a few hours."

"Absolutely," Helen agreed. "Move over, I'm coming out."

"Hey, Evie," Dorie called plaintively. "I need help."

Downstream, Evie slowly got to her feet and started back upriver. "It's so cold and feels so good," she enthused. "I didn't want to get up, but the water's getting deeper already."

"Tides come up fast," Rett agreed. "Dorie's having some tent issues."

Evie headed toward her, saying, "The same way we practiced. You got this."

"What if I do it wrong?" The two conferred over the rolled-up tent and ground cloth, while Helen pulled the little single burner stove out of her pack.

"Do you think we could have a fire tonight?" she asked Rett.

"Probably not," Rett said. "It would be fun, of course, but even this early the woods could be dry."

Helen looked out at the pebbly riverbed. "I don't see anything out there that could burn."

"Right, but a wind could blow sparks into the trees. Let's stick with the stove. Besides, it won't be dark until ten and I expect to be asleep."

"Good point."

After much activity, the other tent was up. Evie went inside to put out sleeping bags, and Dorie wandered toward her sisters. "What do you need me to do?"

"Water," Helen said definitively. "We need water for our meal and we'll need water for the night. Can you head upriver and run some through the filter?"

"That sounds easy," Dorie said dubiously. "Run it through? What does that mean?"

Gripping her patience firmly, Helen said, "Like we practiced. Remember? In the barn?"

"Yeah, maybe," Dorie admitted. "Or really not at all. Can somebody show me?"

"We practiced. That's why we practiced," Helen said through gritted teeth.

"Never mind," Rett said, grabbing the filtration system and heading upstream. "Come on, Dorie. I'll show you and you can be our water guru."

"Water guru?" Dorie giggled. "That sounds silly."

"Very important job."

"Why do I get the feeling you're making fun of me?"

They headed upstream, leaving Helen sorting out food for the evening. First snacks, then dinner. She tossed back a peanut butter protein ball while looking for her dry pasta. She was hungry enough to eat a horse. Or a large bowl of pasta. To heck with the lean protein.

The quiet rose in waves around her. Evie moved around in the other tent, and Rett and Dorie's voices receded and disappeared into the sound of the rote down on the shore, the slight breeze in the evergreens high on the cliff, and the occasional cry of a plover.

As the quiet took over her mind, her body sank into exhaustion. Getting into her sleeping bag was going to be heavenly. Maybe they really didn't need to cook and eat dinner. A granola bar might be enough. Leaving the stove and container of food, she walked down the riverbed to where it widened. A swath of pebbly beach took on the aspect of a feather bed, and she lay on her back, much as Evie had done in the water. The beach, despite the rocks, felt like it was holding her up, and she dropped the exhaustion of the day into the earth below. She sank deeper and deeper into a soft darkness that comforted and contained her.

The sound of laughter awakened her. Sitting up, she dashed her hand across her eyes. "What?"

"Come on, sleepyhead," Evie said. "We need to eat."

"I can't believe I fell asleep on these rocks," she said, getting up and stretching. "Yeah, now I'm hungry, too."

"Rett started cooking, but we decided to let you have a break," Evie announced. "So come on. Time to eat."

A Wolf in the Night

A few hours later, the sisters sat together around the pile of sticks Dorie had insisted on calling their campfire, although it was not lit. The reflected glow of sunset still glimmered on the water, and the moon rose above the cliff face. Helen lay back on her elbows, gazing at the evening sky.

"It's so quiet," Dorie murmured.

"Hmm," Rett agreed, also quiet. Tidal waters poured into the river, the water coming into the muddy channel, but downhill from the campsite. The dull roar of waves on the shore was still audible, and gulls had given way to evening sounds.

A sudden noise from the woods above startled Helen into sitting up. "What's that?"

Tuning in, the sound was clearer. Evie smiled. "Who cooks for you?" she hooted back at the owl.

"What? Who cooks?"

"Listen," Evie encouraged, still smiling. "Doesn't that sound like 'who cooks for you?'"

"It does," Helen said, surprised and intrigued. "Some kind of owl?"

"Barred owl," Rett supplied. "I'm surprised you didn't remember."

"Who else is out in the night?" Dorie asked. "Barred owls don't worry me."

"Nothing to worry about," Rett said. "We'll make sure we put the food away so critters won't have any reason to bother with us."

"Critters?" Dorie asked, high-pitched.

"Lions and tigers and bears, Dorie," Rett said with a grin.

"Oh, you," Dorie scoffed. "You don't need to make fun of me because I don't know what to be afraid of."

"You don't have to be afraid of anything," Evie comforted. "There's no requirement to be afraid."

"Isn't it dumb to be, like, assuming everything's fine?"

"You need to respect nature, but you don't have to be afraid. There's nothing to be afraid of right now, is there?"

Dorie looked around. "I guess not."

"If something happened, then you'd figure out what to do, right?"

Rett elbowed Helen and nodded toward their sisters, deep in discussion. "Look at those two," she whispered.

Dorie looked thoughtful. "Yeah, I guess so. Or somebody would tell me."

"Right. So no reason to be afraid right now."

"That's smart, Evie," Rett said. "It's probably good to talk about this stuff."

"I never slept outside before," Dorie said seriously.

"You'll be fine," Helen said. "It's like sleeping inside, unless you have to get up to pee."

Dorie paled. "Outside in the middle of the night?"

The sisters laughed, and Dorie added, "Okay, no more liquids for me." She tightened the cap of her water bottle and set it aside.

"That reminds me of something." Helen rummaged in her pack and pulled out a flask. "Celebratory libation," she said, holding it up. "Who wants a drink?"

"You carried extra weight?" Dorie sounded shocked.

"A few ounces," Helen said. "Worth it to me."

"Worth it to me, too. I've got a mug," Rett said, brandishing it. "A sip would be lovely." Helen passed her the flask, and it slowly made its way around the group, Dorie declining.

"A toast?" Helen asked when it got back to her. "To sisters together on the trail."

"Cheers!" Evie said, and tossed back her drink, Rett and Helen following suit. Dorie watched.

The darkness grew deeper, with stars and planets brightening. "That's the Milky Way, isn't it?" Evie asked, pointing to the opening between the cliffs where Goose River gained strength. The sky held a swath of glittery light, twinkly chiffon tumbling across the expanse of night.

"Wow," Dorie breathed. "Look at that."

"We can't see it at home because of light," Rett explained. "You have to get away from all the artificial light and sometimes you get really fortunate."

"This feels lucky," Evie said. "So beautiful. Come on, Dorie, let's walk down."

Helen gazed up, feeling herself grow smaller and smaller. They were only tiny little specks on this riverbed, near an enormous body of water that was a speck on a planet. Earth herself was a tiny speck in a massive galaxy that ultimately was a speck in the universe. Her breath caught in her throat, leaving her disoriented and wobbly. All that meaninglessness was too much. She turned away, even as her sisters, drawn like moths to light, wandered toward the mouth of the river, looking skyward.

She brushed sand off her clothing and looked around at their campsite. What needed to be gathered? Rett was tidying the last of the food, and the one pot had been washed and put away.

"I've got to sleep," she said to Rett. "Everything okay here?"

Rett looked around. "Yeah, it looks good. Go ahead. I'll be right behind you."

She needed her little flashlight for her last trip to the designated latrine area, but once inside the tent she clicked it off to let her eyes adjust to the darkness. That sleeping bag looked so good. She rearranged her layers of clothing, tucked things into her pack, and climbed in. The thin pad between her and the rocky ground felt utterly luxurious. She slept instantly.

She awoke instantly, too, with a shock. Where was she? It took a moment to register. That was Rett, breathing regularly next to her. She was cuddled into her sleeping bag, and when she wiggled her toes, she felt wool socks. The ceiling of the tent was barely visible in the dark.

Startled, she caught her breath. The sound came again, the sound of movement, a rattle of pebbles. Someone or something was walking around. Focusing hard, she heard the sound again, along with Dorie's muffled whisper, "Darn!"

She relaxed, pulling the edge of her bag up to her chin. It was only Dorie, despite her insistence on controlling her fluid intake. She hoped Dorie made it back into bed without incident. She turned on her side to go back to sleep.

Even without disturbing noises, she was awake. It was the power of suggestion, but now she had to pee. Could she wait until morning? Not if she wanted to go back to sleep. She stifled a sigh of annoyance, unzipped her sleeping bag as quietly as possible, crawled to the door and unzipped that, too, checking to see if Rett was disturbed. She slipped through the opening and stood.

She stretched, arms high, and gazed up at the night sky. Her tight shoulders complained, but she stretched again, luxuriously. She wondered about morning and taking on her pack once again, but decided that was tomorrow's problem. Instead, she focused on her immediate need and headed toward the designated spot.

Moonlight flooded the riverbed, so she had no need of a flashlight. She wrapped her arms around herself against the cool air and walked briskly upstream, the river lapping at the shore now where before there had only been mud flats or beachy rocks. As she watched the water, the bank grew more pronounced. Right here, she could see the power of the Fundy tides, legendary for their volume and the speed of change. No wonder campers got caught with wet tents while sleeping. But not them, not tonight, anyway.

She turned away from the water to head uphill a bit. While she squatted in the brush, something caught her eye at the water's edge. Something moved on the far side of the riverbed.

Stealthy, she readjusted her clothing and stood, watching. She couldn't make sense of what she saw. A raccoon was possible. It could even be a wolf. Were there wolves along the Bay? She watched, mesmerized, as the grasses across the river moved again. Breathless and slow, her eyes fixed across the river, she retraced her steps to the tent. When she finally arrived, she tossed a glance at the sequined sky, crouched to slip inside, zip up, and finally slide back into her sleeping bag. Rett, hatted and gloved, snored gently. Thin tent walls were no protection against a wolf.

She shivered while waiting for the warmth to come, rubbing her feet together. Impatient, she rummaged for the warm winter hat Rett had insisted on and jammed it on her head before hunkering down again. She curled into a shivering ball.

Later she startled again, hearing a wolf snuffle at the tent entrance. She was still curled tightly, and her shoulders ached, so she stretched out, realizing she was warm and that she'd been asleep. Did she dream about the wolf? In her mind's eye she saw his gold eyes, the slathering tongue, sharp teeth... and realized she was imagining a wolf shifter from a book she'd seen advertised. Give it up, she advised herself. You need to sleep. Sleep.

A Very Early Morning

In the next moment, movement in the tent brought her awake with a start. Helen opened her eyes to see Rett scrambling for footwear.

"Is it morning?"

Rett looked over her shoulder. "Oh, hi. I was trying to be quiet. Sorry. Yes, it's morning. It's light out, anyway."

"That means nothing," Helen grumbled. "It could be four am."

"So go back to sleep," Rett said, unperturbed. She unzipped the tent door and left, zipping it behind her.

Helen closed her eyes against the light, but the damage was done. She was awake. Awake after barely sleeping, she thought bitterly. Getting out of her sleeping bag, she pulled on her nylon pants, another sweater, and a windbreaker. She took a moment to take stock, then stuck her hat and gloves in a pocket before leaving the tent.

"Did you hear anything last night?" Helen asked Rett, who was fiddling with the single burner stove.

"Like what?" Rett asked, looking at the equipment in her hands.

"I dunno. Maybe like a wolf?"

Rett looked up. "There aren't any wolves here."

"Yeah, that's what they say." Helen pulled on her hat and stuffed her fists in her jacket pockets. "But I saw something when I went out, and later I heard it."

Rett shrugged. "Well, whatever it was, it didn't bother anything. Can you figure out how to get this thing going? I'm really attached to the idea of coffee this morning."

By the time they each had a mug of coffee, Evie and Dorie were out of their tent, pulling on outer layers. "We need a fire," Dorie said. "I piled up the kindling and some driftwood last night, but we were too tired."

"We were tired," Evie agreed. "Sure. Let's make a little fire, but down on the beach." They scrambled down to the rocky riverbank.

"Tide's near low again," Rett observed.

"Should be rising," Helen said absently. "I'll go upstream and get some water. You okay here?"

"Yeah. I've got enough to start the porridge."

Helen tossed back the last of her rapidly cooling coffee, gathered up the water bottles, and headed upstream. She had to get up high enough to find fresh water, easy at low tide, but impossible when the Bay flooded the riverbed. Her legs were sore, and she took a moment to stretch. Uphill and downhill took a toll on the hamstrings and the pack had given her sore shoulders. She'd hoped sleep would be restorative, but she'd had little enough. There was no use complaining, though. She gave herself a shake and squatted near a sandy pool to fill the bottles.

A rustle in the grass across the river riveted her. She stared, willing the creature to show itself. That wolf might still be here. A plop in the water made her jump and laugh. Only a bullfrog. She recalled Rett's words. There are no wolves here.

By the time she returned to their camp and set up the water filter, the little fire was crackling merrily down by the river, and Rett was scooping oatmeal into bowls. "Oh, hot!" Dorie said, pulling her fingers back.

"Use your sleeve," Evie advised. "It'll cool off fast. What do you want on it?"

Dorie perused the selection of toppings. "Who brought this? This is pretty nice," she said.

Rett looked around. "Me. We need to fuel up in the mornings. Make sure you put some nuts in that stuff," she added. "You'll need the calories."

Helen frowned. "Not too many calories. I don't want to gain weight on this trip."

Evie laughed. "Not likely. You could eat all day and burn off every bit."

"Eat all day? I like that idea," Dorie said, chowing down on her oatmeal. "Let's go sit by the fire."

They found spots to perch near the little campfire. Evie and Dorie had built a fire ring with stones, and while the tiny fire cast little warmth, the glow was comforting.

"This place is pretty nice," Rett said, gazing downstream. "Look at that sky."

The expanse of sky visible beyond the cliffs was light blue, shading to indigo near the horizon line. "What's that over there?" Dorie asked with a hand gesture.

Helen shrugged. "Nova Scotia?"

"You'd have to see pretty far for that," Evie said. "Maybe it's Isle au Haut. See how the horizon changes?"

Helen squinted. "I can't really tell what's sea and what's land. I guess it doesn't matter." She returned to her bowl. "Congratulations, Rett, on an excellent breakfast, even if it was a lot of calories."

"Did you get some fruit?"

"You brought fruit? That's a lot of water to carry," Evie said.

"Dried fruit. Keeps you regular, Mum used to say." Rett grinned at her. "We don't need anybody exploding on this trip."

Dorie screwed up her face. "Eww. Do you have to talk about that? We already had the lecture on how to shit in the woods."

"It's important," Evie insisted. "We don't want to be contaminating anything."

"I get it," Dorie acknowledged, "but that doesn't mean I like it."

"Nobody has to like anything we're doing, but there are some things we have to do," Helen said authoritatively.

"Like our plan for today?" Evie asked. "Day two. We should check in on how everybody's doing."

Helen scowled. "Everybody's fine. I can see that everybody's just fine, and all we have to do today is what we did yesterday. One foot in front of the other."

"Up the hill and down the hill," Dorie said. "I'm getting the picture."

"I think we need to talk about how we're doing," Evie said stubbornly.

"I think we need to get going," Helen contradicted. "Here, give me your dishes and I'll clean up. You guys get your tents packed up. The water is filtering at the campsite and we have plenty to do before we hit the trail."

Rett looked at her watch. "You do realize it's only six am, right?"

"What difference does that make? The sun is high, we're awake and fed, and we've got work to do."

She gathered their dishes and headed away from the group, ignoring the mild grumbling. It was time to go.

An hour later, they were nearly ready.

"All clear?" Evie asked. "We don't want to leave anything."

"Did you handle the fire?" Dorie asked. "Maybe I'll go give it another stir."

"Good idea," Rett said. "Then come on back and let's get packs on."

"It's finally getting warm here," Helen noted, "and we'll be climbing, so think about your layering."

"Brrr!" Evie shucked her outer layer, tucking her windbreaker into the cords across her pack. "We better get moving before I freeze to the spot."

"Yeah, me, too," Rett agreed. "Come on, Dorie. We're waiting for you."

Dorie dropped the stick she used to stir the ashes and trotted back. "Okay, I'm here," she said, breathless, pulling off her jacket and squatting to slip her arms into her backpack. "Ooooh, my shoulders are complaining!"

"It sounds like you're complaining," Helen said irritably. "It's a pack. Put it on."

Evie took a closer look at Dorie. "Is it too heavy?"

Dorie shrugged it on and stood up to buckle the waist belt. "Nah, it's okay. I think somehow I was hoping it would feel lighter today." She grinned at her sister. "I'm good."

Evie nodded and smiled. "Of course you are."

Helen's irritation grew. This wasn't rocket science. They just had to put on the pack and walk, one step after the other. That's what she loved about hiking. Just do it. Over and over.

"Let's go," Rett said, and started toward the trail.

"Wait," Evie said. "We had a great first night. Let's say goodbye to Goose River."

Helen scoffed. "Whatever."

Evie looked back downriver. "This marks the spot where the Madison sisters backpacked and camped together for the very first time. I'm going to preserve the memory for posterity." She pointed her camera toward the mouth of the river.

Dorie and Rett cheered. Helen shook her head and headed toward the trail. "Okay, let's go."

Her sisters followed, chatting and laughing.

Hiking to Azore Beach

S oon, Helen settled into the rhythm once again. Watching her steps, using her poles, climbing up the steep sides of the river ravine; these became second nature. Unfortunately, that left her brain room to think.

Step, step, step. Climb, step over tree roots, watch out for branches, and climb some more. She made the mistake of looking up. There was no end to the climb. Nothing ahead but hard work climbing this steep bank. Pack heavy on her back, she leaned into the climb, using her poles.

It took a while, but as her legs settled into the work, she became a little happier. This was what she'd asked for, anyway, a strenuous hike with her sisters, the people to whom she was closest.

Was she close to these women hiking behind her?

She considered Rett. So close in age their birthdays almost overlapped, Rett was less than two years younger. She had no memory of life before Rett; they'd been dropped on the planet together. When Evie came along, she and Rett had to play quietly without Mum, but they had each other. When they played school, she was always the teacher and Rett was mad about having to take orders. A tiny smile quirked her mouth when she recalled Rett's red face, and how many times she'd seen that face since. Rett, her dear sister, superb nurse-manager, wasting her life homeschooling and feeding goats. Her ire grew. Perhaps she could help Rett make better choices while on this trip.

What about Evie? All aglow about going off to the States for a PhD when she really wanted a family. It would be too bad for Evie to lose her art in fighting the tenure game. Helen's heart tightened, remembering the mural at the high school. Evie's talent was still unrecognized, so she assumed she had to get more schooling. Helen resolved to do something about that.

"Are we there yet?" Dorie called out, a laugh in her voice. Always the baby, always the joker, Helen thought with disdain. When will that girl grow up?

She stomped on, poles and boots moving, leaning into the uphill. This is me, she thought. It gets harder, I go harder. Working harder and better. Poor sleep meant nothing. Just do the work.

Rett called. "Look! There's light again. There's the top!"

They all put on a bit of energy and soon emerged on the flatland above Goose River and the Bay of Fundy. Trees obscured the water view, but the level ground underfoot felt great.

"Ooh, that's nice on the knees," Rett said. "Everybody okay? Anybody need a snack?"

"We just finished breakfast," Helen objected.

"No, we hiked up a massive incline for over an hour," Rett corrected, "and some of us might need to refuel."

"Fine." She turned away and unbuckled her waist belt. A break could be okay, though she didn't need one. Soon four packs lay on the open ground as people rummaged for food, water, and changed their layers of clothing.

Dorie came back from her solo visit to the edge of the woods, looking puzzled. "I threw up."

"You did? Are you sick?" Rett went into assessment mode immediately. "What's wrong?"

Dorie shook her head. "Nothing's wrong. I needed to pee, but when I stood up, I suddenly got nauseated and threw up."

"Something disagreed with you," Evie surmised. "Oatmeal?"

Dorie shrugged. "Dunno. It never happened before. I'm fine, Rett, not sick. But that was weird."

"It is," Rett agreed. "Eat now if you can, and when we start again, keep food handy. You really needed those morning calories."

"Time to burn some of those calories," Helen called out. "Let's get going."

Evie cast her a curious gaze. "Is there something we're hurrying for? You should let us know, Helen."

She narrowed her eyes. "We need to get going. We're like sitting ducks here."

Rett laughed. "We're nobody's target. We started early, we already did the tidal crossings, so we are not worried about tides right now, and we have time to take a break if somebody is vomiting. Really."

Helen shook her head and walked away toward the tree line. Where was that wolf? And why couldn't her sisters take direction?

Annoyed, she kept gazing into the woods, though she kept an ear tuned toward the conversations behind her. Soon enough, everybody got ready to go again, and Evie called to her. "We're all set, Helen." She huffed a little as she headed back, chin held high.

Evie started off beside Dorie, the two easily chatting. Rett waited for Helen. "Tone it down a bit," she advised.

"Are you bitching about me, too?" Helen snapped.

"Like that," Rett said noncommittally. "Take it down a notch."

"You're so helpful," she sniped. "Like anybody even notices me."

"Everybody notices you." Rett's tone was correcting. "Especially when you're being a royal pain in the neck. Tone it down. Nobody's here to make a fool of you."

Helen, shocked, took the impact of those words on her chest. *Nobody's here to make a fool of you.* She had nothing to say.

Rett nudged her with an elbow. "Come on. Let's make it a good day for a hike."

She nodded tightly and followed.

Hiking made her brain run faster. Rett's words rang in her memory. Nobody's here to make a fool of you, Helen.

I don't need anyone to do that. I've done it myself, more than once. A lot more than once.

Despite her tired body, her mind was super-charged as thoughts, memories and feelings flooded her. She couldn't outrace them, and even the challenging terrain didn't distract her, though after a series of switchbacks, landing at the brook felt like an accomplishment. Or at least a break from her thoughts.

"Listen, guys," Evie said, holding the guidebook. "If we go down this brook a bit, there's a beach, Azore Beach, and we can look for Martin Head."

"Doesn't Martin need it? Get it? Martin's head?" Dorie said with a giggle.

"I'm glad to see you still have your sense of humour," Rett said, "even if your jokes are worse than Mason's."

"No, really," Evie insisted. "Let's go look."

Helen frowned. "I don't think we have time."

"The trail goes there anyway, Helen," Rett said. "Besides, why are we here if we're not going to enjoy the place?"

Helen sighed, but she followed her sisters along Rose Brook toward its outlet. The sky was vast at Azore Beach. Dorie shucked her pack and spread her arms wide into the sea breezes. "Lunch here, please," she said. "Isn't it beautiful?"

"Look right," Evie directed. "It's a clear enough day. There's Martin Head, I think." She pulled out tiny binoculars that hung from her belt and peered through. "Oh, look at this!"

She shared her binoculars with Dorie and Rett. But Helen refused the offer. "Get lunch, you guys. We don't have all day."

Rett gave her a sharp glance, but she resolutely ignored it. It would be on them if they didn't get through this trip.

"It's more beautiful than I ever expected," Dorie said with awe. "I know tourists like it, but I didn't think it would be like this." She gazed on, even after handing back the binoculars. "I did not know I lived this close to a magical place."

Magical? Supernatural was more like it. Helen jumped at a sound, but it was a gull squawking close by. She hunkered down, digging in her pack for food.

Rett sat on a nearby log and pulled off her boots. "Ahhh! That's the feeling," she crowed, sticking bare feet into the air. "Stretch out and breathe, little toesies!"

Dorie snickered. "That looks like a great idea." She parked next to Rett and shed her boots.

"How long do you think we're staying?" Helen asked, trying to keep her voice low and smooth.

Rett gazed at the sky and then checked her watch. "We started so early, we could take a nice long lunch."

"But why? We've got a lot more hiking to do to get to tonight's spot."

Evie wandered back from where she'd been taking pictures. "Isn't this fabulous?" she asked nobody in particular.

Dorie was rubbing her bare feet on the smooth Fundy rocks. "Yep," she agreed, and looked up, smiling. "Nicer than I thought."

Helen's annoyance grew. "Don't get too comfy."

"Relax," Rett said. "We've got time."

"Unhelpful," Helen said through her teeth. "Have you looked at the map?"

"I have." Evie pulled out her copy and approached Helen. "We're heading to Goose Creek for tonight, right? We've actually already hiked the longest leg for today. What's coming doesn't look easy, but then none of it is. We've got lots of time."

"I guess I'm outnumbered," Helen conceded. "Okay. I'll take off my boots, too. Lunch and lunch break."

Appetite urged them to eat, but then the warm sun, plashing water, and solar-heated rocks had an effect. Helen lay her extra clothing on the rocks and reclined, shading her eyes with her arm from the brilliant June sun. Warm. It was so warm. The sounds were soothing, even the quiet conversations of her sisters, and in a moment, she dropped into a deep quiet.

Cougar's Lair

Waking suddenly, she struggled to make sense of what she was seeing, but realized she'd fallen asleep on the beach. The sun had shifted subtly, and her sisters were not in sight. Their packs were, though, so she silenced her momentary fear of being left. She rubbed itchy eyes, then got up to stretch. Her watch was a blank face. She knew the charge would never last four days, but she'd hoped for three. She tucked it away in a pocket in her pack. Now she was flying blind, at least regarding time. How long had they been on Azore Beach? How long until sunset? She squinted toward the sun.

Well, she was no Boy Scout. No watch, no idea of the time, but they weren't at risk of running out of daylight, no matter what. More like running out of energy, she thought wryly and rummaged for another granola bar. She couldn't believe she could eat so much and still be hungry.

While she was chewing, Dorie and Evie returned, chatting away. She cast a glance their way while swigging water. "You guys ready?"

"Sure," Dorie said. "There's Rett, coming back from her walk."

Helen assessed her layers, tidied her backpack, and replaced her boots, while her sisters did the same. "Anybody know where the trail picks up?"

Evie had the guidebook in hand. "It says there's a cairn. Look for a pile of rocks."

"The only thing here is rocks and water," Dorie scoffed, "but look over there. Could that be it?"

Once they got to the cairn, the trail was easily visible. "That's a pretty big cliff," Rett observed.

"Understatement," Dorie noted.

"But we're up to it," Evie encouraged. "The trail switches back. It's okay." She started climbing, sisters following. Helen brought up the rear. When they reached some level area, she looked behind her and down. The empty beach held no evidence of their lunch break.

Evie stopped to take some mushroom pictures, but Dorie bypassed her to keep climbing. Rett and Helen followed, and soon Evie brought up the rear. Helen looked back over her shoulder to speak.

"Good mushrooms?"

Evie nodded enthusiastically. "Some things I've never seen before. They're exquisite. All this beauty in a mushroom."

Just like an artist. No focus on the hard road ahead. Helen stabbed the ground with her pole. Keep moving. That's what they needed.

Once out of the ravine, the trail followed an old woods road, wide enough for two abreast. Dorie and Rett chatted ahead, and Helen waited for Evie to draw close. They walked in companionable silence for a while. When the road opened up into a small meadow, they looked back to see Azore Beach from above.

"Look at that," Evie said, exhaling with amazement. "Sea, sky, all flowing into one."

"Look how high we climbed," Helen noted dryly. "No wonder I'm sweating."

Dorie, across the meadow, followed the trail markers. "These are some old trees." She led them into a dark forest of mature spruce. As the darkness closed around them, Rett howled like a wolf.

"Not funny!" Helen snapped. "It's dark enough in here."

"We haven't had wolves in New Brunswick in over a century," Evie said.

"Helen's worried about the supernatural kind," Rett said.

"Like werewolves? Really, Helen?" Dorie asked.

"No, not really," Helen retorted. "I thought I saw something like a dog at the river last night."

"It's possible," Evie offered gently. "There are coyotes."

"See, Rett," Helen pointed out. "There are coyotes."

Rett shook her head. "The wilderness might be getting to you."

"It's getting to me," Dorie said cheerfully. "I like it a lot more than I ever expected to. It's carrying this pack that wears me out."

"Yeah, well, you're not alone," Rett said. "But if we want to eat...."

"Yeah, yeah, yeah. I get it," Dorie said. "A girl can dream, though. Come on."

Helen's eyes adjusted to the spruce-covered dimness, and bits of the forest came to life for her. A beam of sunlight pierced the canopy, illuminating a ferny growth a few feet off the trail. The chittering of the red squirrel, affronted at their impudence in hiking through his woods, felt familiar and expected. The hike itself suddenly seemed possible.

They began a gradual descent, no doubt toward another watercourse, but Helen didn't bother getting out her map. They had only to follow the trail markers. She kept her head down and hiked. Conversation died out, and only the gentle sounds of the forest were audible.

Her heart lifted as the peace penetrated the thicket of worries she'd brought with her.

The roar of an engine stopped her dead.

"What's that?"

An ATV ground to a halt in front of them. Two helmeted people looked in their direction. The engine stopped and they dismounted.

A sandy-haired man greeted Rett, first in line. "How you doing? You hikin' from Fundy?"

"We're good, yes. Yes, headed west."

"All girls, are you?"

"Women," Dorie corrected. "You?"

Evie stifled a snicker, but the other rider removed her helmet to reveal long brunette locks. "We're only out for the day," she said. "You must be strong, carrying everything like that."

"It's heavy," Dorie said simply.

The man patted the cargo box on his vehicle. "We bring a lot, but not on our backs." He chuckled. "I don't know why you'd want to work so hard."

Dorie looked ready to agree, so Helen jumped in. "It's about the experience."

"Yeah, I did enough of that in the military," the man said, "but you do you. You been watching the weather?"

"Not today," Evie said. "Not much coverage."

"Well, you might check. Forecast is for big rain."

"Great," Evie said. "We'll check when we get into the clear again. Thanks."

"Have a good one," the woman said, replacing her helmet. "It's a nice day for it today, anyways."

The pair roared away.

"I'm glad I'm not on a loud machine. I could even be glad I can carry this pack," Dorie remarked.

Helen's tight jaw softened. "I guess there are different kinds of people."

"Always," Rett said. "I enjoy riding on an ATV. Harry and I rode with a club for a while before we had kids."

"Did you really?" Helen was shocked. "Roaring through the woods, making all that noise pollution?"

Rett shrugged. "It's fun. Like snowmobiles. It's different from this, but I can like them both."

Helen couldn't understand how anybody could like the quiet and the racket. It didn't seem possible. But it wasn't her problem. "Did anybody check the weather while we were in the meadow?"

"We can't do anything about the weather anyway," Rett reasoned. "If it rains, it rains."

"We've been lucky," Evie noted, looking upward. "The weather's perfect. But let's get going. One of us might get cell coverage sometime today."

Helen recalled with regret the hand-cranked weather radio she didn't buy. Rett said knowing wouldn't make a difference, but Helen would prefer to know whether her expectations were realistic. She brought up the rear again as they headed along the trail.

Unexpected things challenged her coping. The separation from Reggie might have been coming for years, and she would have handled it, except for the unexpected blow of Reg finding Juliet. Jake going to hockey school was predictable, but not his distance, or the way he'd been avoiding her. Those things hurt, hurt a lot, not least because she'd not had any time to prepare.

Like what happened in Fredericton when she was barely eighteen. Even as a kid she believed she could cope with anything if she knew about it in advance, but who could have predicted that disaster?

Except — hadn't she predicted it? When she said to Shelly, her roommate, "I'm going to party when we get to Fredericton. Just wait!" she'd meant it. She was going to be somebody other than Helen the good student, Helen the good girl, Helen the big sister who led by example.

She had no idea how a little partying could backfire on her but couldn't help the wash of shame and guilt even now. If only she'd stayed in her hotel room, taken Shelly with her, or simply left when she started feeling funny. But all the "if onlys" in the world couldn't change the facts. She went to Fredericton, but what came back was a shell, not really her. She could only think about getting away, far away from anybody who might know her shame.

Helen gave herself a shake. There was no need to be thinking about that. Here and now. She followed her sisters along the winding trail through the dark forest. It seemed darker than before. Less friendly.

When the trail emerged onto a ridge marked by crevasses, Evie and Dorie, in front, conferred. "I'm just following these blazes, girls," Evie said. "There's a narrow gap between cliffs, but also keep your eyes out for ice inside these caves. They call this part 'Cougar's Lair.'"

"Ice! It's been warm for weeks," Rett said.

"Cougars!" Helen couldn't stop the word from exploding out of her mouth.

"Apparently the sun never gets into those cracks. It's like a prehistoric landscape, eh?"

"I'm checking," Dorie announced, brandishing a flashlight. "No cougars, Helen. Lead on, Macduff."

"Macduff? When did you study Shakespeare?" Evie sounded a little derisive.

"Shakespeare? Never. I just heard that one day and liked it."

Scrambling across the ridge, Helen was acutely aware of the caves to her right. Cougar's Lair indeed. Maybe she'd seen a cat, not a canine. A cougar. You'd never hear him coming. She glanced into the cave as she crossed in front of it, but there was nothing to see, not even darkness. The sun illuminated the back of the shallow chamber. Nobody was hiding there.

Crevasses underfoot and caves to the right and left meant staying focused on her feet and poles. All these dark spaces holding secrets. Helen lifted her chin to look for Evie. Her sister's curly brown hair danced on top of her head in a messy bun. She was up ahead of Dorie and Rett, who were comparing notes while hiking. Didn't anybody else take the dangers seriously? Helen hurried to stay with the rest of them.

Evie waited for Dorie and Rett to catch up, and when Helen arrived, they'd spied the next blaze. "I just wanted to make sure we're going the right way," Evie said easily. "There's a place where we slide between two cliffs. It could be right here. Ready?"

"Let's do it!" Dorie cheered.

Helen's heart was pounding. Slide between two cliffs? Evie picked her way past two saplings barely holding on in the thin soil of the rocky cliff. Then she disappeared into the cliff. Dorie followed.

Helen wobbled.

Rett turned to Helen. "You okay?" Rett's assessing gaze was obvious.

"Of course, I'm okay," she retorted. When Rett disappeared into the crevice, Helen clutched her stomach. Even though she heard her sisters' voices, they sounded far away. Reaching for the cliff wall, she leaned in, a little dizzy. Breath coming fast, darkness closing in from either side, her vision narrowed to a tiny point. She bent at the waist, gasping. A wave of memories left her coughing, choking into her hand, and she leaned hard on the rock. Darkness was everywhere.

The sun, startlingly bright, pierced the cloud cover in a flash that brought her back. She rubbed her palms over her face and knuckled her eyes. Here and now.

"Helen?" Evie's voice was close. When she looked up, Evie was there, smiling at her. "You coming?"

"Yes, right now," she said, lifting her chin. She wasn't in some dark scary place. She was hiking with her sisters. They had just gone around a corner, that was all. She followed Evie between the cliffs to join them.

What Lies Within

"I didn't think we would ever arrive, but here we are." Dorie sighed with satisfaction after taking off her boots. "You were probably right, Helen, about taking a long lunch. We left a lot of kilometres to travel in the afternoon."

"It's still okay, though," Evie said. "There's plenty of light for making camp and getting food and all of that. This is a great campsite."

They'd waited awhile on the eastern shore of Goose Creek until Helen was certain they could manage the ford. The tide was still dropping and they'd gotten across without incident, but she silently criticized herself for not paying enough attention to the tide chart. What if they'd been stuck on the wrong side? They were on the correct side, thankfully, and after following the blazes through the alders, they reached the campsite.

"Looks good," Dorie said. "I'm going to put this tent up by myself this time."

"Sure," Evie said, "but you don't have to. We're all here to help each other."

Helen, tired into her bones, dropped her pack and perched on it.

"Is this where you want the tent?" Rett asked. "Over there might be better."

"Whatever. You pick," Helen said. "Whose turn is it?"

"Does it matter? We'll get it up. You look like you need to sit for a bit."

"Thanks."

Heaving a sigh, she gazed at the rising creek waters, her mind drifting to the darkness that had overtaken her on the cliff. That terrible feeling had followed her into the wilderness. She had hoped to leave it behind. A tear slipped down her cheek. She roughly brushed it away and turned so nobody could see her. No weakness. With an effort, she got to her feet. Time to help Rett make camp.

Later, as the first stars emerged, Evie built a little fire beside the creek. The crackling and sweet aroma drew Helen close, and she dragged a log over to sit. Dorie stretched out on her raincoat. Rett joined Helen on the log.

When the little flame steadied, Evie joined them in the circle. "It's so quiet here."

Helen gazed deep into the fire. The swishing of the creek was the only sound. June was too early for crickets, and even the late evening birds had settled.

"Where's that flask?" Rett asked her. "No, don't get up. Just tell me and I'll get it."

"In my pack. In the outside pocket."

Rett returned in a moment. Helen held the flask but didn't drink, then she passed it to Evie.

"No drink?" Rett asked curiously.

Helen shrugged. "I need to sleep tonight. It probably wouldn't help."

The flask returned to Rett, who took a measured swig. "Delicious. You sure?" She held it out to Helen. She again shook her head.

"How's everybody doing?" Evie asked. "Are the packs getting heavier?"

Dorie giggled. "It's actually getting lighter, but I guess that's because we've been eating so much."

"Doesn't feel any lighter to me," Rett groused. "But it's okay. Manageable. How about you, Evie?"

Evie had a satisfied smile. "I'm stronger than I realized. I can't say I pick it up with joy, but now I know I can do this hike."

"You sounded so sure," Dorie said, "when I got so waffley."

"I had to sound positive, didn't I, so you didn't waffle right out."

"I guess. I'm really glad I came," Dorie offered. "Which I never thought I'd say."

Helen let their talk drift over her. The evening darkness gathered around them, and she tilted her head, listening into the woods.

"Earth to Helen! Come in, Helen," Evie said, in good humour.

Startled, she jumped and snapped, "What?"

"We're just checking in. See how everyone's doing." Evie's voice stayed even, unperturbed.

"I'm fine," she snapped again. Her sisters gazed her way. The fire popped, and a frog started singing up the creek.

"Helen —" Rett began.

Helen interrupted. "Sorry. I'm fine, really. Except I didn't get much sleep last night, and today has been really long. Really long." She took a long shuddering breath, shocked to find tears forming. Rett moved closer on the log.

The frog abruptly quieted. Into the silence, the sound of ragged breathing came with intense pressure on her chest. Darkness closed in fast, until all she could see was the licking flame of the campfire.

"Helen!" Her shoulder got a rough shake. "Come back," Rett said.

Turning her head to look at her sister restored her vision, eased the pressure. She drew a deep breath. "Yeah, I'm here. I'm okay."

"Are you gonna tell me what just happened?" Rett was in no-nonsense mode.

Hell, no, she wasn't. "I told you, I'm just tired. More than I expected because of no sleep. I should hit the hay now. You guys should consider it, too," she said precisely, and got up.

As she headed away from the fire, she listened hard. What would they say about her? It didn't matter, really. Everything was fine, her, the hike, all of them. Fine.

She prepared for bed with all her layers, but the tent was overwhelmingly dark. She flicked on her little flashlight. That was better. No bad memories could hijack her when she had her light. She slid down into her sleeping bag, socks, jacket and hat already on. Tucking in her elbow, she kept the flashlight in her hand and slept.

Whatever awakened her, it happened late. Her light was off, but she was unbothered, as starlight or moonlight illuminated the roof of the little tent. Rett's even breathing beside her was comforting, and she turned over to settle back into slumber, but to no avail. Her uncooperative body needed to go outside, despite having limited her water intake. She unzipped the tent and slipped into the night.

The full moon overhead cast light into the campsite. The creek, full with the tide, glittered. A cold breeze hastened her activity. She resolutely avoided looking around; if there was a wolf, he'd have to come and get her. She wasted no time getting back into the tent. As soon as she cuddled into her sleeping bag, she slept again.

A pattering on the roof of the tent woke her. "What's that?" a sleepy Rett asked.

"It could be rain. Let me look." She peered out the screened window at the end of the tent. "I can't tell. It's not bad, anyway."

They scrambled up and out, layering for the cold. Helen topped her layers with rain gear, pulling her hood over her head. No point in getting wet if she could avoid it, though hypothermia was unlikely.

She headed toward the campfire site from last night, followed by Rett. "Did you guys stay up late?" she asked.

"Not really," her sister replied, "but you were down for the count when I went to bed. I turned off your flashlight, by the way."

Helen, abashed, said, "I might have been freaked out by the dark last night."

"You were a little freaked out, period. Are you going to talk about it?"

"No. And thank you for not prying."

"Better today?"

Evie walked up. "Good morning."

"Yes, better," Helen answered shortly. "Hi, Evie. We're going to get the coffee going."

"Ahhh," Evie said happily. "Nothing like coffee when you're camping."

"I kind of liked Helen's scotch," Rett threw in.

"Was there any left?" Helen asked, wondering who had her flask.

"There could be a drop or two," Rett said with a grin, "but never fear. You don't know what I've got tucked away."

Dorie arrived, dishevelled and sleepy. "Looks like a good day," she said.

"Looks like rain to me," Helen contradicted, looking up. "Get your rain gear on before everything gets wet."

Dorie gazed at the sky. "Yeah. Okay. Come on, Evie."

"You got breakfast?" Rett asked. "I'll get the tent packed up before things get really wet."

"Yes. Good idea."

The gathering clouds were drippy, but not drenching. They could eat and pack without getting soaked. The weather looked a little ominous, though, so Helen wasted no time in heating water for porridge and coffee.

Evie and Dorie finished packing up their equipment and turned to help Rett. "Helen, do you want me to pack up for you?" Rett called.

"No, I'll do it," Helen said, looking at the sky. "Food's almost ready."

"What are we rushing for?" Dorie asked in general. "We're outside, it's going to rain, we're going to get wet. That's just fact."

"You're right," Evie said. "But if we can keep our clothes and tents dry, we'll have a chance of sleeping dry tonight. It's worth rushing a little, even though we'll be hiking in the rain."

Hiking in the rain didn't sound like fun, but it came with the activity. Part of the deal. No adversity, no adventure, isn't that what the consultant said? Even without wolves in the forest, this hike had adversity aplenty. Why not rain? Helen steeled herself for an uncomfortable day.

When they were nearly ready to go, Evie asked them to wait a moment. They stood in a circle with their packs beside them, adorned with rain covers. "This looks like obedience class." Dorie chortled. "If you can imagine dogs being as well-behaved as those backpacks."

"That's quite an imagination you've got there," Rett said, smiling. "Charlie never learned how to behave. He just picked it up from the kids."

"Listen, guys," Evie said. "Let's finish our check in. How's everybody's energy? Nobody with blisters? Sore shoulders?"

Dorie considered. "My shoulders are good. I'm good."

"I found out I need to eat more often," Rett said. "Yesterday I got tired early, and it turned out I just needed some food."

"We're burning a lot of energy carrying that pack up and down all day," Evie said. "Let's make sure we remind each other to keep snacking."

"Not a problem," Dorie said with a bounce. "I like to eat."

"Helen? How are you doing?"

"Better," she said without thinking, then realized what she'd said. "Sorry about being so snappy last night. I really needed some sleep."

"Did you get some?" Evie seemed genuinely interested.

"Yes, pretty good. No more wolves." And no flashbacks, she didn't say.

Rett cast a critical glance over her. "Make sure you eat enough," she said. "Do you have snacks you can reach without stopping?"

"Yes, and we all have full water bottles, right?" Helen put in. "Evie, are you good?"

"I am," Evie said. "No blisters, no energy drop, and I'm having more fun than I expected. Today's going to be a slog, though. What's on the map for us, Helen?"

She felt more relief than irritation at Evie's leadership takeover but it was nice to be consulted. They gathered around her and the map.

"We wanted to make Brothers Brook for our third night," Helen said. "That's a decent day's work. It's likely to be harder if this rain intensifies."

"There are some things to see, too," Evie said. "Waterfalls called Tweedle Dum and Tweedle Dee. And Martin Head is supposed to be spectacular."

"If we can see it," Rett said dryly. "That depends on the weather, too."

"Right. We could keep Wolf Brook in mind for a fall-back position if we decide Brothers is too far. That depends on how we feel," Evie added quickly.

"It makes sense to stay flexible," Helen said. "But let's get going, so we can cover some distance before the rain gets serious."

A Hike in the Rain

They started up the incline from the brook, complete with the usual switchbacks. By the time they got to the top of the hill, the rain had intensified. Helen shrugged deeper into her raincoat, grateful for the hood and the drawstring that pulled it snugly around her face. Rain dripped off her hood, but her face was dry.

"Well, we might not get the views of Martin Head I hoped for," Evie said, once they gathered on top of the cliff. "This isn't perfect hiking weather."

"It's okay," Rett said. "Let's keep going."

The trail wound through a big stand of hardwoods, all still a bright spring green, though the leaves were full. When the trees thinned out, the bay spread out before them, but the horizon was lost in clouds. The rain was pounding now, water puddling underfoot. Evie, in the lead, walked toward the cliffs, looking to the right. She returned to the group, shaking her head.

"No view today." Her shoulders were down.

"We'll come back," Dorie promised. "This will not be my last hike."

Evie brightened. "Actually, you can get here pretty easily. You don't have to hike for two days. There's an ATV trail and shorter hike according to the guidebook."

Helen didn't really care about Martin Head. She attended to putting one foot in front of the other while the rain streamed down. If she thought much about anything, it would be the bad stuff that made her lose her breath and lose focus, so she didn't. Only walking today. One foot, the other foot. Her running litany worked for hiking. Here and now.

It had been her mantra from grade twelve, but when she got to Halifax she learned about running. Pounding the pavements gave her power, self-reliance. She felt safe, too, despite other women questioning her sanity to run alone. Safety was in knowing yourself. Staying in the moment. One step, another step, another step.

She did her work the same way, studying, applying to law school, completing legal training. Don't look back. Stay in this moment, do this one thing. Hindsight brought you right into the yucky memories and feelings, and looking too far ahead was just a recipe for worry. Here and now.

Despite her best efforts to leave the yucky stuff behind, it stayed with her. Her return to Stella Mare had cracked those memories wide open. The pain of Reggie's abandonment and losing her house and practice, even all that shame, was nothing against the darkness and terror dogging her steps even on this hiking trail.

Wait! Stop thinking about that! One step, another step. Keep taking your steps.

Taking the last position on the trail meant Helen had a great rear view of her sisters. It was funny how similar they were when seen from behind; perhaps she looked like them, too. Despite Evie's certainty of her difference, she was absolutely a Madison sister. Helen noticed something in the set of their hips, obvious even under layers of rain pants and raincoats even carrying full backpacks. We are all Madisons.

What had gone wrong between them? She remembered a time when Rett was practically her best friend. As a teen, she would never have said such a thing, but Rett was the one she confided in, the one who heard about all the things that bothered her in high school, all the worries about the other girls, and the boys she might have liked. The confidences were reciprocal, too, though Helen recalled being a little dismissive of Rett's thirteen-year-old angst. "You'll get over that," she remembered saying. "That's middle school stuff. Wait until you get to high school."

That memory stung a little. She was an annoying big sister even then, but later, things got very bad. Heated. She and Rett couldn't get along for more than five minutes, and family dinners were characterized by Mum and Dad having conversation with Dorie and Evie, because Rett and Helen were too angry to be civil. Oh, that was a rough time.

It could be time to unpack some of that. Helen slogged past the alders and up to a plateau. She probably had some amends to make. Her gusty sigh might have been due to finally reaching a flat area.

The hikers grouped up on the plain. "Snack time?" Dorie asked happily.

"If you're hungry," Rett answered. "You might even have to fuel before hunger, remember?"

"Oh, right." Helen dug in a pocket for the trail mix she'd stashed earlier. "The rain means we're working harder, too."

"How could you tell? All of this is more work than my body has ever done," Dorie said. "I am finding the whole thing kind of satisfying, I have to admit."

"You are just weird," Rett said. "Hiking with a heavy pack in the pouring rain is not on my list of satisfying activities."

Dorie shrugged and grinned. "Once you're in it, you might as well enjoy it. You guys ready to go on? What's coming up, Oh Keeper of the Guidebook?"

Evie looked cheerful. "Well, we've got to find another cairn to show the trail to Brandy Brook. But before that, we can take a brief detour to that waterfall I told you about."

"Oh, I don't know," Helen said. "A detour to a waterfall on a rainy day? What's the point?"

Rett stared at her. "What's the point of any of this? It's not like we're going to get to the hotel and have a hot shower. I say we should see and do all the things we want to, even if it is raining."

"A waterfall sounds great," Dorie added. "Especially with all this water coming down."

Rett was right. Early arrival at the campsite would make nothing better. There wasn't a dry spot on the Fundy Footpath for them to sleep in.

"I don't know what I was thinking," Helen admitted. "Okay, let's go find the waterfall."

The descent toward Brandy Brook was slippery and treacherous. Step after careful step, she proceeded, using poles, but her heel slipped in the mud, throwing her off balance. She dropped her pole and grabbed for a sapling, but missed. She landed on the ground, ankle twisting under her, pressed down by the weight of her pack.

"Rett!" she called weakly toward her sister's back. "Rett!"

She fisted her poles and tried to push herself to stand, but slipped again, this time landing on her butt on a rock. Painful, yes, but better than breaking an ankle. She moved the twisted part gingerly. "Rett!"

Her sister turned, gave a shout, then headed back uphill toward Helen, Dorie and Evie following. Helen's ankle throbbed, her butt hurt where she'd contacted the rock, and she was mortified. Why did she have to be the one to get hurt?

"Twisted?" Rett asked, sliding her pack off her shoulders and then helping Helen get out from under hers.

"Yes," she said through gritted teeth. "It hurts."

"Yes," Rett said. "I bet. Can I move your ankle around?"

"I can move it," Helen said, and demonstrated, grimacing. "It moves okay, it's just — it hurts."

"Moving is good," Rett reassured her. "I don't want to take your boot off because it's probably going to swell up and you won't get it back on."

"That makes sense, I guess."

"Yes. Only it's going to swell in the boot and that's going to hurt." Rett gave her an appraising glance. "You slept good? Ate enough?"

She nodded. "Yes, I'm good enough otherwise. I can't tell if I can put weight on this thing, though."

Evie looked around. Helen had slipped on a steep downhill. "If we can get down about thirty meters, it's less steep," she said. "From there, we can figure something out."

"Okay, sure," Rett said. "Can you girls take her pack? Slide it down?"

Helen was confused. "Why are they taking my pack?"

Rett reached to help her stand. "Because you've got enough to do to get yourself down this part of the trail."

With her poles in her left hand and Rett lifting from the right, Helen got up on one foot. Careful, so careful, she thought. She rested her injured foot on the ground, then leaned in.

"Hey, hey! Go slow," Rett advised, still holding her up. "How are you feeling?"

Helen assessed. "I'm okay. Just the ankle."

"Not dizzy, not nauseated?"

"No, not that bad." She allowed a bit more weight on the foot and shrieked. "Okay, that was bad. But let me try with my poles. Maybe that will help."

"Okay. I'm going to let go. See how that is." Rett stepped away.

"Don't go too far." Helen's voice was small. She leaned on her poles and shifted her weight forward. Could she take a step?

Well, she could shuffle and use poles to keep herself upright, mostly. How would she ever carry her pack like this?

Rett was apparently a mind-reader because she said, as if Helen had spoken aloud, "Don't worry. We need to get to that flat place right now. I'm here if you need help."

Nodding tightly, Helen proceeded. Rett watched before tugging on her own backpack to follow Helen's slow descent. The others waited below in the open space.

Tears started with each step on her right foot. I'm not crying, she told herself. That's just the pain. Slide, shuffle, slide, shuffle. A few more steps to the clearing. Evie clambered back up the trail to offer her arm as support.

"I've got this," Helen said. "But stay right in front of me, please." The three of them crept down the last twenty feet of steep descent with Evie leading, Helen shuffle-sliding, and Rett following behind. Finally they reached where Dorie waited with three packs.

The sigh of relief when they landed was collective. The landing spot was small, though, with another steep descent to follow. Rett dropped her pack with the others and turned to Helen. "Well?"

"It's okay," Helen said. "It hurts like crazy, but not any worse than before."

"Dorie, where's that first aid kit? We've got some painkillers," Rett said.

"I'll get it." Dorie handed it over. "I bet you wish we still had the scotch," she said. "I'm sorry we drank it all."

Helen made a sound that was half laugh, half sigh. "Shouldn't mix them," she said, her voice tight. "Painkillers sound like a good thing right now."

"Is it too early for lunch?" Evie asked, looking at her watch. "I can't tell anything from the sky."

"I can tell it's raining," Dorie said.

"Funny girl." Evie said. "Seriously, we need a break to let that medicine work, and we should eat."

"Eating is a good idea," Rett said. "Here, Helen, take these, and I'm going to put this ice pack on, even over your boot."

"Ice pack? We have ice?"

"Cold pack. Whatever. It's a chemical that works like ice. Don't think about it."

Helen perched on a fallen tree, leg extended, heel resting on her pack. The cold pack was on her shin above her boot. "I can't tell if this is doing anything," she said to Rett.

"Don't question the nurse," Rett said firmly. "Elevation and cold. Your boot is providing the compression."

"Isn't the fourth thing rest?" Evie asked.

"Can't do anything about that one," Rett said. "We work with what we've got."

"I'm keeping you guys from the waterfall." Helen had a sudden realization. "Isn't the side trail near here?"

"Evie, you want to go? Helen's got to hang out for a bit, so there's time for a side trip." Dorie sounded excited.

Evie glanced at Helen. "You okay with that?"

"Why not? I'm stuck here for a bit." Why not go without me? Leave me alone here with my injury. Every woman for herself. It was hard not to feel sorry for herself.

Rett glanced at the younger women. "You girls go ahead. I've seen enough water for now. Besides, I have a waterfall coming off my hat."

"We won't be long," Evie promised. She and Dorie started downhill and veered off to the right. Their voices grew fainter.

"How are you doing?" Rett sat near Helen as the rain continued to fall.

"Oh, you know. Been better." Helen tried for humour.

"Yeah, I know," Rett said. "This trip is a challenge."

Yes it is, Helen thought. "Even for you?"

"Really hard work, all those ups and downs. When you get somewhere good, the clouds close in, and you can't see anything."

"When you're on the downhill path, you slip and twist your freaking ankle."

"Yeah. Challenging like that."

A moment passed. "What about being together?" Helen asked. "Sharing a tent is close quarters. It's been a minute since we shared a room."

"How long for real?" Rett asked. "Over twenty years."

Helen moved her foot. Yes, those painkillers were working. Her ankle still hurt, but the pain was dull, not piercing. "What do you remember?"

"About sharing a room? Not much," Rett said. "We had some big fights about space. You taped a line down the middle of the room. I had to jump to get to my side from the door."

"I did," Helen said, rueful. "I wasn't the nicest person."

"Suddenly. You changed suddenly," Rett noted. "We got along, and then we didn't. I was so confused. I must have made you mad, to make you hate me, but I never figured out what I did."

Helen's tears started, but this time, the pain was emotional. "I'm so sorry."

Rett shrugged. "It was a long time ago, but it hurt. You would never tell me what I did wrong."

Waves of fatigue pressed down on Helen. "You didn't do anything. It was me," she said. "Something happened, but you didn't do it."

Rett's gaze was curious. Before she said anything else, Evie and Dorie appeared in the woods above them. "Hey, you guys!" Dorie called. "We found another path."

They dropped to the clearing to join Helen and Rett.

"Nice waterfall?" Rett asked.

"The best. Look at the pictures I got," Dorie invited. Rett left Helen to confer with Dorie.

Relieved, Helen switched gears. "Evie, let's review the map. We might have to reconsider some things."

"Sure." Evie sat beside Helen. "Here we are, above Brandy Brook. Obviously, the waterfall is off over there." She gestured north. "We were planning to make Brothers Brook, with Rose Brook as a fallback position."

"It's so far." Helen's heart sank. Was her injury going to torpedo this trip? Like the debate competition had torpedoed her relationship with Rett all those years ago?

"It was already a big hiking day, and we didn't figure in the rain and certainly not somebody getting hurt." Evie looked across the map. "But we can figure something out."

"Maybe we need to call it," Helen said quietly, so Rett and Dorie couldn't hear. "Stop right here."

Evie looked her in the eye. "If you think we need to call it, we will. But based on the map, nobody can get here to pull us out, really. Except by helicopter or search and rescue."

"It's really not that dire," Helen said.

"The other option would be getting picked up at the beach if we can make it to Brandy Brook."

"Rescued by sea? That's a little extreme, too. I only twisted my ankle." She grimaced at the very thought. "That does not sound good. What else?"

"Well, it depends. If we're going to try to stick it out a little longer, we could aim for Quiddy River. Before we get that far, there's an old road, so Chad or somebody with a truck could probably come pick us up. So a few more kilometres of hiking before getting rescued by road."

The idea of calling Chad to pull them out of the forest was mortifying, though not as bad as the Coast Guard or Search and Rescue. "I really hate that idea, too."

"Of course," Evie said kindly. "This trip was your idea, your baby."

Helen tried to flex her ankle. "And I guess my failure."

Evie looked horrified. "No failure. You slipped in the mud. That could happen to anybody."

But not me, she thought. "Well, I guess the question is whether I can get to Quiddy River."

"Only a couple of kilometres. If you're good, we go on. If not, somebody can drive in to get us."

"It's only two kilometres." Helen tested her ankle.

"Remember, distance doesn't tell you much about terrain or elevation."

"I remember," she said irritably. "I'm the one who landed on her butt."

Evie chuckled. "Is that Tylenol working?"

"You know, it is," Helen said. "Maybe we should give this a try."

Evie called Dorie and Rett over, and the four discussed the options.

"We won't really know what Helen can do until she tries it out," Rett said. "Promise not to push past big pain, though. No martyrs on this trip."

"I have no intention of being Saint Helen of the Fundy Footpath," she agreed. "I'll complain if things get worse."

"In the meantime, let's repack a bit," Evie said. "Who has a little room?" She started to unload Helen's pack.

"Wait, I can do it," Helen said.

Rett glared. "Let us do this for you. Tomorrow you can carry stuff for me if you insist."

When they finished, Helen pulled on her pack. Remarkably light, it contained her snack and the first aid kit. Somehow everyone else had squeezed her items in.

"I don't feel right not doing my part," she complained.

"You are doing your part," Evie explained patiently. "You're hurt, so your part is getting yourself to the next spot. We're all responsible for each other."

Helen subsided. Besides, even her light pack put pressure on her foot. And would this rain ever let up? She was damp inside her jacket, too, from the sweat she generated before the painkiller started working. She poked her poles into the ground.

They continued the descent to Brandy Brook. Rett took up position behind her and Evie glanced back now and then. She was comforted by their presence.

Crossing Brandy Brook

Getting down to water level left her ankle throbbing again. The relief of stopping was cut short when she saw the brook, roaring with the runoff from the storm.

"This is supposed to be an easy crossing," Evie said when they gathered on the east side. "I don't think they meant in a hurricane."

"Is this a hurricane?" Dorie jumped in, high-pitched. "A hurricane?"

"No, no," Rett said hurriedly. "Evie just meant it descriptively, right, Evie?" She gave Evie a meaningful look.

"Nobody mentioned a hurricane to me," Evie declared stoutly. "I'm sorry I used the word. It's just been raining a lot."

Helen gazed at the rushing brook. There were stepping stones, and it looked like an easy enough crossing even with the high water, if you could put weight on your foot. Her sisters would make it across easily.

Evie looked at Helen and then at the brook. "It's not very wide," she noted. "But I think we'd all do better without too much to carry."

"If we can get the packs over, you mean," Rett said. "Maybe...wait. I got this." She went to the brook, looking upstream and down. "I think this is the place," she called back over the sound of the rain and water. She stepped onto the first stone.

She was agile, Helen thought, for somebody who never went to the gym. Within a few steps, Rett was waving her pole from the other side, then shucking her pack and returning across the water.

"What are you doing?" Dorie demanded. "You were already there."

"Give me your pack," she said. "I can take it across. Then you guys can support Helen."

"Okay, but I don't really get it," Dorie said, but she slid her pack off and handed it over. Rett crossed again, fleet-footed, in a moment returning to get Evie's pack. When she returned the next time, they gathered to look at Helen.

"What? I'm doing the best I can," Helen said, wondering why her eyes were brimming again.

"There's no blame here," Evie said. "Let's just think it through. Rett, what can you tell us about this crossing?"

"You can see where the water is deepest." She pointed it out. "Once you get to that big piece of granite, it's quite shallow and a lot more still. The only really tricky part is getting yourself over that main channel without losing your balance."

"I saw you using your poles," Dorie noted.

"Yes, they helped a little on the far side, but when I tried to put a pole in the streambed, the water pulled it hard. So use your poles only on the far side. Otherwise, you really just have to jump a bit."

Helen blew out her breath. Jumping didn't seem possible, but neither did dying on this side of the brook. Or, more realistically, waiting here until the water went down, which might be never, based on how much rain was falling.

"It's going to hurt like crazy," practical Rett said, "but I'm 99 percent sure it's not a broken ankle or foot, so you will be able to bear weight."

Ninety-nine percent. Helen nodded. "I was doing some weight-bearing to get down this hill."

"It will hurt, and we'll ice it and rest after the crossing. Now, though, I'm more concerned about you keeping your balance," Rett went on. "You know, not falling in."

"I'd really rather not fall in," Helen agreed, "but if I do, I get wet. That's all."

"More wet," Dorie corrected. "We're all wet already."

"Not my underwear," Helen added with a grin. "So far."

"I think I have a plan," Evie said. "What do you think about this idea?"

A few minutes later, Rett crossed the brook, carrying all their poles, to wait on the far shore. With Dorie in the lead, Helen in the middle, and Evie bringing up the rear, the three sisters were linked by a rope around Helen's waist and grasped by Dorie and Evie. Dorie, gazelle-like when unburdened by her pack, leaped into the brook, landing on the first stone, then looked back. Helen gave her a nod and she went on.

Helen held the rope in her left hand, balancing on her left boot. Her right toe was touching the ground, but she knew she'd have to lead with her right foot. One step at a time, one step at a time. Right now, this is the step. She leaned, reaching with her right foot for the first flat stone. A firm landing, but oh, the pain! Her ankle buckled, and she listed left, letting the waves of pain flow through her injured foot. Ahead, Dorie had reached the middle rock, beyond which the water rushed, whitecaps and all. Helen looked back to see Evie's encouraging glance, then leaned into her next step.

Yes! Shooting pains reached her hip, but she nailed the landing. No slipping, no collapse. Good job, Helen, she heard her mother saying. Good job. She panted a little, waiting for the waves of pain to ease. Dorie, now across the rushing channel, turned back to watch, rope still in hand.

Helen gripped the rope with her left hand and felt a comforting tug in each direction. Dorie ahead and Evie behind, sending strength along the length of the line. You got this, she said to herself. The sound of rushing water filled her ears, and she gazed at the current swirling, crashing, and dark under the white foam, rushing away downstream, grabbing up logs, brush, anything in its path.

"Helen!" Evie's voice penetrated her fog, and she looked up toward the landing rock. Dorie's worried face was beyond it, in the shallows. She gave the water one more glance. Grim, she leaned into her leap. Her right toe touched the landing rock on the edge and slipped off. She threw her arms forward, releasing the rope, grabbing for the rock, but the rushing water sucked her into the center of the stream.

Time moved slowly in the moment of falling. I slipped, she thought dully, and I missed. Her face scraped along the rock under the water. In another brief moment, though, she was aground, Dorie and Rett grabbing for her arms and pulling her out downstream from the stepping stones.

"Are you okay?" Dorie asked anxiously.

"Come on, let's get you to shore." Rett grabbed Helen, half-carrying her to the shore where Evie had landed. Dorie followed.

"I fell in," Helen said stupidly. "I can't believe I fell in."

"You sure did," Rett agreed, easing her down to sit. "The water looks shallow, but you almost disappeared."

She touched her face gingerly. "I felt like it."

"Let me see your face," Rett said. "You got up close and personal with a rock. You're going to have some spectacular bruises."

"Souvenirs," Evie added with a smile. Helen managed a faint smile in return. Ooh, that ankle hurt.

"But is she okay?" Dorie asked again.

"I'm good," she said firmly. "I'm wet and my ankle hurts, and my face had a close encounter with an alien rock, but no problemo." She sighed again.

"Chill, Dorie," Rett commanded. "It's going to be fine."

"I need a snack," Dorie said. "I bet you do, too." She rummaged for granola bars and handed them out. Rett continued to minister to Helen's face and Evie sat on her pack to watch.

"More painkillers instead of food," Helen suggested.

"Both," Rett ordered. "I wish we could make a fire, dry you out a little."

"I have dry socks," Helen said, "but I don't know whose pack has them."

"I've got dry pants," Dorie added. "We can share."

Evie jumped up to get the fly from her tent to provide some cover from the rain, and everyone pitched in, helping Helen strip down and put on dry clothes topped with rain gear. It was no easy feat, with the ground muddy and rain still coming down, but they made it happen.

"Sorry about your right foot," Rett said. "You'd rather have dry socks on both feet, but you need to keep your boot on."

"I get it. I'm amazed that I could change pants with a boot on my foot, but I guess that was good luck."

Dorie nodded. "Good luck and zippers. It's time for some good luck. This day has been full of the other kind."

"Well, adventure," Evie said. "That was more adventure. Do you think we can move ahead?"

It was late afternoon and they were barely two kilometres from their last campsite. "It's not been a very productive day, has it?"

Rett laughed. "Helen, we're hiking. We're hanging out together doing stuff. That's productive. You know, in a way."

"In a way I'm not used to," Helen agreed.

Evie brandished the map. "Helen and I talked about options. We're already on the way to Quiddy River. In a little while, there's a possible road out."

"Are we assuming we need to abandon our trip?" Helen chose her words for effect. "I'm no worse just because I fell into the water."

"Abandon is a loaded word. We have an injured hiker," Evie said. "That's a good reason to change plans. We've already hiked a lot and camped for two nights. It's hardly abandonment."

"I think I'm going to be better," Helen announced. "Let's not decide right now. Let's keep going and see how things are."

Rett narrowed her eyes; Helen narrowed hers in return. "I'm no quitter, Rett Madison," she said tightly.

"No Saint Helen either, right?" Rett reminded her.

She relaxed and laughed. "I promise. But honest, dry clothes can make you feel almost human again."

"We have lost a lot of time today," Evie said. "No matter what, we have to leave this place, so let's get going."

Reflection at Quiddy River

They started away from Brandy Brook, following the inevitable uphill trail. As they emerged onto the headland, the sky lightened. The cliffs to the left fell away to the Bay, and as the clouds drifted away, visibility improved.

"Martin Head!" Evie shouted in the lead. "Look!" She headed toward the cliff edge, camera poised.

Rett caught up with Helen. "Have you noticed?" she asked, pulling her hood off to shake her head. "It's not raining at this moment."

Helen looked at the sky. "Blue over there. The sky's clearing, thank goodness."

"You're walking pretty well," Rett observed.

"Not too bad," Helen said. "Of course, it's mostly flat here, the sun is showing itself, and suddenly everything seems more possible."

"Amazing how that works, eh?" Rett smiled. They continued walking.

"I could even put my stuff back in my pack," Helen offered.

Rett shook her head. "Let's not push our luck. We're all doing okay."

"The old road is coming right up," Evie said, returning. "We could get picked up here. What should we do?"

"I'm doing well," Helen said honestly. "I'd really like to continue the trip. Let's keep going."

"Okay," Rett said. "Let's keep going."

"No, wait." Evie stopped her. "I'd like to hear from everyone. If Helen's good, that's great, but this day has been hard for everyone. Let's take a few minutes."

"I never mind a little break," Dorie agreed, shucking her pack. "Snacks?"

"Girl, I think you have a tapeworm," Rett told her. "Keep it up, though, because you're doing great."

Dorie looked pleased. "I'm doing okay. Once I get past that morning yuck, everything seems great. I packed a lot of snacks, too."

"Did you have morning yuck again today?" Evie asked. "You didn't mention anything."

"We were busy coping with rain," Dorie said. "Besides, it's not a big deal because it goes away. I'm fine."

"Rett?"

Rett gazed at the toes of her boots. "I'm kind of proud of us, how we're handling the hard parts. I'd like to continue if we can." She looked up. "That's me."

"Thanks, everybody," Evie said. "So we go on."

"Wait." Helen waved a hand. "What about you? How are you doing, Evie?"

Evie paused. "Well, my legs are tired after three days. I will be happy to sleep tonight, and I probably won't ever want to eat oatmeal again after this trip, but I'm good. I'm happy to be in the woods with my sisters, some of my favourite people in the world."

"Aww," Dorie said, and gave Evie an awkward hug.

"Ooh, rain gear hug!"

"Is it safe to shed a layer?" Dorie asked.

"I'm willing to risk it," Helen said, peeling off her raincoat. "We might be able to dry some things out later."

"Optimist," Rett scoffed, but they tucked away their rain gear and hiked on.

Helen's ankle felt almost normal. Evie's words stuck with her. Some of my favourite people in the world. Why on earth would her sisters be her favourites?

Helen's busy mind flipped the idea around and around, and soon she wondered why she didn't count her sisters among her own favourite people. Or did she? Did she even have favourite people?

Well, Jake, of course. Naturally, your child would be a favourite. Dad, too. Honestly, she'd never considered Evie that way, or Dorie, either. They were just sisters. Sisters who had been in conflict for years.

Rett's practised clinical gaze returned to her mind. When Rett narrowed her eyes, Helen's eyes narrowed, too, in an automatic response. It was entirely possible they had fought so long it was the only way they could be together.

But no. Not anymore. This trip demonstrated their ability to get along. All the sisters.

Sisters, like the way Dorie led her across the brook, looking back to ensure her well-being. Evie insisting on checking in for everybody. Her sister Rett's hands, cool and firm, pressing on her ankle, cleaning the scrapes on her face. A warmth grew in her heart. If only she'd had sisters with her in Ottawa, maybe things wouldn't have gotten to such an extreme.

Ottawa.

Jean-Louis' face came into her mind, his wrinkled hands holding hers across the bistro table. His bright blue eyes, golf-tanned face, his steady kindness. Superimposed immediately was Sarabeth's grim visage, telling her she had to leave the firm. Then Reggie, wrapped around Juliet as always in her imagination. Her last walk through the wood and glass house, heel clicks echoing in the soaring empty space.

Her memories faded as she looked ahead to see Dorie's neon-orange pack cover, and Evie's lime green. Her sisters, carrying her load for her. She felt Rett's gaze behind her, and knew she was being watched, assessed, to see if she needed help. This was what it was like to know somebody had your back.

The afternoon distance wasn't shorter, but the group moved faster now Helen could use both feet. It was later than usual when they had travelled far enough inland to find the Quiddy River campsite.

"Water's easy to find," Dorie chirped. "Let's see if there's any dry wood anywhere." She and Rett headed into the forest.

Evie set up her tent, then helped Helen set up the other one. Helen blew up the sleeping pads outside the tent, then shoved them through the door. She wasn't taking her boots off until she could sit for a while.

Rett and Dorie returned with sticks and water, and Evie started the little camp stove to heat water for pasta.

"Pasta again!" Dorie said. "Wonderful!"

Rett snickered. "There's nothing like hiking all day to make any-thing edible sound delicious. What's going on that pasta, Evie?"

"Mushrooms and Alfredo sauce," she replied, shaking a packet. "Rehydration is magic."

It seemed like magic when Helen's bowl filled with fragrant, creamy deliciousness. "I've got bread, too," Evie said, rummaging. "Tear off a piece."

The sisters dug in. Helen had never tasted food so delectable. She shoved in the first bites, then made herself put the bowl on the ground. She leaned into tugging at the laces on her right boot.

"It's time for the unveiling," Rett said.

"I'm not too excited about it," Helen said. "It could be gnarly." The sisters watched with interest as she loosened the boot and pulled on the heel. Rett jumped in to assist.

"Ouch!" Once freed of compression, the throbbing returned. "Oh, that hurts."

"Cold pack," Rett said, holding out her hand.

Helen dug the first aid kit out of her pack, then submitted to Rett's ministrations. "I'm glad you know how to outfit for first aid," she said to her sister. "Even if it hurts like.... like a monster. Or something much nastier, but I'm trying not to swear."

"The cold will help." Rett was firm.

"Why is it so hard to believe you?"

Evie built a small fire from Rett's gatherings, and they drew near. "I'm hanging up my rain gear," Dorie said. "Helen, I'll hang your wet clothes, too."

"It will only get wetter after dark," Evie reminded her. "It's not like doing the laundry. Dew settles on everything."

"Right. We don't have a lot of time to dry things out, but it'll be okay," Rett said. "Everybody's got dry socks, right?"

"Well, not quite. My dry socks had to go into wet boots," Helen said apologetically. "One wet boot."

"I brought extras," Evie said. "I'll share. Put these on."

Helen was overcome. Warm, dry socks felt incredibly luxurious. She didn't deserve these sisters.

After cleaning up, they sat around the struggling fire. Dorie poked around with her flashlight and unearthed a stash of driftwood covered by leaves, dry despite the day of rain. Triumphant, she carried an armload to the fire and added a piece.

"Dorie to the rescue!" Rett cheered from her place on the ground.

Dorie looked surprised. "That's a first. Usually it's Dorie the screw-up."

"Nah. You've been great on this trip. I had my doubts, but you've been a super camper." Rett was clear.

"Wow, that's nice. Mostly, I feel like I don't belong with you guys. You know, the tag-along baby sister, very annoying."

Helen, listening, wondered if she'd contributed to Dorie's feeling of separation, alienation. Probably. She'd not been much of a sister.

Evie scoffed. "It's funny, isn't it? I always thought you were the chosen one, the baby everybody loved. I got left out, not allowed to play with the big girls. Told to take care of my baby sister."

Dorie chortled. "I remember how much you hated that. I always wanted to play dolls."

"You were three and I was fifteen. I just wanted to hang out with Rett. And Helen, before she left for school." Helen caught Evie's glance in her direction.

"You two shared a room," Rett remembered, "but you always wanted to bunk in with Helen and me. I didn't think we'd even fit three girls in, even though my three kids have shared a room occasionally."

"They're not teens," Evie said darkly. "The most unfair thing was that you got to have your own room after Helen left, and I was still sharing with Dorie. I was mad at Mum for years for not letting me move in with you."

Rett laughed. "I didn't know."

"Mum said I'd have my space when you left for uni, Rett, but I didn't want my own space. I wanted to be with my big sister. You."

"Sorry, Evie," Rett said. "I was so happy to have a room of my own, I don't think I knew you wanted to share."

"Well, we were kids," Evie pointed out. "So even if you knew, you probably wouldn't have offered."

"Probably not," Rett agreed. "Especially after the way Helen and I used to fight. It was terrible that last year you were home," she added, turning toward Helen.

"Then you all left. I was the only one," Dorie said plaintively. "I had the dogs to play with. Mum and Dad were not really into little kids as much, and who could blame them? By the time I hit middle school, Mum was over fifty."

"Funny, I hardly ever think of them like that," Helen said. "Maybe because they were young when I left home. Pretty young, I mean, like not much older than I am now."

"Young is relative," Dorie said. "Some of us are actually young, and some of you believe you're still young."

"Snarky!" Rett called it. Dorie giggled.

Helen's conscience pressed on her. "About that last year at home," she said. "I, uh, I think I want to tell you about that."

The fire crackled, and Dorie poked at it with a stick. "I'm going to put on another log," she said to nobody.

"In October of grade twelve, I went to Fredericton with the debate team."

"Dad's got the picture of your team holding the trophy, right in the living room," Evie reminded her.

Helen shook her head. "I'd forgotten, or kind of forgotten, until I saw that picture in January when I got back." She shifted around, wondering where the courage was coming from – or remorse, maybe. She eyed Rett. "Are you sure that flask was empty?"

"Keep going," Rett said. "Tell us."

"It's all tied up with Reggie and moving," Helen said frantically, "and I don't know if I can tell you all of it."

"Breathe," Evie said from across the circle. "Breathe. There's no pressure. Say what you want to say."

"No, I want to hear it all," Rett said clearly. "There's been something wrong for months, and you've never really told us why you're back. I want to know."

A war erupted inside Helen. Shame begat anger that made her lift her chin and say, "I'll decide what to tell you." Immediately flooded with remorse, she added, "You deserve to understand what I've been taking out on you."

Evie peered at her in the deepening dusk. "We've got you. You're our sister. There's nobody closer than that. Not boyfriends, not children, not parents."

"That's the problem," Helen said, frantic again. "I'm supposed to be the big sister, leading by example. The one you guys look up to. That's what I was always told."

The group was silent. In shock? Helen looked around to see Evie's kind eyes, so like Corinne's. Dorie smiled and Rett's eyebrows knitted together.

"How do you see me?" Helen asked, her voice shaky. "Maybe I don't want to know, but I think I have to."

The crackling fire, the swish of the little current in the river, and the gentle sounds of the forest readying for night filled the silence after Helen's question.

"Never mind," she jumped in. "That was a lot to ask."

"You've been larger than life," Dorie began. "Because you were older, and besides, I thought Corinne was your sister. Evie was my sister, Rett, too, but I didn't really believe in my big sister Helen who lived far away."

"You didn't believe in Helen?" Evie asked, laughter in her voice.

"Kind of like Santa. Is he real if you hardly ever see him? Helen was like that. Remember, I was only two when you left the house."

"Two is so little." Helen was moved at the thought, recalling Jake at that age.

"When you came back, I was so hopeful. I wanted to have a relationship with this kind of legendary sister."

Helen's heart sank. "And?"

"It hasn't come naturally, that's for sure." Dorie was clear. "We don't have much in common besides the same parents. You're a successful lawyer and I clean kennels. You're wealthy, and I'm perpetually scrambling for grant funds. You have all this education, and I dropped out of university."

The sinking sensation became an actual pain in Helen's chest, squeezing her heart. "I...I..."

Dorie shrugged. "It's not your fault, and besides, we're here, right? Working on our relationships?"

She sniffed and nodded, vowing internally to do better.

"I wanted to be your friend, like Rett," Evie said. "You were the larger-than-life Madison sister, and I honestly thought I was adopted, and in fact, I wished for it. At least then I could understand why nobody liked me, and why nobody was like me."

"What do you mean nobody liked you?" Rett asked sharply.

Evie sniffed. "I don't want to rehash all this, but it was how I felt as a kid. Helen, you left when I was fourteen, barely conscious of the world outside Stella Mare, and you were a shining light. A beacon of what I should have been. A truly good person. Instead, I embraced my inner goth. You two were the Madison girls. I was the 'are you sure you're a Madison?' girl."

"Evie, that's horrible," Dorie said plainly. "Did somebody really say that to you?"

"Only once," she said, "but it stuck in my mind for years."

"You know you're not adopted, right?" Helen asked. "I remember when you were born."

Evie chuckled, a comfortable, comforting sound. "I don't worry about that stuff anymore. When you moved home, I hoped we'd become friends. I really hoped you weren't the perfect human that Dad and Mum told us about."

"No chance," Helen said.

Rett stirred the fire with a long stick. "Sounds like there were a lot of illusions, but I didn't have them. By the time you left, I was glad to see you go, and I'm not sure I've gotten over being dumped by you."

"Dumped?"

Rett looked at her with hard eyes. "Dumped. At least it felt that way. We'd done most everything together until you hit grade twelve, and then splat. Nothing. Only fights."

Helen waited. She'd been thinking about it, too.

"You were great last fall," Rett said, and there was a catch in her voice. "I needed your help, and you really helped, in more ways than you probably know. When you came back, even though I was mad you hadn't told me you were coming, I wanted us to be proper sisters again. But that hasn't happened. You don't let anybody in, Helen. It's hard to be close to somebody who works so hard to keep you at a distance."

Helen felt battered by the words, by all their words, but they also rang with truth. She sniffed and wiped her face with her sleeve. Nobody could see in the dark, anyway.

"Sorry to be so blunt," Rett said. "You asked."

Helen swallowed hard. She knew she deserved every word.

Sisters in Shame

"I did ask." Helen sat in the silence, letting the evening sounds sink in, slowing her heart rate and breathing. Her sisters were honest. She had to be honest, too.

"You're right, Rett, about me trying to keep a distance. It seemed safer. There are things I've done I don't like to think about. I don't like myself when I think about them, so I don't tell anyone. It's shameful, so I have to keep my distance. Keep up appearances. It's exhausting. I've been trying to be someone you look up to. But if you look up, I look down.

"The big sister is supposed to lead by example, but I panicked on the first night, had a couple more panic moments on the second day, got injured today, and failed at leading this group."

"Oh, not failed," Evie began.

Helen held up her hand. "Let me say this. Please. Today, with all of you helping me, today I felt like I belonged to you. Belonged with you." Tears overflowed her eyes. "I want us to know each other."

Rett patted her shoulder, and Evie reached over with a tissue. She saw Dorie's warm gaze when she looked up. "You deserve the truth."

"Whatever it is, it'll be okay," Evie said.

"Well, not if she murdered somebody," Rett disagreed. "Or stole a lot of money."

Dorie had eyes like saucers. "She didn't do that."

Helen choked out a laugh. "No, I didn't. But thanks for putting my sins in context."

Rett peered around the campfire. "Any cookies?"

"Protein balls," Evie offered. "They're chocolate."

Rett took one and leaned back on her elbow. "Okay, go."

Helen's emotions fought, but the snicker beat out the shame. "Okay, guys. My life has been kind of a mess. You already know Reg left me."

"Because of his cheating heart, right? The other woman?" Dorie spoke briskly.

Helen sobered and gazed at the fire. "Not really. It was more about the fighting. He'd tried to get me to go to counselling, but I knew better. He said he'd given up on our marriage before he started seeing Juliet. I shouldn't have been surprised. From here, I see the breakup as mostly my fault."

"No," Dorie said robustly. "It couldn't be."

"Yes," Helen said. "I didn't have time for him or Jake. I just worked. I even refused to go on a trip to Barbados he planned for our anniversary, two years ago."

"Barbados?" Dorie's eyes were like saucers. "Why wouldn't you go?"

She looked at the fire to avoid those eyes. "Things were, well, it wasn't a good time. I had a lot going on at work." She looked up. "The same thing I said about everything."

"I'd have figured out a way," Dorie said firmly.

"I should have," Helen agreed. "I should have done a lot of things."

Silence settled around the circle. Helen's throat tightened, but she squeezed out, "I did a lot of things I shouldn't, too."

She looked at each of them. Dorie frankly curious. Rett direct and appraising. Evie with deep brown eyes, soft and kind. Like Corinne's, yes, but also like Stephen's. Maybe they were a good match.

"Are you going to tell us?" Rett asked.

Shifting the position of her leg, she heaved a sigh. "Yes. But give me a minute." She pulled up the collar of her fleece jacket and put her hands in the pockets.

"Something's going on with me on this trip," she said. "I've been remembering some things."

"This is like pulling teeth, Helen. Just spill it," Rett griped. "Whatever it is, it's okay."

"Remember when I went to Fredericton for the debate competition?" She directed her question to Rett. "I did something awful. I went to the Campbellton team's hotel room. They were drinking. I did, too."

"That's not awful, that's normal," Dorie said. "That's what kids do."

"I didn't, never. The whole thing made me so ashamed. I couldn't tell anybody."

"So what? You drank. You were eighteen."

"Almost," Rett inserted. "Tell us what happened."

"I left the party and went with a guy to somebody's room. I was pretty well out of it, and I went with him, and there were more of them, three altogether, I think three. Three I can remember."

She choked up as the scene replayed in her mind. Darkness closed in, and she caught her breath, willing herself not to be swept into the memory. Pressure on her chest, the smell of wet wool. She gasped.

A branch popped in the fire, waking her to here and now. She shook her head and lifted her chin. Right. Here and now.

"Oh, no," Evie said on a sharp breath.

Rett slid over on the log and put her hand on Helen's shoulder. "You didn't tell anybody?"

Helen looked through watery eyes. "Not until this minute. It was so terrible, and all my fault. I knew better than to let it happen."

Dorie stood up on the other side of the fire, hands on hips. "That wasn't your fault!"

Evie shook her head. "You didn't cause that."

Rett moved in closer, wrapping her arm over Helen's shoulders. "I knew it."

"You knew?"

"I knew something like that. You had a big reaction to something."

"I guess so. I thought I hid it well." She recalled days under the covers with her dog.

"If taking to your bed is the same thing as hiding it," Rett remarked. "You certainly never talked about it with me. What about Mum?"

"Oh, no. It would have killed Mum. I couldn't shame her like that."

"Oh, geez," Rett said.

"Mum would be so ashamed of me," Helen said, little sobs interrupting her words. "Getting divorced, and now, maybe the worst...."

"There's more? Helen, a terrible thing happened to you when you were just a kid."

She looked at Rett. "I did a terrible thing, you mean. And I did more. I was spending a lot of time with a man in Ottawa."

"Reggie was moving out. What's wrong with that?"

Jean-Louis' handsome visage came to mind. "He was a client."

Her words met with stunned silence.

Rett asked, "Your client?"

"Oh, of course not, no! He was married to my partner's client, but they had an open relationship. And besides, we never…" Helen's voice trailed off. "You know."

"You never slept with him," Rett filled in.

"I don't get it." Dorie was blunt. "What did you do that was so terrible?"

"I let him give me gifts, take me to expensive dinners, and even take me away for a weekend." Her chest felt crushed by shame. "He was married. Married to one of my partner's biggest corporate clients. She complained to my partners, and she might even complain to the Law Society, and so I can't work as a lawyer right now."

"Did you do something wrong? Sorry to be dense, but I'm not getting it," Dorie insisted.

"Sounds like optics to me," Rett said. Helen knew Rett understood that; her sister's nursing position had been damaged by optics.

"Maybe it is optics, but that's not the point." Helen sat straight up, pulling away from her sister's grasp. "It was poor judgment."

"You're a little rough on yourself," Rett said. "Lighten up."

"Aren't you listening? I'm trying to tell you. My life is full of poor decisions and bad judgment. Like thinking this trip was going to solve something."

"I knew it," Rett said. "I knew we'd end up fighting."

"Wait a minute." Evie's calm voice entered the conversation. "Helen's trying to tell us something important. Let's listen."

"I don't think I want to talk anymore."

"That's up to you," Evie said. "If you're done, though, I have something to say."

Grateful to have the focus turned elsewhere, Helen listened.

"Did you guys ever think Mum might have had unrealistic expectations?"

"Never," Dorie said emphatically. "Mum was the best."

"What do you mean, Evie?" Rett asked. "I kind of agree with you, but say more."

"She honestly thought we should try to be perfect. Look perfect, act a certain way, be upstanding all the time. She hated it when we fought. I remember more than one lecture about needing to carry yourself with confidence, being a beacon to others. All that stuff."

"Sounds familiar," Helen agreed.

"It felt so impossible," Evie sighed. "I was just never going to be a leader of anyone, and I didn't like being looked at, much less being a beacon. I knew I was letting her down, but I didn't know how to fix it."

"She could be rough," Helen put in. "Maybe you didn't see it, Dorie, but I remember her being pretty demanding. You—any of us—were at risk of not measuring up. When I came home from the debate trip, I was sure she could see my black soul right through my chest. I couldn't bear having her tell me it was my fault. I already knew it."

"She was exacting." Rett spoke precisely. "You knew where the line was, and you had to be right there, toe on it. Not a step across. She loved us, but she expected a lot."

"It's weird how after somebody dies, you say nothing remotely critical about them, even if it's absolutely true. Dad would not like this conversation," Evie added.

"I'm not sure I like it." Dorie fiddled with her jacket. "It seems disloyal to Mum or something."

"She was wonderful," Helen said. "She was the best at bringing people together. She took great care of people and dogs, and she was fun to be with."

Rett added, "She demanded a lot of her kids, too."

"I think she valued our achievements because she stayed so close to home," Helen remarked.

"Like living vicariously?" Evie asked. "She sure was proud of her lawyer daughter and her nurse manager daughter."

"Not so much her artist daughter?" Helen asked.

"Not so much," Evie agreed. "At least that's how it felt."

"But she loved you!" Dorie objected. "She was always telling me I had to grow up to be like my sisters. All the wonderful things you did."

"That's what I mean," Helen said. "She put pressure on you, too. Maybe that's just part of being a mother."

Rett frowned lightly. "I hope I'm not pressuring my kids, but I probably am."

"I don't blame Mum for my mistakes, Dorie. Don't think that. She made it hard to talk about failures, though."

Rett peered through the gloom toward Helen. "Trauma, too. You didn't fail when you went to Fredericton. You were attacked. That wasn't your fault."

Helen shook her head. "I shouldn't have been drinking. Shouldn't have gone with that guy."

"Still not your fault." Evie was staunch.

"Well, we disagree," Helen said. "I was terrified that the story would come out, and I'd have ruined myself and my family. I had to leave and stay away."

"You were successful at that," Rett said dryly. "Twenty years."

"I missed so much. I didn't even realize it."

"You got a lot, too," Rett reminded her. "Your practice, your house, your marriage. Jake."

"Hmmm. I guess." She rubbed her chest; thinking about Jake hurt.

"I stole some money," Dorie said abruptly.

Helen swivelled. "You did what?"

"I took money out of Mum's wallet, and I took some money Dad had in a drawer." Her words tumbled out. "They never knew it was me."

"When? What were you thinking?" Rett demanded.

"Ages ago. I was probably fifteen."

"Dorie, why?" Evie probed.

"It was a dare, sort of. This kid at school made me pay, or he'd tell everybody about the time I peed my pants in grade one."

Shocked silence. "In grade one?" Rett was the first to speak.

Dorie coughed and then laughed. "I can hear how ridiculous it sounds. It was so hard in high school. People could turn on you in an instant. But the bad thing was stealing."

"No, the bad thing was bullying and extortion," Helen said. "Did you tell Dad? He would have stopped that."

"I couldn't tell Mum or Dad that I stole money. I gave that kid ten bucks, but I used the rest to buy beer," Dorie said, shamefaced. "Somebody's brother got me beer to take to a party. I wanted the other kids to like me."

"No wonder you didn't tell," Rett said. "Bullied is bad, but Dad would not have liked you buying beer at fifteen."

"Do you guys remember that embezzling case a couple of years ago?" Dorie said. Rett and Evie nodded, but Helen didn't recall. "They put the money in my account to make me look guilty. That didn't scare me, but I was afraid Dad would remember when money went missing at home and ask me about it." She hung her head. "I still feel lousy about it."

"Guilt is miserable," Helen said fervently.

"It used to be a lot worse," Dorie said. "For years, if I was awake at night, I'd think about how I stole from Mum and lied. I had a terrible conscience about it."

"As you should," Rett said, but there was a laugh in her voice. "Was that the worst you did?"

"I also smoked dope in high school under that big oak tree," Dorie added promptly. "But honestly, stealing money from the parents felt so much worse. It still does."

"So, are we baring all our secrets?" Rett asked. "Because I've got a couple."

"Do tell," Dorie urged. "Take the spotlight off me, please."

Rett shifted on the ground. "Yeah, well. Helen knows last year I was sort-of, kind-of enamored of that Jürgen guy that lives next door. I actually let him kiss me."

"You didn't let him," Helen reminded her. "He took advantage."

"Ha!" Rett said, pointing at her. "You can see it when it's somebody else. Right?"

Helen subsided. "Point taken."

"Anyway, that was yuck, but not the worst I've ever done." She drew in a big breath. "When I met Harry, he blew me away. He was like nobody I'd ever dated. Scared me to death at first. I just kept thinking this is it. He was so much my perfect match, I was afraid. Like maybe I'd miss something. So I went out and out and out. The first six months I was dating Harry, I was also out every other night. I'd go dancing at clubs in town and go home with different people."

"You mean like sleeping around?"

"Helen, you sound like Mum, I swear. Nobody says that anymore," Dorie said.

"Every night?" Evie sounded awed. "Wow, Rett. You really have a past."

"I'm not proud of it, but it's true. I feel a little ashamed of it. Since we're sharing."

Helen asked, "Did Harry know?"

"He did. I was clear about not being exclusive."

"Obviously something changed," Helen said, a question in her voice.

"Well, my grades fell, but that's probably not what you meant." Rett grinned.

Helen snickered. "How did you get from the Tinder Queen to married forever with three kids?"

"Well, for one thing, it was a long time before Tinder. But honestly, it was simple. Whenever I was with somebody else, I thought, you're not Harry. They might be great, but they weren't him. It got so I couldn't be bothered with anybody else. I only wanted Harry."

"That's so sweet." Evie's voice was soft.

"You going home with some guy. A lot of guys. Wow! You are a woman with a past," Helen said, her smile widening.

"It's not me now, that's for sure. But it was for a few months when I was young."

"You tested the waters before deciding. That sounds kind of smart." The worried tone came from Dorie.

"It was right for me, but not for everybody, Dorie. You don't have to do what I did."

"It kept you from FOMO. You know, fear of missing out. You know Harry's the one for you."

"That's how I looked at it, but can you imagine Mum? She'd die a thousand deaths if she knew her daughter was exploring."

"She'd approve of exploring the Fundy Footpath," Helen said, "but not exploring your sexuality."

"I wonder if that's true," Evie mused. "We think Mum had high standards for us, but what was she like when she was young?"

Rett snickered. "Dorie's a small-time thief, Helen had an affair that didn't even include sex, and I was briefly promiscuous before giving it up for full-time monogamy. What a shameful bunch." She laughed again. "What about you, Evie?"

"I'm not sure I can measure up," Evie commented. "In trying so hard to look bad, I didn't have time to be bad. I looked like a wild thing, all the hair dye and the piercings and the tattoos. They were not exactly commonplace back in the day. At least not on a Madison in Stella Mare."

"What I remember is you never looked happy," Helen recalled. "Even in Christmas pictures."

"I figured I should embrace my differences. But the only really bad thing I did was I got a real tattoo. When I was only fifteen."

"You did? What did Mum say?" Dorie.

"Mum never knew," Evie confided. "It's not a place she'd see."

"Oooh, where?" Dorie.

"On my lower back, way down low," Evie said. "I drew the design, and I saved babysitting money to pay for it, and I had to get a friend to work on it because I couldn't go to a pro without parental permission."

"Can I see?" Dorie was persistent.

"When we get home," Evie promised. "I don't want to take off any layers right now."

"Okay, we have a tattooed renegade to add to our shameful ranks," Rett said cheerfully. "Those Madison sisters, you never know what you're going to get."

"We Madisons." Evie was firm. "Sisters in shame." She giggled and Dorie joined her.

"We're a motley crew, for sure," Helen said. She exhaled with something that felt a lot like relief. "Thanks, everyone. Thanks." She lay back, cradling her head on her arm. These sisters. Her sisters. All of them, together.

Before Dorie drowned the fire and they headed to bed, Helen and Evie put their heads together about the next day. Evie had an idea.

"We could just hike to this place above Little Salmon River and head out. When we get coverage, we could ask Chad to come and get us."

"I hate cutting it short," Helen griped. "Especially because of me."

"I know," Evie said, tilting her head.

"I really wanted us to cross that big suspension bridge together. The one at Big Salmon."

"That looks exciting," Evie agreed, "but we made so little distance today that we won't make it there before our food runs out. We'll have to come off the trail early, no matter what. It will be tomorrow above Little Salmon or the day after."

Helen put weight on her injured ankle. "By morning, I'll be back to hiking with a full pack."

"Do you mean you can't decide tonight?"

"I guess that's exactly what I mean." She smiled at Evie. "Thanks for interpreting for me."

"Let's decide all together in the morning. For now, we better get some sleep."

Flexible Thinking

Helen slept immediately and didn't wake until morning. The sounds of the water and a breeze flowed into a dream: her mother was tucking her into bed, under a quilt full of stories.

"Tell me about this one," she invited, as her mother sat on the edge of her childhood bed.

"That was your Aunt Hannah's graduation dress, and it was so beautiful. My mother made it herself, and later sewed it into this quilt for my babies. Here's a piece of the fabric I used to make my wedding dress." Her mother fingered the light blue lace. "Here's Auntie Corinne's baby blanket."

"Everybody is here, aren't they?"

"All the girls are here," her mother said, brushing her hand across the quilt. "All the women from my family. Your family on my side. Grandma Sarah's own wedding dress, here. My sister Annie's christening gown and her graduation dress, right there, side by side."

"How do you remember?"

"It's in the love," her mother said, gazing at the quilt and then at Helen. Such a loving glance Helen caught her breath. "It's the feeling that goes with each scrap. The love your Grandma Sarah sewed in, and the care we take with the quilt, and the fabric of everyday life with your sisters and your aunt and your grandmother. All the women together, keeping each other safe and warm."

She leaned over to kiss Helen's cheek and left the room. As she opened the door, the sound of rushing water and wind in the trees got louder.

Helen opened her eyes to the inside of the tent.

Caught in the memory of the dream, she held onto the sense of being cradled by her mother, and a warmth from last night, knowing her sisters knew her story. They were bound with strands of love and connection. How odd that sharing your worst moments brought people closer.

Delicate little snores came from Rett, so she got up quietly. As she pulled on layers for the cool morning, she noted with pleasure her foot was nearly normal size, and her boots went on easily. She stirred up the ashes from last night to start a little fire with the extra wood they'd collected. The smoke floated straight up, telling Helen the breeze had died away. Perhaps it had only been breezy in her dream. The sky was clear; no more rain. Thank goodness.

She got busy making coffee. Dorie made her way to the fire, looking sleepy. "Good morning."

"It is. This will be a minute."

"Yes. Thanks for making it." Dorie squatted down and rubbed an arm across her face.

Helen looked at her, really looked. Here was her baby sister, looking like a little kid, hair all mussed, eyes half open. She could see the child in her, the little one who adored her Big Helen so long ago. "How was your night?"

"Ugh. Not good. I spent half the night worrying about Dad finding out what I did, and the other half wondering why I can't come clean."

"Come clean about taking the money, you mean?" Helen filled mugs for them.

Dorie nodded miserably. "You guys won't tell, right?"

"What's said on the trail, stays on the trail," Helen declared staunchly. "But that doesn't mean you shouldn't tell him. You'll feel better."

"I can't see it. He'll be so disappointed." Dorie sipped gingerly at the steaming mug. "Are you going to tell him about you?"

Gut punched. "Tell him what?"

"You know. What you told us."

Helen's mind swirled. About Jean-Louis? About her workplace?

"About what happened to you in high school," Dorie explained.

"Oh, I don't know about that."

"Come on, everybody drinks in high school."

"Is that what you meant? I thought you meant, well, the assault. I don't need to talk to Dad about that. If Mum were still alive, she might deserve an explanation for my behaviour. Dad wouldn't have noticed."

"Rett noticed."

"She sure did," Helen agreed. "I have amends to make there."

"What does that mean, making amends? I mean, I understand the basic meaning, but in this case, what do you mean by it?"

Helen considered. "It's about harm. In the law, we have remedies when somebody is harmed by another persons' actions. The victim seeks a remedy. In relationships, we can make amends. If I hurt you I can try to mitigate that, both by acknowledging my responsibility and by trying to undo any harm."

Dorie's forehead wrinkled. "Amends means to make it up, not just apologizing. I could return the money I took."

"Yes. Or maybe not. It depends on you and Dad deciding together." Helen gazed into the sky. "I need to make amends to Rett, to undo the harm I did to our relationship by my behaviour." She focused on Dorie's face. "Actually, to all you sisters. Same thing. I realize this entire trip is about making amends."

Dorie sipped and pondered. "I didn't think of the trip like that. More like trying to find out why we can't get along and fixing it."

"Do you have an answer?" Helen asked with a smile.

"Yes. It's me. I'm the problem." Dorie sighed.

Helen grinned at her. "Wrong. It's me. I'm the problem." They giggled.

Conversation over by the tents drew Helen's attention. Evie and Rett chatted as they rolled up sleeping pads. "I have to make things better," Helen said, almost to herself.

"Isn't that what's going to happen?" Dorie tossed back the rest of her coffee. "Now that we've all bared our souls?"

"Is stealing a few bucks from Dad really the worst, worst, worst thing you ever did?" Helen felt laughter bubbling.

Dorie shook her head. "Probably not. There was an incident right after I met Chad, but everybody knew about it. Also, there were moments when Mum was dying when I wasn't a very good person. Rotten, to be honest."

Helen gave her a quick shoulder hug. "Everybody was under strain. Nobody can be wonderful all the time."

"How's the coffee?" Evie asked, looking in the little pot. "Oh. Gone." She filled the pot from their water supply. "Is this the last of the coffee?"

"It is," Helen said. "Tomorrow we'll be without coffee."

"Hey, you two," Rett said. "How's that ankle?"

"Good. I'm ready for a full pack today."

"Thank goodness," Rett said. "I'm ready for a break!"

"We wanted to talk about that," Evie said. "We have a couple of options for finishing this trip. One is to head to the access road a few kilometres from here and get Chad or Dad to pick us up."

"Then we'd be finished with camping!" Dorie's voice was filled with dislike.

"Right. Also finished with hiking," Evie pointed out. "We have to get to the access road, but it's not too far."

"What other options?"

"We hike to Little Salmon River and camp there tonight. Tomorrow, we hike up Walton Glen. Chad collects us at the Walton Glen information center, to give us one more night and another hiking day."

"Walton Glen? I never heard of it," Rett said.

"Neither of those gets us to cross the big suspension bridge at Big Salmon River." Helen's disappointment lay heavy on her.

Rett looked up. "You really wanted to do that? It's not such a big deal. I hiked it from the other end once."

"Well, it is to me," Helen said.

"If it's a big deal to Helen, I want to do it, too," Dorie said loyally.

"I wanted us to cross it together," Helen said. "I figured we'd be different somehow, coming over that bridge at the end of this trip."

Evie was studying the map. "I don't see how we can do it, honestly. That's a lot of kilometres and we're not fast."

"We'll be fast today," Dorie said, looking upward. "The day is clear and we're up early."

"Helen's ankle," Evie said. "Plus we're tired. I'm tired."

"You're right, we're all tired. My ankle is fine, though. I don't want to give up."

"Maybe we can try it," Rett said. "Reconsider when we hit that ATV trail. Helen will have a good idea then if she's okay. No Saint Helen."

"No Saint Helen," she agreed. "If I'm fine, we'll keep on to Little Salmon. That's reasonable."

"Nothing about this trip has been reasonable, you guys," Dorie said darkly, "but it has been fun. Much as it pains me to admit it."

They hurried to eat and pack. Dorie was right about the weather; it was as perfect a long June day as they ever came, and Helen peeled layers away before starting out.

Rett watched her as she slid into her full pack and stood. When she tested the bad foot, nothing hurt, so she gave Rett a thumbs up.

"Where's Dorie?"

She stumbled back to the site, waving a toothbrush and water bottles. "Threw up. Again. It's like an everyday event. But I'm good now. Got all our water."

"Let's go."

The climb up from the campsite was arduous, and Helen was pleased to find her feet well under her. The woods trail had dried out overnight, and her footing was sure. In fact, she felt better than she had for the entire trip. Probably because of taking a day with a very light pack. Her sisters were probably extra tired from hauling her stuff as well as theirs. Guilt landed on her shoulders, but lightly, like a feather.

Well, she was doing her part now. Cheery, she followed her sisters along the trail. It was good to be out in the woods, good to be with people you liked, good to be hiking.

As she climbed, thoughts arose. Maybe they could make the entire trip. They needed more food; food turned into energy, and another day or two on the trail would get them over the suspension bridge. Helen imagined the picture. Four sisters, leaning over the bridge happy and smiling, knowing that they'd conquered the Fundy Footpath. Chad or Dad could resupply them. Why not?

Evie, in the lead, disappeared from Helen's sight as she gained the false plateau. Dorie followed. By the time Helen was up into the woods at the temporary top, the next incline showed itself. More up and up. Her glutes burned. She'd be stronger for all this uphill walking but going home wasn't such a terrible idea.

She had to laugh at her attitude change. Fifteen minutes ago, she was plotting to complete the trip, and now she was ready to bail. Maybe somebody could pick them up, take them home. Her ankle was stable, and when she finally reached the real top of the plateau, walking was almost easy. Her shoulders were a little tired, but her legs were strong.

They reached the ATV trail sooner than Helen had expected. Dorie dumped her pack and called for a snack break. By Dorie's watch, they had been hiking for over two hours, but the time had passed quickly.

"Come see this," Evie called. "It's a great big hole."

Rett snickered. "We went hiking and saw a hole." Her grin evaporated when she got to the site. "That's massive," she said and breathed sharply. "I take back my snarky comment." Dorie, Evie, and Rett stood at the rim of the hole, marvelling, but Helen was less interested.

"This is the ATV trail, Martin Head Road," Helen called. Brandishing her map, she added, "Here's where we make our decision."

"Let us enjoy the moment," Rett said. "Ease up."

"Yeah, yeah." She wandered in their direction. It really was a big hole. "How do you think that happened?"

Evie had the guidebook. "It's a sinkhole."

"That's not an explanation," Helen objected. "It could hold a truck. Many trucks."

"Or campers," Dorie said, shuddering. "I don't feel so safe here on the edge."

Helen gazed deeper into the hole. How easy it would be to fall in, to sink into some subterranean level where nobody could find you. To disappear. The only problem was if you wanted to come back. How would you get yourself out of such a hole?

"Come on, Helen," Evie called. "Don't get too close."

"Yeah, we don't want to lose you again," Rett said.

She looked over her shoulder at her sisters and stepped away from the edge. "No worries. I'm here."

When they regrouped, Helen waved the map. "Let's talk about what's next," she prompted. "Let's continue. My ankle is fine even after a couple of tough kilometres. I say go on."

Dorie sagged back against her pack. "I don't know. I'm more tired than I thought possible. More tired than ever in my life."

Rett squinted at her. "You still throwing up?"

"Yeah, but that's not a big deal. Once or twice a day. Afterwards my stomach is fine. But I am tired. So tired."

Helen and Rett shared a look and a silent agreement not to say any more. Rett spoke. "That's important. If you're too tired, you can't be careful on these trails."

"We finished the coffee this morning," Evie reminded them. "I don't know about the other supplies."

Helen rummaged. "Not great. We've got supper and some snacks. We sure ate a lot on this trip."

Cheerful, Rett said, "Supper and snacks. That's not bad. We could stick it out one more night, if Dorie's got the juice for it. Does that work, Evie?"

"Who's in charge of this trip?" Helen snapped.

"Nobody's in charge, but Evie's been handling the map stuff," Rett said. "Keep your panties on."

Helen handed the map to her sister, trying to quell her rising trepidation. She didn't want to give up now. It was bad enough they would not get to cross the suspension bridge, but to leave after only three nights was quitting. It would be her fault, too, because she'd slowed them down. They couldn't quit because of her.

A little noise made her look toward Dorie, asleep on the ground, head on her pack. She snored again. "Dorie! Wake up!"

"Let her rest," Rett said. "We're not going anywhere yet."

Evie laid out the map for them to see. "Let's talk about this idea of hiking up Walton Glen. We can do that."

"Andrea never said anything about Walton Glen," Helen objected.

"We didn't ask her," Evie explained. "It's not part of the Fundy Footpath, but it's accessible from the Fundy Parkway. So Chad could come get us once we climb up."

"That makes tomorrow a big hiking day," Rett said. "Do we have the energy to do today and a big day tomorrow?"

"Our food supplies are going to be tight," Evie said. "Our other option is to head down this ATV trail now, call Chad when we get a signal, and head home today. We'd have to hang out and wait for him, but we'd be home tonight."

Helen thought briefly of home; a hot shower, clean clothes, food that wasn't dehydrated. But she was no quitter. No way. "I vote to stay another day."

"Me, too," Evie said. "I'd love to see Walton Glen from the bottom."

"I'm not sure," Rett said. "Dorie? Dorie, how are you feeling?"

Dorie struggled to wake and sit up. "I'm good."

"Good enough to hike today and tomorrow? A big hike tomorrow?"

Her shoulders dropped even though she nodded. "Yes."

Rett turned to Helen and Evie. "Okay, I'm in. We agree. But we're going to have to watch our supplies. Tomorrow's hike is going to require some calories."

The Gift You Want

After lunch, they continued, knowing Little Salmon River came next. Hiking under her full pack was almost normal now. With only today and tomorrow left, Helen focused on the experience. Okay, the experience had a lot of up and down, up and down, but she enjoyed the woods. The clear June day was perfect. The squirrels, songbirds, and their footsteps provided the soundtrack to peace.

As she approached the top of a hill, loud voices carried down. She picked up the pace, curious. She reached the top tight on Rett's heels, and the two of them joined Evie and three men, hikers by the look of them, coming from the other direction. Dorie was nowhere to be seen.

They might be fifty, not as old as Jean-Louis, but one had silver hair under his cap and the other two were balding. The short guy chatted to Evie as she and Rett approached. "So, yeah, we came down through Walton Glen. Stayed at Little Salmon, then last night at Wolf Brook and now we're heading out. My buddy's picking us up."

"This is Jerry, Tim, and Pete." Evie introduced the three to Helen and Rett. "Pete knows Dad."

"Yep. We coached hockey back in the day. James was in charge, though." Pete's infectious smile made Helen smiled back.

"I bet," she said.

"It's New Brunswick for sure, when you meet people out on the trail who coached with Dad," Rett said, smiling. "Or might be related."

"That's possible, too," Jerry nodded. "My grandmother grew up in Stella Mare."

Dorie returned from the woods to be introduced. "You're going home?" she asked, awe in her voice. Helen gave her a sharp look. She might be more tired than she let on.

"Two days of this terrain is enough," Pete said. "And that rain came down so heavy on our first day out. I wasn't sure we'd get down the river, but it all worked out."

"Tell us about Walton Glen," Evie said, glancing toward Helen. "What's it like?"

"Challenging." Tim spoke for the first time. "But the most beautiful place I've ever seen."

His colleagues nodded. "Lots of competition for beautiful spots around here," Jerry said, "but the ravine is unbelievable. Eye of the Needle and all that rock. Makes a great story, too. You know, bragging rights."

Rett laughed. "What do you mean?"

"The ravine hike was a big deal," he continued. "Had to wade through waist-deep water while the rain came down. A great day in hindsight."

"Much better in hindsight than it felt at the time," Pete added. "Where have you been?"

"We started in Fundy Park," Helen said. "Three nights on the trail. The rain slowed us down some."

"Where are you going?" Tim's curiosity was on his face.

Helen paused, and Rett answered. "Our original destination was Big Salmon, but we're making a course change."

"Oh, you were doing the whole thing," he said, nodding thoughtfully. "Well, it's a big hike, no matter how much you bite off. All those ups and downs."

"I'm happy to go home," Jerry said. "Backpacking is great and so is going home. We'd best be getting on. We have a shuttle to meet."

"Do you have any coffee?" Evie blurted out, then blushed. "Sorry. We just ran out."

Pete laughed. "We do. And some other food, too. Do you need it?"

"We packed extra, and we're going home early," Tim explained. "We have plenty to share."

Rett leaned in. "That would be great. Happy to take it off your hands."

What was wrong with these girls? Evie was crazy to take food from strangers. Helen raised her eyebrows in Rett's direction, but Rett shook her head and reached for the supplies Pete handed over. "I'll tell Dad we met you," she said warmly. "Thanks so much!"

"Are you sure about this?" Helen asked, once the men had gone. Rett tucked the food in the top of her pack.

"Why not? They had extra and we didn't have enough. We'll need it to hike tomorrow. It's okay, Helen. You can take help sometimes."

"Sketchy guys on the trail," Helen muttered.

"Guys on the trail aren't sketchy," Rett said. "They were backpacking, just like us. Give it up, Helen. You want to keep going. They're helping us keep going."

It was hard to let go of her cynicism, but Rett was right. Either she trusted those men, or they didn't have enough food to fuel them to hike out of the woods.

The rest of the day passed comfortably. Only the steep climb down to Little Salmon presented difficulties. Once again, they slowed their descent, keeping their feet carefully under them.

"Whew!" Dorie blew out a big breath when the trail widened enough for them to gather to stare down the next big descent. "That's steep."

"This is the longest elevation change on our trip," Evie said. "At least the trail is dry."

Helen fervently agreed. She'd injured herself a week ago on a similar descent. No, not a week. It was only two days, impossible though it seemed. Time had telescoped, and the day of the week was elusive, irrelevant. Somehow they had already camped three nights, with their final night coming right up.

"Watch your step," she reminded them, as they picked a path down the steep slope. Little Salmon River, and their final campsite, lay at the bottom of this descent. Tomorrow they'd hike up the tidal river through the ravine. Their next climb would lift them out of Walden Glen Gorge to the end of the journey.

When they landed on the flood plain, Dorie hooted a cheer. "The last big downhill! We made it!"

"We did. Now let's get things organized," Rett said. "I, for one, am looking forward to eating again. Where are those snacks?"

After fortification, Dorie and Helen found a tent site, consulting the tide chart, and the sisters worked together to get tents up, collect firewood, and filter water. Once the chores were done, Dorie opted for a nap, Evie carried her camera downstream, and Rett checked on Helen's ankle.

"Are you really here to watch me take off my boots?" Helen asked dryly. "I can make a show of it." She pulled them off with a flourish, slid out of socks, and wiggled her toes in the fresh air. "That's so good."

"Let me see," Rett said, looking closely. "It's still a little swollen. Ice again."

"It's fine. I don't want to."

"Ice it," Rett said firmly. "Prevention. Tomorrow's a big day."

"They're all big days," Helen groused. But she got the cold pack to apply to her ankle. Rett was just as correct as she was annoying.

Any food was delicious when you were hungry and eating outdoors, Helen thought for the thousandth time. Shovelling in pasta with peanut sauce and Evie's foraged greens, she relaxed. Even if they weren't going to cross the suspension bridge, they had accomplished something big. Together.

Still, something was missing.

She couldn't tell what it was. She longed for the power she could feel when she imagined her sisters crossing that suspension bridge. Something about moving into a new world, one they hadn't yet entered. But now they weren't going to do that. There was no new world.

She tried to talk herself out of her funk, but it didn't work. Nothing had changed, not really. Rett was still annoying, Evie too calm and quiet, and Dorie still immature. They were the same, and so was she. Nothing had changed.

Doing all the right things hadn't worked. Even though she'd felt the closeness in her dream this morning, felt her sisters' support when she crossed the stream. Even telling them her deep secret, the one she thought better hidden. She couldn't get any more real. She was being the best big sister she could be. It wasn't enough to transform things. To transform her.

"It's our last night," Dorie said dreamily, gazing upward. The sky had darkened slightly, but night was hours away. "Remember what Andrea said about what you take home? Everybody will take something different. The gift you get might not be the one you want, but it could be the one you need."

"Deep, Dorie," Rett said with a laugh.

"Deep, but a great thought," Evie added. "Did you get what you wanted from this trip?"

"I did," Dorie said. "I got to hike in the woods. Got to sleep outside. Got to get eaten alive by black flies."

"You did not," Helen snapped. "We had enough bug dope for everybody."

"Just kidding," Dorie said, facing her. "It makes a good story. But really, hiking taught me I'm strong. If I can hike this trail with that pack, I can do anything. I never had to take care of myself, but now I am certain I can. I amaze myself," Dorie said with a giggle.

"You guys all amazed me," Helen admitted. "I expected to be great at hiking and help everybody. It turned out I needed the help."

"That's only because you got hurt," Evie said loyally. "It could have happened to any of us."

That might be true, but she still should have done better. It was hard to feel successful when you were the reason to cut the trip short.

"What did you get, Evie?"

Evie smiled. "I'm not entirely sure, but I think I got to take responsibility in a new way. To lead from the center, if that makes sense."

"Yeah, I can see that," Rett said. "You stepped up in a few ways. Did you get any good pictures?"

"Oh, so many," Evie gushed. "I'm looking forward to seeing them on my computer. I'll have a great photo journal of our trip. Rett, what are you taking home?"

Rett looked over at Helen. "What I wanted was to get my best friend back." Helen's eyes smarted.

"And?" Evie prompted.

"I wanted too much," Rett said, "but relationships take time. There are no miracle cures. Overall, it's been a good trip, and I'll never see the night sky the same way. I'll always know the Milky Way is there, even it I can't see it. Just like I know my sisters are with me, no matter what."

"Aww," Dorie said, and Evie patted Rett's arm. Helen offered a tight smile.

Evie turned to Helen. "I know you're disappointed about the bridge. I hope Walton Glen will make up for that."

"Oh, well," Helen said. "It's just an idea." She tossed a pebble in her hand. "I wanted to feel like we did something important together. To be connected."

"Did you get what you wanted?"

Helen shrugged. "The trip's not over yet," she said. "Rett keeps telling me tomorrow is a big day."

"Tomorrow's hike is going to be over the top." Intense, Evie leaned forward. "We'll hike up the riverbed, over those boulders, making sure the tide is with us. As we get closer to the top, the river's carved out this ravine with cliffs over 300 feet high. There's this narrow place between cliffs. I've only seen it from the top or in videos, but they say the hike is unbelievable. It's going to be epic."

"Spoken like a true Generation Y or whatever you are," Helen said. "While us old Millennial folks are just going for a hike."

"It's a pretty cool hike," Rett put in. "It's a great way to finish our trip, even if it's not what we planned on."

Dorie poked around in the food pack. "Hey, those guys gave us some chocolate. This is excellent!" She waved a bar around. "Who wants some?"

"I would, but I think I need to turn in. I wish I could stay up with you girls, but honestly, I'm about done in." Helen pushed herself to her feet. "Good night."

Upriver

E arly to bed worked out well if you wanted to rise with the sun. On the last day, the earliest light coincided with high tide, and Helen sat by the river watching the water flow, wrapped in her warm clothes and nursing a tiny fire. She did not know, nor did she care, about the time. There was nothing there except the wash of water, the sounds of seabirds, and the sun creeping over the cliff top to light the valley. Soak it in, she thought. Keep it to remember always. This could be her gift.

Her sisters joined her in the quiet. Dorie sat to her right, and Rett and Evie to her left. The water flowed upstream and down, tide and current in opposition, but soon they could see the tide changing, turning and heading back to sea, the river current winning this round, at least. Tide rose or fell, pushed or pulled on the river, always in motion. You could say always in conflict, but rise and fall, push and pull were necessary. There was no push without a pull, no rise without a fall.

Such deep thoughts only disturbed Helen's peace this morning, so when Dorie leaned into her, she pressed back with a pleased smile. With a start, Dorie leaped to her feet and dashed off.

"Time to throw up," Rett said quietly.

"Do you think she knows?" Helen asked.

"Knows what?" Evie asked.

"I don't think this is the day to bring it up," Rett warned quickly. "We've got a strenuous day."

"They've all been strenuous," Helen retorted.

"Is something wrong with Dorie?" Evie asked with more intensity.

Rett gazed off to where Dorie had disappeared. "Nothing's wrong. Not wrong."

Comprehension dawned on Evie's face. "Ohhh. You think...."

"Shh!" Rett admonished as Dorie returned.

"Sorry. I won't know what to do when I get home and don't throw up every day," she said with a little smile. "Fortunately, once it's over, it's over."

"It must be time to get going," Helen remarked, and went to start breakfast.

Leaving the campsite was bittersweet, the lure of getting home in a push-pull with the pleasure of her sisters' company in this exquisite setting. The easy hiking helped. They travelled up the riverbed, hiking along as it widened with the dropping tide.

It wasn't long before the hiking got more strenuous, with large boulders, steep riverbanks, and slippery footing.

"Good timing," Evie commented. "Look at the high-water mark. We'd never have gotten through here a couple of hours ago."

"Dumb luck," Helen admitted. "I forgot to check the chart."

The valley grew deep. The steep walls of the ravine let in only a little light, but there was room to hike along the sides of the river. As the elevation increased, the rocks became slabs and platforms. In places the river was narrow and fast; in other places, it widened out into pools where the surface was highly reflective. Evie, in water shoes, walked through, poling carefully when the rocks were slippery. Helen stayed toward the shore, more confident in finding a path on the ground. They conferred frequently, looking for the easiest path upstream.

A couple of hours into the hike, they took a break. "Bless those three guys," Rett said fervently, as she bit into a chocolate chip cookie.

"These are wonderful," Dorie agreed.

Evie had the map. "It looks like things get a little tighter up here," she said. "We have to go through the Eye of the Needle. That's where those guys said they got so wet."

"Eye of the Needle, eh? Like the Lord of the Rings stuff," Dorie said.

"It's coming up. I hope I can get some pictures," Evie said.

"I'll help," Helen offered. "Let me know what I can do." The Eye of the Needle sounded very epic, as Dorie might say. Intriguing and maybe even exciting. Maybe she'd find her gift there.

They continued to climb up the ravine, marvelling at the rock walls, the vegetation growing out of the least bit of soil, trees reaching for light at the top of the cliffs.

"Hey, look at this," Dorie said, on the other side of the narrow channel. "We really are going to have to get in the water to get through."

Helen boggled at the sight. There was the rock wall, and the slice through which the water flowed. Nothing on either side except sheer rock climbing to about two hundred feet. Ten feet above the water's surface, the walls came close together. The water flowed through the needle's eye.

"Fall back, I guess, and make a plan of attack," Rett said. "Dorie, how much room is over there?"

Dorie, looking around, said, "Looks like more here than there. Come on over."

Rett and Helen perched on rocks to pull off their boots. Tying them to their packs, they crossed the river.

Helen gazed at the rocks. Water rushed through the gap, and though she knew the trail continued on the other side, it was easy to imagine being crushed while trying to pass through. The massive cliffs took on more meaning the longer she looked. The slot with pouring water looked tiny, but that's where they were headed. Right through the needle's eye. Her heart was in her throat.

Rett, always practical, shouted over the roar of the water. "From here, it looks completely doable but it's a little deep."

"Not too deep," Evie said, coming up to the shore. "Our packs will have to come off, though. Carry it on your head," she added. "I saw a video once."

"Packs on our heads. Aren't we something?" Helen said with a grin. She watched the slice in the rock as if it might share a secret. Thigh-deep water flowed through it. It might be waist deep on Evie, but certainly passable. Rushing water made it hard to hear her sisters, and she couldn't tell whether it was louder above the eye or below. Regardless, they were hiking upstream, so there was no fear of an unexpected drop. And unlikely that the eons-old cliffs would choose this moment to crush together, despite her imagination.

Excitement bubbled in her belly as she took off her pack, secured her poles, and practised carrying it on her head. "Oh, yeah," she said. "We've got this."

"These rocks are probably slippery," Evie shouted over the noise, "and your hands are going to be busy."

"Well, what are we waiting for?" Dorie asked, her voice high. "Let's do it."

"Let's go, Madisons!" Rett held out her arm and the four sisters fist-bumped.

Helen checked for her belongings; yes, everything was attached to her pack. Her sisters' voices receded as she looked up and up, finally finding the sky, a wedge of blue high above the spruce-topped cliffs. For a moment out of time, the rush of the water slowed. She turned in a circle, gazing toward the blue slice above the steep dark rock and deep green spruce. The ravine was a cathedral, and the Eye of the Needle, that narrow passageway, a portal. Moving through it would change her. She would be different on the other side. Now was the moment.

"Are you coming?" Rett called impatiently. "We need to do this together. All together."

"Right there," she said, hugging her pack and heading toward the water.

The Gift You Get

"I think we should get in here," Evie said, "and then watch out for each other as we go through. It looks wide enough, but you can't tell how deep any of it is."

Perception heightened, Helen gazed into the water before the needle's eye. The rushing sound got louder. The water was green, with wispy foam no doubt from a rocky upstream bed, and deep. At least knee deep right here. "Let's go!"

"Oh, cold!" Dorie exclaimed, and each of them gasped as the water climbed up their thighs.

"Mostly spring run-off." Rett had to shout to be heard over the rush of upstream water.

"It'll be fine. We just have to get adjusted."

They set off upstream, hugging packs. Evie was first, and as she slipped into the narrowest place, she hoisted her pack to her head, wobbling a little. The water was at her hips. Rett and Dorie, both taller, had water to mid-thigh. They rounded the near corner and Dorie shouted, looking back. "The water's pushy!"

Pushy? Helen followed, lifting her pack overhead as she strode through the thigh-deep stream. The high cliff walls loomed. Just like before, her field of vision shrank, as darkness pressed in from all sides. She squinted but kept moving. As she rounded the rocky corner, the rock met overhead. The Eye of the Needle. In the next step, she would pass through the portal of change.

She slipped through the slice in the rock. The sudden rush of water at her hips threw her off balance. Reaching for the riverbed with her left foot, she fell into a deep pool. Icy cold water closed over her head. Flailing her arms, her face broke through and she gasped, but more cold water rushed over her, sinking her again.

It's just cold water. No need to panic. Her foot touched a rock and she pushed off toward the surface. Then someone grabbed her, pushing her down into the dark, pressing the breath out of her. Darkness closed in, her throat clutched, and she sank. Hands clutched at her, grabbing everywhere.

Her hip hit a rock and she scrabbled for purchase. Someone grabbed her legs, held her down. As she choked for air, her back hit the rocky riverbed. Rage bloomed.

You bastards! You won't get me this time. Get off me.

She kicked, hard. Kicked again. Again. No panic. Clean, clear fury. She fought her attackers, pushing hard with her arms and her feet. When her feet landed solidly on the riverbed, she reached up. Her face breached the water and she coughed, then drew a big breath.

She was here, now. Cold, wet, here and now. On the upstream side of the slice. She was as present as she'd ever been. She'd just come through the Eye of the Needle.

"Dorie, help me!" Rett's voice sounded close, and Helen felt a hand on her arm, a welcome hand this time. Rett's other arm went around her shoulders, and Dorie tugged on her hand, crying.

"I'm okay," she said. "I'm okay. It's no big deal, really. I just fell in."

"Bring her over," Evie called from the little shoreline, barely audible over the rush of water. Helen was surprised she needed Rett and Dorie to support her, but they half-carried her to the beach. They let her slide down to sit on the pebbly verge.

Laughing, she shook the water from her head. "Did you see that?" she shouted, jubilant. "The Eye of the Needle! We did it."

"We sure did," Evie said, concern in her voice. "Are you okay?"

"I'm wonderful," Helen said simply. "Wet and cold, but wonderful."

"I'll be right back." Rett left, heading back toward the water.

"I'm glad you're wonderful." Evie looked her over. "Your pack took a little swim."

Rett dumped a pack beside them. "Mine and Dorie's are here. Your pack is downstream. I'll head back to get it."

"I can do it."

"Sure you can, but I'm going to do it instead. You hang out with Evie."

"Want me to come?" Dorie asked.

"Yes, please," Rett said. "Evie, you've got this, right?" she gestured to Helen and the makeshift campsite.

"You go ahead. I'll get some tea or something going."

Within minutes, Helen sat wrapped in Evie's fleece jacket, Rett's fleece pants, and Dorie's dry wool socks. A tiny fire sparked near her feet. "Why does this feel so familiar?" Helen asked. "Helen falls in and everybody has to dry her out."

"It's okay," Evie reassured. "We love you."

"I slipped," she said. "The water wasn't too deep, but my foot slipped off a rock and I fell into a pool. Somebody was grabbing me. But I didn't let him."

Evie shook her head. "Rett and Dorie got you out."

Helen knew better. She'd fought off her attackers and stood up on her own. That memory would never bother her again.

Evie squatted in front of her. "Can you sip this tea?"

Helen obediently took the mug, wrapping her fingers around it. The spreading warmth filled her. She could see Evie, feel the rocks and the sunlight pouring down, and hear the rush of water. All of her senses were heightened, sharpened.

"I had a moment out there," she said. "The cliffs got to me."

"Like the wolves got to you?"

"Like that." Helen sighed. "I guess it might be time to deal with my history."

There was a shout, and Rett and Dorie rounded the cliff, coming again through the Eye. Dorie carried Helen's dripping pack.

"Victorious!" Evie said, jumping up to greet them.

"How's our hypothermia patient?" Rett asked, shaking water off her lower half.

"I'm much better, thanks," Helen said. "Not shivering as much."

"Well, we should all take a few minutes to dry off," Rett suggested. "We're not done yet, but we need a rest and refuel after our adventure."

"Early lunch!" Dorie crowed. "Always up for food."

"Except in the mornings," Evie reminded her.

"That'll get better when we get home," Dorie said. "It's just a camping thing." She sat, pulling off her water shoes.

Rett sat beside Dorie. "We're at the end, almost the end, of this journey."

Helen looked up. That was a pretty darn tall cliff they'd have to climb, so no, it wasn't the end.

"When we get up there, it's back to regular life, real people, cars, all that," Rett said. "Now is a good time for truth."

"Truth?" Dorie looked askance. "About what?"

"Think, Dorie," Evie urged. "Why do people throw up in the morning?"

"And you're so tired," Helen put in. "So tired, even though you're the youngest."

Dorie shook her head. "I don't understand. Do I need a doctor or something?"

Rett sighed. "She's hopeless. Never mind, Dorie. Everything's fine."

"Wait, you guys. This is like when I was little. You have a secret and you won't tell me."

"It's not our secret," Rett said.

"Well, it isn't mine," Dorie snapped. "I don't know what you're talking about."

"Has anything been late?" Evie asked in her quiet way.

Dorie gazed, uncomprehending. Rett turned to Helen. "This is what you call a pregnant pause."

Dorie answered Evie. "Well, yes, I'm late, a couple of weeks late. I was kind of worried about what to do if it started while we were camping, but did you say pregnant? Pregnant?"

"It's a question," Rett pointed out. "None of us has an answer."

"Wow." Dorie breathed out, her face a study in wonder. "Maybe that's it. Maybe."

Rett gave her a rough side-hug. "Well, good for you. Maybe."

Dorie, wide-eyed, gazed at each of her sisters. "Maybe. That's not the gift I expected from our camping trip."

"But what a great idea!" Evie put in, jumping up to hug Dorie.

Helen leaned in, too. "Whatever you're hoping for," she whispered to Dorie, "that's what I hope for you."

"Well, I'm hoping it's not some great cosmic joke," Dorie said. "I could get used to the idea really fast." She was smiling nearly ear to ear. "Now I can hardly wait to get home."

"Speaking of truth and secrets," Helen put in, "I need to tell you something."

Looking up, she saw each of their faces. Evie, unfailingly compassionate, Rett, clear and assertive, now looking attentive, and Dorie, open and sweet. "I brought more than a little baggage on this trip," she said. "I told you all the stuff about my work and Reg. All the things that have gone so wrong lately.

"I didn't tell you about my episodes," she went on. "I've been having these moments where I kind of lose my way. Everything closes in, my vision even goes dark, and then something happens, like I lose my footing, or slip in the mud. And before that, it was the first night, when I thought I heard wolves."

She looked directly at Rett. "Am I crazy?"

Rett didn't answer her question. "Were these episodes, as you call them, happening before the trip?" Rett's face was grim.

Helen heaved a sigh. "Yes."

Rett blew out a frustrated breath. "For Pete's sake, Helen."

"It started last fall. When things were awful at home, but they got worse when I got back to Stella Mare."

"Wait, I don't understand," Dorie said. "Is this high blood pressure or something? Like Dad?"

"No," Rett replied grimly. "Helen's been having flashbacks, but she didn't see fit to tell anybody."

"It wasn't anybody's business," she retorted sharply, but immediately backed down, "except now I realize I put you at risk."

"I still don't get it," Dorie insisted. "Flashbacks from those guys hurting you twenty years ago? How can that happen?"

"It happens," Rett said. "She should have told us. There's enough danger on the trail without somebody dissociating."

"I should have trusted you to get it," Helen agreed. "Instead, I plowed through. I know it was wrong to drag you on a backpacking trip when I couldn't even rely on myself. Plowing through always worked before."

Rett's eyes softened. "Well, sort of. Now I understand why you came back." She sat on the pebbly beach beside Helen and took her hand.

Helen's eyes grew damp. "Really? Why?"

"To finish it. To let it go, finally. To get yourself back."

"Maybe," Helen agreed softly. "But what I really wanted was to get my sisters back."

Re-entry

From the little beach, the trail up the cliff wasn't easy to find, but Evie was persistent and finally located something that looked right. Clothes had dried quickly, lunch had been delicious, and getting started on the very last leg buoyed their spirits.

Helen felt lighter than ever. She followed up the group, as usual, watching her sisters hike. Dorie took the lead, chattering about the wildlife, the rocks, the steepness of the climb and giggling with no provocation. Evie followed, sure-footed and calm. Rett hiked immediately in front of Helen, glancing back periodically with a smile.

Reaching the top felt anticlimactic and a little disorienting, but good. The trail to the visitor center was wide, more like a road. Voices carried through the woods. When the path forked, they chose the overlook trail, heading away from the parking lot, back toward Walton Glen.

"I really want to see it from the top now," Dorie enthused.

"Worth it," Evie agreed, and they headed toward the precipice, along with other tourists and even a couple of people in hiking gear.

"You've been out," a woman commented, looking at Helen's pack.

"We have," she agreed happily. "Started in Fundy Park, did the Footpath, and just came up from there." She gestured down into the ravine. The woman's eyes glowed. Jealousy? Helen smiled privately.

"How was it?"

"It was amazing. These are my sisters." She gestured to the others, a sense of pride swelling her chest. These women. Her girls. The woman started talking to Dorie, and Helen gazed over the ravine. Was it possible that they had been down there a few hours ago? Had she shed her demons coming through the Eye of the Needle? It felt that way, but time would tell.

"Come on," Evie called from the path. "Chad's waiting for us."

The kilometre walk along the wide trail to the visitor's center was easy, and they chatted excitedly. "What are you going to do first?" Dorie asked.

"Hot shower," Evie said firmly. "With a lot of soap."

"That sounds good," Rett said, "but I think I'll hug the kids first. Let 'em give Mum the sniff test."

"I vote for pizza," Dorie added. "Or a nap. Or French fries."

"Really?" Rett shook her head.

"After the drug store, of course," Dorie amended with a grin.

The blue van with the dog sanctuary sign sat in front of the visitor's center, Chad leaning against it with the white poodle at his knee. Dorie and Rett headed straight toward it, the poodle delirious with joy. Evie and Helen detoured to use the bathroom.

Helen let the hot water pour over her hands for a long time, soaking in the feeling. When she stepped outside to pick up her pack, she took in the busy scene. There were cars in and out of the parking lot, walkers, adults and kids and dogs, all heading in different directions. She loved them all, including all the sounds of habitation. Beneath those sounds, the gentle susurration of the wind in spruce branches was insistently present. A chittering sound made her look up to see a red squirrel complaining from a high branch. So-called civilization was here, but the real world was right underneath it, just needing to be noticed. She headed for the van, now full of sisters, packs, Chad, and the poodle.

Miles down the Fundy Parkway, they approached the Big Salmon visitor center. "Look!" Dorie pointed. "There's the suspension bridge."

"The one we're not on," Helen said plaintively. "Sorry about that."

"We got to do the Eye of the Needle instead," Rett said sharply. "Don't forget that. If you hadn't gotten hurt, we would never have done that."

"Somebody got hurt?" Chad asked. "So that's why you needed a ride? I thought you just got tired."

"Yeah, Helen did," Dorie said.

"You okay?" He turned to look toward her.

"I am, yes, but it slowed us down a lot."

"And we almost ran out of food, Chad," Dorie said breathlessly. "That would have been a disaster!"

"But we met some nice campers who gave us their extra," Evie put in.

The story is growing, Helen thought. "Now we're in the next phase of the trip," she said to Rett. "Telling the stories."

Rett smiled at her. "The stories are the best part," she said. "Or at least the most lasting part."

Helen shook her head. "I want our connection to be the most lasting part." She reached for Rett's hand and gave it a squeeze.

"That's a given," Rett said casually and winked. "We're good."

Dorie prattled on in the front next to Chad. "Thanks for coming to get us," she said. "You'll never believe what I can lift now. And I've been throwing up every day." She tossed an arch look at her sisters in the back seat.

Chad gave her a concerned glance, but immediately returned his attention to the twisty road. He manoeuvred the van past the bridge and down a steep grade, then turned into the parking lot at the Parkway Visitor's Center. Rett's vehicle awaited at the far reaches of the parking lot.

"There's our getaway car," Rett pointed out. "Except we had to get away sooner."

"Not sooner. Just from a different place on the trail."

"How did you get hurt?" Chad asked Helen.

Before Helen could reply, Rett spoke up. "Helen twisted her ankle in the mud," she said easily, "so we had a slow day and got behind. But we got to hike up Walton Glen, and that was amazing."

"You did great," Chad said. "I'm impressed."

"I'm impressed, too," Dorie added. "I keep telling myself we did it. Yay, us!"

"Chad, you won't believe the pictures I got," Evie said. "There was a guy with a drone taking video at the overlook, too."

"I've seen some footage of that ravine," Chad said. "I wouldn't think you'd ever hike down there."

"We hiked up, not down." Dorie said. "It was a whole lot of up."

Chad, usually undemonstrative, put an arm across Dorie's shoulders. "You've been sick?" he asked, looking into her face.

"Not sick, just throwing up," Dorie said lightly. "I'm sure it'll be fine now that we're back to normal, right?" She looked around the group.

"Throwing up in the morning, Chad," Rett said meaningfully.

"Every morning," Helen added.

"But I'm fine," Dorie protested. "A little tired, but we're all tired."

Chad looked at Rett, eyebrows up.

"We'll be stopping at the drugstore on the way home, Chad," Dorie said, grinning. His face was a study in surprise and wonder.

"Well, I've said all I'm going to say," Rett announced. "Let's get going." She dug in her pack for her keys. "Right where I left them," she noted with satisfaction, and clicked to unlock the SUV. They helped move the gear.

"Well, I guess this is where we leave you," Helen said to Dorie and Chad. "Thanks, sister, for everything."

She reached to hug Dorie, who seemed to melt into her arms. Then Rett and Evie were in the mix, too, a big group hug right there in the parking lot overlooking the Bay of Fundy. Helen could feel each one of them, Evie, soft and kind, Rett, angular and assertively caring. Dorie–oh, Dorie was dissolving into tears.

"I don't know what's wrong with me," she sobbed. "I just love you guys."

The group hug got tighter around Dorie. Helen lifted her head enough to catch Rett's eye. "Kind of weepy, isn't she?"

"Weepy, tired, and throwing up," Rett noted over Dorie's bent head. "That's our girl."

Dorie lifted her face, the rest of her wrapped in their arms. "You guys are making me crazy. I'll let you know as soon as I can."

"You do that," Rett said. "Listen, we all have a long drive, so let's wrap this up."

"Not sure I want to let go," Helen murmured. "But one, two, three..." They released the hug all at once, laughing.

Through her own sniffles, Helen said, "Who's up for pizza at my place tonight?"

"Sorry," Chad said. "James already put his hand up. Said to tell you supper's at the homestead, and the pizza's on him."

Helen looked at Rett. "Let's get going, then. Pizza at Dad's house!"

Rett drove, Evie rode shotgun, and Helen stretched out in the backseat. Not too tired, she thought, but then a wave of fatigue washed over her. The next moment, Rett was calling her name.

"Come on, Helen, this is your stop."

"Right. Got it. Thanks." Grabbing her pack from the back of the SUV, she dragged herself up the front steps of her townhouse, then fumbled for her key. Entering, everything felt unfamiliar, like she'd been away for a year instead of four days. It smelled unfamiliar, like cleaners, and a faint tinge of perfume. Not like spruce and salt air. Helen dropped her pack at the front door and headed upstairs to her shower, shedding clothing as she went.

"Mmm mmm," she murmured, stepping into the steaming spray. Oh, soap. Heavenly. Hot water flowed over her aching shoulders, poured down her scratched-up legs, slid around her still-swollen ankle. Nothing had ever felt so good.

Jake

Helen sang in the car on her way to the airport. She nearly danced into the small terminal, heading toward the gate where she'd always arrived on her brief visits to New Brunswick. Once at the arrivals area, she alternated pacing with scrolling her phone.

Jake would be a special guest for Mum's party. She felt a blush of shame she'd not been to the solstice gathering since her mother died, though Dad and the sisters celebrated annually.

Now Jake was coming to join his family for this event. She was excited and anxious. How would they get on? She hadn't seen him since late January, and conversation had been strained.

Passengers deplaned on the tarmac, climbing down portable stairs. Helen peered through the narrow window at the trickle of people. There he was! Tall, taller than she expected, and broad in the shoulders, her son lifted his carry-on with ease, trotted down the steps, smiled at an old man who spoke to him. Then he was out of sight as the line of passengers entered the building.

She hurried to meet him, catching his eyes as soon as he entered the building. She tried to contain her face-splitting smile, but it burst through. "Jake!"

"Mum, hi." He was hugging her or she was hugging him, and what she noticed first was his size.

"You're huge," she said in awe, pulling back to look up at him. "You grew a lot."

He grinned. "Great, isn't it? I'm half a head taller than Dad now, too."

"I bet you are. Is that a beard?"

He rubbed his chin self-consciously. "I haven't shaved for a couple of days. Off season, you know."

"Amazing. Grandpa won't believe it. Did you check a bag?"

"Nope. Only this." He hefted his duffle. "I've gotten good at packing."

"Hungry?" She gave him the side-eye.

"I could eat."

"Good. That's a side effect of growing a lot."

They found a nearby diner. She gazed at him over the rim of her cup as he made short work of a full farmer's breakfast, plus a giant cinnamon roll. Finally, he sighed and put his napkin down.

"Thanks, Mum."

"The least I can do. The refrigerator is full at home, but we might not have made it there," she said, smiling.

"How far is it? I want to learn my way around New Brunswick while I'm here," he said.

"Good." Helen approved. "You can use the map to navigate us home if you want. Or your phone."

"Old fashioned map," he decided.

"It just so happens I've got one," Helen said. "Are you ready? We can head out."

She steered the car out of St. Jacques and pointed it south at Jake's direction. She knew the way, but it was fun to hear him make sense of his surroundings.

"So where was your hiking trip?" he asked, looking at the map. "I want to hear all about it."

"Look up the coast from Stella Mare." She gestured with her chin, hands on the steering wheel. "Once you find Fundy National Park, you can see where we hiked."

"Oh, yeah, there it is," he said. "Looks like an event. You used a different map than this, I bet."

"Maps, guidebooks. Evie even had a compass, but we didn't use it. You're right, it was an event. The Fundy Footpath is full of adventure," she said with a smile. "I found out adventure requires adversity, though."

"Sounds like what they tell us in physical training; what doesn't kill you makes you stronger."

Helen snickered. "That's rough. Does your coach really say that?"

"Nah. He has different words, but the guys say this. Keeps us working harder."

"If it's true, I'm a lot stronger than I was." She looked toward the passenger seat. "I'm so happy to see you."

He smiled back. "Me, too."

The conversation flowed easily, to Helen's delight, on the drive to Stella Mare. As they drove the twisty road down the peninsula, Jake looked around. "I remember a little bit," he said. "At least I think I do."

Stricken, she said, "I wish I'd brought you more."

He shrugged. "I'm here now. I can't wait to see Grandpa in person. And meet the dogs."

"Oh, Grandpa's got the dogs, for sure," Helen said. "Dorie will fix you right up if you want to hang out with dogs."

"Yeah, that's cool, a dog sanctuary. I want to see it."

She smiled at this almost-man, her son, so adult, so open and interested in finding out about his family. So different from the way she'd arrived last winter, prepared to change everyone else.

"Hey, is that the way to Grandpa's house?"

Helen twisted the steering wheel. "You bet it is. We'll be there in a few hours, but first, our house. I hope you like it."

She watched him take in the new space, the big windows overlooking the harbour, the back deck, the kitchen. She'd even bought a big television, though she didn't care to watch it much.

"Nice house, Mum," Jake said, checking it out. "I like my room, too."

"Is it as nice as your room at Dad's?" She hated herself for asking, but the words were out.

"I'm not that much into comparisons," he said mildly. "When is this beach party? Is there time for me to walk downtown?"

"Sure. The party is at four, but we'll go to Grandpa's house about three. I have things to do, so yes, go walking. Fill yer boots."

He squinted. "Are you really talking maritime now?"

She chuckled. "I thought that might get you. No, just for fun. Can you pick up a couple of things for me?"

"Yep. Do you want me to make my famous devilled eggs?"

"You're famous for devilled eggs? That's excellent."

"Something about dosing them with hot sauce," he added. "But I could go easy on the old folks."

She wondered what teenage devilled eggs would look like and immediately squashed the thought. "Of course you can. Get another dozen eggs at the market, will you, and give yourself time."

"You bet. See ya."

Before the Party

S he and Jake arrived at Dad's house before anybody else.

She led the way into the kitchen, petting big dog heads and snatching brief glances at Jake, as if he might disappear any minute.

"Jake! My boy!" James emerged from the living room. "Whoa! Where's my grandson, and who's this big guy?" They clasped hands and James patted Jake's shoulder. Jake leaned in for a hug, and James gave a gratified laugh. "Look at you. All grown!"

"Yep, I got bigger," Jake said.

"You can't see all that on FaceTime," James grumbled. "I've been missing crucial information."

"FaceTime?" Helen inquired.

"Me and Grandpa talk," Jake offered. "How are you, Grandpa?"

James sat Jake down at the kitchen table, poured him tea, and soon the conversation leaned into hockey and hockey school.

Helen wandered into the living room. How often had Dad been video chatting with Jake? What else had she missed?

She trailed her fingers across the photo wall as she walked, touching first her parents' wedding picture, then baby pictures of her and the sisters, dressed in touchingly frilly little outfits. She didn't remember ever wearing an outfit like that except for photos. When she came to the school pictures, she stopped. There was Rett, happy and exhausted, getting her field hockey tourney trophy. Next came Rett's certificate in sciences. Beside it, as always, the photo of the debate team just after their win in Fredericton.

She gazed at the girl she'd been, and tears welled up. Poor young Helen, so afraid of disappointing her family. Not knowing she could count on them even when she herself fell short. When that picture was taken, she was certain going home would cure her shame, guilt, and terrible memories. Instead, they had followed her. She carried them with her in dreams and waking nightmares. Throwing herself into work kept them at bay, but she had to stay busy. Otherwise, they'd haunt her mind. She spent twenty years staying just ahead of her demons. When her work disappeared, she moved to Stella Mare, but the memories followed. Intensified. Threatened to overwhelm.

But no more. She narrowed her eyes. She left those miserable demons in the Eye of the Needle. Gone for good. She nodded to her photo. "You're okay now," she whispered. "Everything's okay now."

"Helen! Where's that girl?" Rett was in the kitchen, loud. "Jake's here! Hey, kids, come see Jake!"

"Jakey's telling me about school. Helen's here somewhere." James was a little quieter, but not much. How did I never notice my loud family? Helen smiled to herself.

"Helen!"

"She's in the other room," James told her. "You're cheery."

"You bet I am. We're going to have a great day. Mason, this is Jake. You were like three years old the last time he saw you."

"Mason," her son greeted his cousin. Helen stood still, listening. These were her people. She imagined Jake shaking Mason's small hand, treating him like a big kid.

She looked again at the photo. That seemed so long ago, and her real life was here, now. She turned on her heel and headed to the kitchen.

James sat smiling, while Jake and Mason conversed over a pile of vegetables on the table. Rett was moving things around on the counter, making room for a cake and breadboard. The twins bounced around with their hands full.

"Auntie Helen! I've got bread," Maggie said importantly.

"I have the strawberries," Callie added. "For the shortcake."

"Who's making shortcake?" Helen asked. "That sounds delicious."

"I think Dorie," Callie said seriously. "But the best part is the whipped cream."

"Right. Who is doing that?"

"You?" Maggie asked.

"Not me." She looked at Rett. "I thought Stephen had the food all managed."

"He does, probably," Rett said, "but I knew somebody would need a cake, the strawberries are from our garden, and shortcake, well, 'tis the season. Harry and Stephen have been doing a lot of prep work, but I still like to add my touch."

Mason was leaning on the table, enthralled by Jake, who still sat beside his grandfather. Evie pushed through the back door with grocery bags.

"Need any help?" Helen asked. "I parked in your spot again. Sorry."

"No, I'm all set," Evie said. "Besides, Chad and Dorie were right behind me." The kitchen door opened again to let them in, along with the white poodle. Chad glanced at the crowded, chaotic kitchen. "I'm going to put this back outside," he said to Dorie, hefting his cardboard box, and left.

"Hi, everybody," Dorie said, breathless. "It's like Grand Central here."

Rett scowled at her. "When have you ever been to Grand Central?"

She shrugged. "I saw a meme."

"She's got a point. Why does everybody have to show up here?" James asked irritably. "Can't you just take your stuff to the beach like everybody else does?"

Dorie leaned over to drop a kiss on his head. "Oh, you love it. All the noise and dogs and people."

James scoffed, but then his face softened into a smile. "You're onto me."

"Besides, this way we can figure out what we forgot before getting to the beach," Rett said practically.

"But we still always forget something." Evie waved a clipboard. "Stephen said he kept a list. Does everybody know what they're supposed to do?"

"Not really. This is my first time, you know." Helen shifted on her feet. "Jake made devilled eggs and I made Mum's potato salad."

"Perfect," Evie said, marking her list. "It's going to be fine."

"What is?" Stephen said, backing through the screen door. "You know, it looks like a party out there." He nodded toward the backyard. "Six cars? Seven?" He carried a large stockpot.

"Yummy, your mussels," Rett said. "Put that right here on the stove."

"Is this all really going to the beach?" Jake asked his grandfather.

"That's what they tell me," James said. "Seems to work out every year. It's so good to have you here this time, and your mum, too." He patted Jake's shoulder, then abruptly left the table, heading to the living room. He wasn't quite out of the room when Helen noticed he wiped his eyes.

Jake, stricken, looked at her. "What did I do?" he whispered.

"Not a thing," she whispered back. "It's okay." She patted his shoulder, then followed her father into the living room. James stood by the window, hands in pockets.

"Dad? You okay?"

He sniffed and turned her way. His fine white hair haloed his shadowed face. "Just missing your mother, Helen. She would have been so proud of you and that fine boy of yours."

"Oh, Dad." The lump in her throat tightened her voice. "I wish I'd brought him to all of these picnics. I'm so sorry about that."

He shrugged. "You were busy. It was a long trip."

"Don't make excuses for me. Let me be sorry. I wish I had done better, and now I will."

Lifting his chin, he gazed at her face. "I believe you are already, daughter."

Eyes wet again, she reached for a hug. She held him carefully. Yes, it wasn't like hugging your daddy when you were a little girl, but it was still pretty good.

"Dad! There you are." Dorie came toward them. "I have something to tell you."

Helen looked at her. "Should I leave?"

Dorie shook her head. "Absolutely not. Dad…"

"What is it, daughter?"

"Listen, Dad, when I was fifteen, I stole some money from you," she said rapidly. "And Chad and I are going to have a baby."

"What? What did you just say?"

Helen, too, was taken aback. "Dorie…"

"Dad, I'm so sorry. I stole money from you."

"Dorie, did you say a baby? You're having a baby?" James' voice was loud. He laughed and grasped Dorie's shoulders. "My little thief, having a baby! Get over here, girl." He hugged her, hard.

"Dad! Thief?"

"I knew about that money years ago. But you're having a baby! Where's that man of yours?" James looked around, then tugging Dorie by the sleeve, he headed for the kitchen. "Chad? Where's Chad?"

Dorie, tugged along, looked back over her shoulder at Helen. "He's taking it well, don't you think?"

Helen laughed. "Congratulations, Dorie. Wonderful news."

General racket ensued from the kitchen, where Chad was apparently being pounded on the back as Dorie explained the situation to the twins.

"Helen! Where'd you go?" Rett was calling. "We need you in here."

"Coming!"

Summer Solstice

Somehow by four, they were at the town beach, marking out a place for the bonfire ("did you get a permit, Stephen?"), hauling over the picnic tables and coolers, putting out the food and greeting others as they arrived.

"Evie, give it up," Rett insisted. "Stephen said he'd handle it, so relax and have some fun. Come on, give him that clipboard."

"I don't know," Evie said, giving Stephen a measuring look. He smiled at her and wrapped an arm around her shoulders.

"We can do it together," he said.

The kids, including Jake, were dispatched to help find driftwood for the bonfire. James sat in a circle of his friends, while families with children filled up the beach with sound.

Helen walked toward the glistening water, waves gently washing the shore. This part of the cove was close to the bay, and the breeze off the water held a fresh, salty scent, like on the bluffs above the Bay of Fundy, but different.

She felt connected to her mother here. It was impossible for her to be dead, when she could almost hear her voice, feel her touch in the breeze, catch the scent of her. Her tight chest kept her from taking a deep breath, but she sighed deeply and tears filled her eyes.

Mum. I've been so afraid. Afraid of disappointing you.

The breeze off the water caressed her face, like her mother's hand in that dream. Her cheeks grew wet.

I have so many regrets. I've tried too hard at some things, and not hard enough at others.

A sandpiper skittered across the beach ahead of Helen, peeping as it went.

You taught me to be in the here and now. I have used that advice for everything, but it didn't save me from flashbacks. Only I could fix that.

For the first time, Helen wondered if her mother had ever questioned herself, ever wondered if she was equal to the challenge of raising four daughters. What was it like to know your child had been hurt, and to be unable to make it better? Helen's chest eased a bit.

Here and now, Mum, you're gone. The girls and I are the ones who are left. But we're not girls anymore. We all needed you and you left too soon; not your choice, I know that. But I think I've been trying to make up for your absence.

I wanted to be the ideal everything, daughter, sister, wife, mother, lawyer. I won't be getting any awards, but I'm finally learning to be a better sister, a real sister. I'll be here for Dorie and that baby, and I'll still be here when Evie gets to have babies, and be Auntie Helen to all the kids, Rett's included. I'm here for Dad, too, and I'll make sure Jake doesn't miss out on his Madison family.

I miss you so much. I'm trying hard to be here and now. Be a sister. Be a better mother. Be a good human. It's all I've got. I hope it's enough.

A far-away sailboat moved silently across her field of vision, entering the cove from the Bay of Fundy. The freshening breeze helped it scud lightly across the water, skimming the surface, white sails like wings. Her gaze followed it across the horizon.

Mum might be gone, but here was the sailboat, the sandpiper, the breeze. The sun, dropping lower, sparkled off the water, making diamonds out of beach sand.

She was certain, now, something had changed. She was different. She felt it. Softer. Gentler on the inside. How had that happened?

It didn't matter. What mattered was being here and now. She smiled and turned back toward the party.

"Mum!" Jake's voice. "Come help us!" He carried an armload of wood, and his little cousins followed, equally laden.

"Sure," Helen called back. So much for her outfit, but so what? She was fortunate to carry driftwood on a beach in Stella Mare with her son and his cousins. Fortunate to help build a fire for her family. Lucky to share a meal with her sisters. Blessed to be celebrating her mother, who had borne and raised them all. Helen felt like she was floating, floating on a sea of love and goodwill. It wasn't hard to enjoy the party.

There was food, drink, speechifying by James, and music. A couple of guitars played for a sing-along, and Helen even shook the tambourine. When darkness finally crept in, it was time to light the bonfire. Harry invited Jake to torch the gigantic pile into flames, which started small but grew fast. Helen gazed, mesmerized, as the crackling got louder and flames licked upward.

"What is it about a fire?" Dorie asked, coming up beside her in the growing gloom.

"About a fire and kids," Helen added, nodding toward the group of children being kept at a safe distance by Chad. "Jake was always poking the fire when we camped."

"I'm going to lodge a complaint," Dorie said. "You girls all got to play with fire when you were kids, and I only learned how last week."

"At least you were safer, playing with fire at twenty-four. Jake could have singed his hair any number of times."

"You and Reg camped." It was a statement.

"Yes, I guess we did," Helen said. "I had forgotten, but we did, at least a few times. Probably before Jake was six."

"What happened?"

"Oh, I decided to be the youngest person in my firm to make partner."

"Good decision?" Dorie's face held curiosity.

Helen shook her head. "Not from here. But at the time, you think you know what's best."

"Yeah. I guess I'm going to have to consider parenting decisions."

She side-hugged her sister. "You sure are. Welcome to the club."

"I'm glad you're going to be here," Dorie said. "I'll need a lot of help."

Helen's heart was full. "I'm honoured that you think I could help. I've made a mash of motherhood myself."

"Oh, I don't know." Dorie gazed toward Jake at the fire. "He's turning out pretty good."

"In spite of me, I'm afraid."

Her sister scoffed. "Take the credit. You're his mother."

"Thanks. Is there something else we need to be doing here?" She looked around. "It's been a very full day."

"Nothing left to do," Dorie told her. "We hang out to see the end of the sunset, watch the fire, and go home. Tomorrow we get to clean up all the dishes and stuff."

"There's always that part," she said, smiling. "I can help. Jake, too."

"We're counting on you."

Home is Where the Dog Is

S he and Jake were the first to arrive on cleanup day. James sat at the kitchen table with coffee and his newspaper.

"Good morning, daughter. Pull up a chair."

"We're here to help, Dad," she demurred, though Jake sat at the table. James tapped the plate of Evie's cinnamon rolls. Helen sighed.

"Okay, I'm sitting. Bribed with pastries." She poured coffee for Jake and herself. Jake poured sugar into his mug. She watched without comment, then turned to her father.

"It was a great party, Dad."

"It was. But I want to talk about something else." He folded the newspaper and laid it on the table.

Her stomach flipped and she glanced at Jake. "See how he talks to me, Jake? I feel about twelve years old right now. Like I'm in trouble."

Jake laughed, but James scoffed. "You should, daughter. This is serious business. What happened on your hiking trip?"

"What do you mean? We hiked, we camped, I twisted my ankle, I fell in more than once, and the sisters hauled me out. We told you."

James set his cup firmly on the kitchen table. "You girls are different now. Could be the outdoors that did it."

She squinted. "Different how?"

"Did you hear yourselves yesterday? All that talk, all that planning, party fixing, cleaning up, and nobody yelling."

She laughed. "You mean no fighting? Come on, Dad, you told us we had to fix that." She got up to put her cup in the sink.

"Hiking and camping fixed it?"

"I guess so."

"I wasn't sure all four of you would come back from that trip, to tell the truth," he said. "Jake, you should have heard those girls going at each other."

"Oh, yeah?" Her son looked at her with a grin. "I bet they were mean."

"Jake doesn't need to hear this."

"They were some nasty. Like a bunch of teenagers. No offence to teens, Jake."

"Dad, really. We were not like teenagers."

"Anyway, it seems better now. Thank you for that."

She sighed, leaning against the sink. "Could be because Dorie's pregnant. But we didn't know then. There's something about having sisters to bail you out."

"You mean literally, huh?" Evie walked into the kitchen from her tiny office. "More like haul you out of the drink."

"That was some seriously cold water," she said with a mock shiver. "I hope I expressed my thanks."

"You did," Evie said. "Is there more coffee?"

Helen poured her a cup. "Jake, you want to tell them about our new project?"

Jake's face lit up. "We're getting a dog."

Evie's eyebrows lifted. "A dog? Helen, really?"

"Dorie's pups are ready for homes. Jake and I are going to find one we connect with."

"There it is. More evidence," James pronounced with satisfaction. "You changed out there on that trail, missy."

"I probably did. It's hard to see from the inside out."

Evie looked over her cup. "I can see it, too," she said matter-of-factly. "It's actually in your face. Your lips used to be squeezed. You're more relaxed."

"My lips?" Helen pursed her lips. "I guess an artist would notice a detail like that. They don't feel different."

"It could be my imagination," her sister offered, "but I don't think so. It's like your life got easier."

"It did, for sure. Now we're getting a puppy to make sure it doesn't stay that way."

"I'll help, Mum," Jake said. "I can't wait. You know I've wanted a dog my whole life."

James gave Helen a glare. "Do you hear that? That boy's been needing a dog. It's a good job you're finally going to fix that."

"It wouldn't have suited our lifestyle," she started, but backed away to agree. "You're right. It is a good thing to do. We'll have fun."

Helen, Evie, James, and Jake washed dishes, put away beach furniture, and reorganized after the big party. By early afternoon, the house was back in order, and Helen and Jake prepared to leave.

"How long is Jake staying?" Evie asked, out of Jake's earshot.

Helen glowed. "He asked to stay all summer. Said it's more fun here than he expected."

"That's wonderful. And you really are getting a pup."

Helen nodded. "I'm sure Mum would be horrified to know that he got to be sixteen years old without having a dog. Now he can't, really, because of boarding school, but this is the next best thing. He's also volunteering at County Rescue. His school requires some kind of civic engagement during summer, so it works all the way around."

"Do you remember puppies? They're so much work, so much mess," Evie said in warning. "But a dog will be good for you once you get through the puppy part."

"I'm up for it. I have Dorie for support." Helen smiled. "Besides, Dad said I'm a new woman."

Evie shook her head. "You are different, I'll grant you that. Good for you. I'm glad Jake will be here all summer."

"Oh, me, too," she said fervently. "It feels like a second chance."

She hugged Evie and headed to the car. Second chance at being the mum she wanted to be. Second chance to be the daughter and sister she'd like to be. This was an opportunity she hadn't expected and didn't deserve.

On Sunday, they went to Dorie's place to meet the puppies. It turned out to be a family affair. Jake drove under Helen's supervision, and as they pulled down the long driveway to the barn, she pointed out the only place to park. Her father's truck, Rett's SUV, even Corinne's little EV were already in the small lot. As Jake carefully backed Helen's car into a spot, another car came down the driveway, Evie waving vigorously from the passenger seat. Helen waited for her and Stephen while Jake headed straight for the barn. When he opened the door, little girl squeals were audible.

"I didn't expect the whole crowd," Helen said to Evie. "What's going on?"

Evie chuckled. "Everybody wants to help Jake pick out a puppy. A new dog in the Madison family is an event."

Helen gave her the side-eye. "Are you sure it's not everybody waiting for me to mess up? You all know I haven't had a dog for a long time."

Evie shoulder-bumped her. "Nobody wants anybody to mess up. Come on, Jake's probably picked one out already."

"I'm getting prepared," Stephen said. "For when Evie and I decide to add to the family."

Helen's eyebrows went up. "Really?"

"He means a dog, Helen," Evie said. "Back down."

"Not only," Stephen said warmly, an arm around Evie's shoulders. "But we can start there."

Inside the Old Friends Dog Sanctuary, it was too warm, with so many people and dogs milling around. Helen felt the heat as soon as she stepped inside, but Dorie was on the job.

"Okay, guys, I'm going to take these pups to the play yard on the west side. Go out that door and meet us there."

"Where's west?" Mason asked. Dorie was busy herding pups, but Harry leaned down and pointed. "Come on," Mason shouted to his sisters, and the three kids headed outside.

Jake helped Dorie round up pups and assist them out the kennel door into the play yard. The other adults streamed out the door and around the side of the barn.

The sun was bright, but there was shade for the dogs beside the old building. Dorie, Jake and a milling mass of little dogs were inside the fence, with Mason, Maggie, and Callie hanging on the outside, attended by Rett and Harry, James, Corinne, and Alice. Helen, Evie, and Stephen found a place along the fence to watch.

"How many are there?" Helen asked. "They're in continuous motion and I can't even count them."

"Come in, Mum," Jake invited. "You have to play with them, too."

Dorie pulled open the gate to let Helen enter. "He's right. Come on in to meet the pack."

Mason excitedly pointed out a puppy. "See, Callie, that's the one you like."

"No, that one's mine," Maggie argued. "Callie likes the black one."

"We're not getting a puppy," Rett reminded. "We have Charlie. This is for Jake."

"I know, Mum, we're pretending," Callie explained. "We all picked out our favourites. Maybe Jake will like my puppy."

Rett looked at Helen. "Did you hear that? No pressure, though."

Jake sat on the ground, puppies climbing about and over him. Dorie pointed her phone camera at the scene, but Helen watched him interact with the little dogs. Quiet, patient, and calm. This was how he'd always been in the hockey goal, too. Deceptive to the other team, who might mistake his demeanour for slowness. No, Jake wasn't slow. He was patient until it was time to move, then lightning quick and accurate.

She sat, too, and watched, barely aware of the conversations going on behind her. The puppies were amazing, all of them. Jake turned to smile at her, his hands full of puppy. He rubbed his cheek on the little dog's head.

"Check this one out," he said, and put the dog in her lap. Her hands automatically stroked the little head, fingers touching the velvety ears, one down, one sticking up. The tiny dog turned around on her lap and curled into a sleepy ball.

"Not too excitable, is he?" James noted.

"Look at the ears, Dad," Helen said softly, to avoid waking the puppy.

"Look at that," James said in agreement. "Just like old Maple, there."

"What?" Rett was on it. "What's like Maple?"

Helen pointed out the ear that stuck up. Dorie, watching, said, "I thought you might like that."

"This is a sweet pup," Helen said.

"Yep," Dorie agreed. "Smart, too. We did our puppy testing last week, and she was top of the group."

"See, Mum," Jake said. "She's smart. And a girl."

"You don't have to convince me. I'm already sold. Here, you hold her." She handed over the sleepy pup.

Jake got to his feet. "I think I'm ready," he announced. "They're all great, but I think this is the one for us. Right, Mum?" His open smile warmed her.

"Right. She's perfect."

Jake carefully carried his pup out of the play yard and bent over so the kids could see and pet her. "You picked a good one," Mason said approvingly.

"Thanks," Jake said, glancing at his mother. "I'm glad you like her."

"She reminds me of Charlie when he was a baby," Mason said. "He didn't jump around and bite too much. It was good because we had babies at our house." He jerked his head toward the twins.

"I'm not a baby, Mason Brown!" Maggie insisted.

"Not now, but you were when Charlie was a puppy," Harry intervened. "Did you pat Jake's new dog?"

Mollified, Maggie nodded. "She's cute."

"Charlie's a very good dog," Helen told Mason, "so I appreciate your take on this pup."

"Ha!" James said behind her. "Charlie is a good dog. Didn't realize you noticed." She glanced over her shoulder but didn't comment. Her father patted her shoulder and winked.

"Okay." Dorie bustled up. "Here are the instructions they use at County Rescue for adoptions, and you already got a crate and bedding and food, right?"

Helen took the proffered papers. "Yes. The pet store clerk was overjoyed to polish my credit card at nine this morning."

Dorie smiled at her. "You'll be a great dog mom. Lots of experience."

"Jake's the primary parent," she said, looking at her son with the puppy. "He's in charge, at least for the summer."

"Shared custody, right, Mum?" he said, grinning up at her. A quick stab in the chest—why should her son have to have experience with shared custody?—but then she grinned back. "We'll be good co-parents, Jake."

"It was brilliant," Dorie whispered. "He'll never want to go back to school."

She scoffed. "Oh, yes, he will. That boy lives for hockey."

"Maybe now he'll have another thing to live for," her sister noted. Jake watchfully handed the puppy off to Mason, who held it carefully for the twins to pet. "Or another great reason to come here for vacations."

"Honestly, I never thought of that." Maybe I have changed, she thought. Dorie gave her a meaningful glance.

The puppy was asleep on Jake's shoulder. Helen asked, "Did everybody get their pats in? I think it's time for us to take our new family member home."

Everyone followed Jake and the puppy to the car where he gently settled her into cozy bedding. "Can you drive, Mum? I want to sit in back with her."

"Of course," she agreed. Standing at the open driver's door, she surveyed the small crowd gathered to see them off. "Okay, guys. We'll send you pictures."

She glanced around. Dorie, to her right, was surreptitiously wiping a tear. "What's up?" she asked.

"Oh, nothing," Dorie sniffed. "Nothing." She leaned in, and Helen found herself holding her baby sister as she cried on her shoulder. "I don't know what's wrong with me," Dorie wailed. Helen patted her back while Rett slid closer.

"You're just pregnant," Rett stated.

Evie reached over to pat her back. "Lucky you," she whispered.

Helen whispered back, "You'll be next." She smiled at Evie, whose misty look of longing was unmistakable.

"Girls, girls," James said. "What's all this hugging?"

"Your fault, Dad," Helen said, over her sister's shoulder. "You said fix it."

"Hmph. I only meant stop fighting. I didn't mean all this mushy stuff." He grumbled, but his eyes were alight. Rett reached out to grab his elbow and pulled him into the hug. "You girls are too much for an old man," he said, but let them squeeze him before he extricated himself.

Helen whispered, "You guys are the best."

"You bet. But it's time to go," Rett said. "My kids need lunch and so do I. Harry?" Harry nodded and went to corral their three kids.

The group broke apart, heading for their respective cars.

"See you Friday for pizza," Helen called. "We'll bring the dog." She climbed in and started the car.

"Does that happen every Friday night?" Jake asked. "Pizza?"

"Pizza at Grandpa's house," she said with a smile. "Then we all watch a kids' movie."

"I think I'd like that," he said, looking out the window.

"I bet you will."

About Annie

I write under the name Annie M. Ballard, and my women's fiction is set in the Canadian Maritimes, where I have settled after growing up in New England and living all along the East Coast of the US, plus Louisiana. The history of each place I've lived has been a part of what fuels and inspires my writing. I'm interested in how the geography and culture of places influence the people and the stories they tell about themselves.

My first book was about an American who came to the Maritimes to find the father she never knew. It's an exploration of place and the meaning of family, The Sisters of Stella Mare series is about four sisters from the same small fishing and tourist village, based on a real New Brunswick place. I capture realistic life experiences with an emphasis on how strong communities support us even in our most dire moments, and a focus on how everyday experience can be transcendent. Most of us live large lives within our own frame and that's what I want to share.

Website: https://anniemballard.com.

Subscribe to the newsletter for more updates. http://subscribepage.io/newsfromannie

Books by Annie M. Ballard

A Talisman of Home (2021)
Angels in the Architecture (2022)
Sea Stars Christmas (2023)

Sister of Stella Mare series
Four sisters, four books....Dorie, Evie, Rett and Helen, each one on her own path, finding her way home. Can be read as standalones.
A Heart for the Homeless (2022)
Domestic Arts (2022)
A Home out of Ashes (2023)
The Helping Heart (2024)